Melville C Keith

The Young Lady's Private Counselor

Melville C Keith

The Young Lady's Private Counselor

ISBN/EAN: 9783337371630

Printed in Europe, USA, Canada, Australia, Japan

Cover: Foto ©Andreas Hilbeck / pixelio.de

More available books at **www.hansebooks.com**

THE YOUNG LADY'S PRIVATE COUNSELOR.

THE

Care of Mind and Body.

—BY—

MELVILLE C. KEITH.

A book designed for young ladies, to aid them in
acquiring a life of purity, intellectual culture,
bodily strength and freedom from many
of the ills and annoyances of life that
custom has placed on the sex.

ALSO,

*STUDIES FOR YOUNG LADIES ON SUBJECTS CON-
CERNING THEMSELVES.*

BY MANY MOTHERS.

PREPARED AND COMPILED BY

MELVILLE C. KEITH, M. D.

MINNEAPOLIS, MINN.:
BUCKEYE PUBLISHING COMPANY.
1890.

PREFACE.

The favorable reception of "SEVEN STUDIES FOR YOUNG MEN," and an often inquiry for a corresponding work for the girls, first brought out a desire for the present book.

When his two daughters made their visit to the Normal School there was a desire to place something in their hands that could assist them in the care of their bodies.

A PRIVATE MENTOR.

Although there are numerous works for girls, none on certain subjects are plain enough to certain minds. The book has been written, therefore, as if the writer has been speaking to his own girls, and not with the idea of lecturing or of speaking a piece. The style is not to be chosen for its bluntness, but the book can be taken as a desire to do good to those whom he will never see.

The idea of different articles from different pens of ladies who have been successful and happy mothers, and having these articles embodied in the work, was an after thought, and has delayed the appearance of the work in book form for some time. But to those who believe such messages are *sent*, this will not be an objection but a help, when they receive the book.

These essays have been unchanged. Instead of giving their names, the state they are from is signed at the bottom of their essay. Noble and valuable thoughts will be found in these articles. Every article is from a mother *of girls*, and is written *to girls*.

As for the style, it is a book for the closet and for *thought*, and is strictly the thoughts of a parent for the child, with the best interests of the child at heart.

THE AUTHOR.

The Young Lady's Private Counselor.

CHAPTER I.

THE TWO NATURES.

It is evident that there are in every person two distinct and separate natures and that, in many instances, these natures are most strangely at war.

They alone are happy who understand the relation of these TWO NATURES to the control of the mind and body.

We know this of ourselves without asking any one about it.

Our desires are not the same at one time as they are at another time, yet we think we are the same person at one time that we are at another time.

These contrary conditions may be because we may be under one influence or nature at one time, and under the other nature at another time.

We shall call these two natures:

1. *The bodily.*
2. *The spiritual.*

The bodily nature demands many things which are not good or expedient for the body to possess.   There are appetites and desires which, if gratified, will bring on a penalty, and this penalty will be death.

The bodily nature is of a self-limited existence.

We may be able by proper methods to make this bodily life longer or shorter; stronger or weaker; easy or uneasy; healthy or sick; pleasant or unpleasant.

The bodily nature demands food, clothing, shelter and air.

The spiritual nature also demands sustenance, clothing and growth.

Many persons have never become acquainted with their spiritual nature, and others have never taken the trouble to have their spiritual nature born or nurtured. Others have their spiritual nature so warped and dried up that we can hardly tell whether they have any spiritual nature or not.

The ones who are safe in this life are those who are acquainted with both of their natures and have their bodily nature fully under the control of the mind or this spiritual nature.

The most unhappy of all persons are those who have never had their spiritual nature born and are under the control of their bodily nature. Such persons are materialists, of the earth, earthy.

These persons are the ones who are constantly desiring something they have not. They desire some article of diet, or some article of dress, or to go somewhere, or to hear something, or, in short, to gratify some of their bodily nature, while they do not know that they have a spiritual nature which is capable of enjoying life a thousand-fold more happily and more continuously than the bodily nature can ever become capable of enjoyment.

Persons who have not allowed their spiritual nature to grow, or who have neglected to furnish their spiritual nature with food and growth are those who are constantly seeking something to feed themselves with and do not know what is the matter with them.

We find these spiritually starved natures in all classes and in all the walks of life. They are the theatre goers; the gamblers; the wine drinkers; the card players; and the gossips of the neighborhoods. They are the *wanters* of your acquaintance, the unfortunates of the world. They would rather have thirty pieces of silver to jingle than a friend.

The ones who, under any circumstances, are those whom you consider happy are those who have conquered the bodily nature and are governed by their mental or spiritual nature.

The bodily nature is still desiring some other thing just beyond it, never satisfied.

As this book is to deal principally with the bodily nature, we may profitably examine the double natures at this time and state that, without this understanding, happiness or contentment is impossible.

THE SPIRITUAL.—It is quite certain that there is no happiness for the spiritual nature in the enjoyment of the body.

The happiness and contentment of the spiritual must come from the growth and enjoyment of the spiritual.

We must have something tangible for the spirit to take hold of and to rest in. Not that the body should be neglected, but the spirit is of more importance. The spiritual is not born when the body is, but at some period after.

When we are "*born again*" very few can positively tell. But after the spirit is once born, there is a desire for the spirit to constantly grow. The free spirit desires to know more of spiritual things and we are as constantly finding some new thing for the spirit to feed upon.

The true food for the spirit is the Word of God. This food has been provided for us to feed upon in advance, just as the coal and oil for our heat and light are found in the earth where it had been placed by the Maker of the earth thousands of years ago.

This food for the spirit is all found in the Bible and is not found anywhere else, but the means of digesting this prepared food is in the spirit which is in harmony with the Spirit of God, which is called the Holy Spirit.

These two acquaintances are sufficient to feed the spirit of man as long as the man lives. All the supplies of spiritual food are drawn from these two sources. We may be nourished and feasted by admiring the sublimities of nature or in contemplating the wondrous works of God—His mountains, valleys, oceans and landscapes, but the true supply of *spiritual* food can come from no other source than the Word of God and the Holy Spirit.

When we have once accepted this we shall never cease to grow daily. We shall be kept. The Lord will hold us in His hand. We shall be His children. Our spiritual nature will be fed from him day by day. The bodily nature will be in abeyance. We shall be free from the desires of this world. No one can taunt us or worry us about the affairs of this world, because the affairs of this life will be beneath our care. What we may need we shall have without our having to fight for it or without our having to worry about it.

This condition is what the Lord meant when he said: "Seek first the kingdom of God." If we have our spiritual natures fed we will be found *in* the kingdom of God. We shall be daily dependent on the Holy Spirit and the Bible for our supply of daily food, and we shall not have to be very anxious to know where the next supply is coming from, because we shall know that the Spirit and the Book will provide. This truth is of the very first importance. We must have our spiritual natures fed. They must be fed from the Word of God. We can not find the Word of God out of the Bible. With the Bible comes the Holy Spirit. With these two supplies we shall have an abundance of food and as constantly grow. We shall have all our spiritual natures in good order and in the way of life. As children, we shall grow up in the light of "Our Father, God.".

If we do not have these spiritual natures of ours in good condition, no matter what else we may have, we shall be unhappy and miserable. Unless we have these spiritual natures born and fed and growing, we can not understand the truths of life when we see them.

The first advice we would give, is to settle your mind on this great subject and have your spiritual nature resting on the great God, "the Maker of Heaven and earth and all that in them is," your Maker and mine.

You may think this is not "counsel." It is. You can not keep anything in this life unless you have some spot to place away what you may get. There has to be some place to place your earthly possessions.

You can have no room for anything spiritual in your head or in your body unless you have your spiritual nature in a receptive condition. You do not have to wait a moment. Follow the teachings of the Master and go into your closet, shut the door and pray to the Father who is in secret and

He shall reward you openly.   This is a spiritual act, forcing
the body to become obedient.   Or, you can simply *look* and
satisfy the spiritual nature.

If you are not in the habit of praying, you have to commence and you do not need any one to tell you that a prayer
is asking of God something you may wish.   This *desire*
to be obedient to God is born of your spiritual nature.
Your bodily nature desires to eat, sleep, and grow fat.   God
is your Father.   He is your Maker.   He is your Preserver.
And no matter how young or how old you may be, God is
now ready to hear your petitions and as ready to answer them.
He made you and formed these two natures.   He asks obedience from you, as His child.   The organizations of man are
not needed.   You may think so.   But God and the spirit
are not found in man's material societies.

There is a great deal of this supposed need of a church
to join.   But we tell you that the great majority of
the societies and organizations are not helps to holy living,
but are hindrances.   We tell you more.   If you have a desire to live in the best manner to produce the best results for
your spiritual nature you would best keep away from these material organizations, societies and bands, and the people who
are wedded to the material and earthly brotherhoods or sister-
hoods.   We are most sorry to tell you this.   We feel that
we are antagonizing many good and true friends.   But we
know that we are right.   The so-called societies and bands
of human fabrication are not beneficial to your spiritual life.
The people who are in those societies are not truthful, and
too many of them (but we do not say all of them) have
joined those societies for the purpose of being helped in
their bodily and material life.   We acknowledge that help is
needed.   But we tell you that the help one gets from the
common society is not the help that helps.   The help which
is needed is from the power of the Holy Spirit, and is not to
be received from the association of the people who frequent
the societies and weekly gatherings of the multitudes who go
to obtain the same thing.   They lack this help of themselves,
and, as they do not have it, they certainly can not and do not

give it to you. They can not help your spiritual nature. The only way by which you can be helped in this gaining of the Spirit, is to read the Bible and pray to God. We might tell you that some holy men or holy women could help you, but they can not and it is not of any use to deceive you when this hand shall be dust.

There is no real help outside of the Bible and the answers to your prayers. This is the fact and the sooner you realize this the sooner you will educate your spiritual nature. You may imagine that some scapula, some image, some prayer to some saint, or to the deity who may be supposed to preside over your nativity, or a prayer to the Virgin, will aid you in your endeavors to lead a holy life. But this is all a mistake. These saints are all dead and they can not help you. Christ is our only authority for the way to act. He said:

"But thou, when thou prayest, enter into thine inner chamber, and having shut the door, pray to thy Father which is in secret, and thy Father which seeth in secret shall recompense thee."

We think we are correct in saying when you have done this and when you have learned to depend wholly on the Father for assistance, you will acknowledge that all the societies made by men can not help you.

There are some things which we hesitate to say, and yet we know for your own good you would better learn them now than by and by when the tempter comes.

Many of your worst temptations will be from the so-called churches. You will grow worldly and selfish by thinking that the churches and church people are what you should be generous to.

You should be generous to the entire world. Every person in this world who is one of God's children claims your help. If you are once tied to a society, that society will be the boundary of your life. If you do not ally yourself with any human organization, but depend wholly on the Lord Jesus, you will be IN THE CHURCH—although you will not belong to any human organization.

This is our experience. The society of man does not help

you but develops the earthly, and they do your spiri ual nature hurt. These societies must have money; must have
your labor; the earnings of your hands; the toil of your
body. You must dress. Ten thousand things come up that
lower your standard of living to the Master. And we think
it is best to keep from all entanglements with all human societies, all human bands, as it is known to be a human society, and the work of human hands. Do not allow the
spiritual to depend on earthly charity for food. Go to God.

Perhaps you are a church person, so-called. If you are
really desirous of serving God you should lose no time in
seeing whether the body of men known as the human
churches are correct.

Take one single point. The traditions of this so-called
church tell and teach you to pray to the Virgin Mary.

At the same time the church professes to believe on the
Holy Bible. Very well.

Take your Catholic Bible (there is no material difference
in the Bibles—the Spirit of God is with the reading of
either of them) and turn to the first epistle of Paul to the
Thessalonians, fourth chapter, and commence at the thir-
teenth verse, and read to the end of the chapter.

Here you find that the good are "*asleep in Jesus.*"

They are "dead in Christ," and "shall rise first." When
shall they rise?

You will see that they are going to "rise" when the
"Lord shall descend from Heaven with a shout."

They are not yet risen. If they are not yet risen why should
you pray to them? Think this over carefully and with
prayers to God and prayers to Christ, and ask God to
help you.

Let me tell you, my Catholic reader, that one of the
reasons of your unhappiness and of your not having answers
to your prayers, is because you do not pray according to the
teachings of your Lord and Master, Christ. All of your
prayers to the Virgin are of no value, and you have now, although you may not read another word, a full reason why you
should look into the Bible and see for your own self whether

your so-called church is of God or is it of man. We tell you, if you desire to find God, and if you desire to have some help for your spiritual nature, you should see that you go to the only place where there is any help, and that place is the Bible, and to the closet as taught by Jesus, and in sincere prayer to God. All your prayers to the Virgin are an abomination to God and are a part of the idolatrous system known as the Roman church. We tell you still more. If there are any of the human organizations which are under more misfortune than any other, we can show you that the members of the Roman Catholic church are the ones.

The time has come which has been looked for, when God cries out: "*Come out of her my people.*" And we tell you without any hope of reward or of fear, that the time is here when the good people of all denominations are coming out of the churches and belonging alone to the church of God and wholly trusting to the saving grace of the Holy Spirit, which does not have to have any human organization to assist it in its work. No earthly organization can help your spiritual nature. God can alone satisfy and provide for you.

So we go back to our first point,—that if you desire to help your spiritual nature you must depend on two sources, and those two sources are the Bible and the Holy Spirit. Let all the human societies alone.

When you are free from these societies you are ready to depend on the Spirit of God. As long as you are in these human societies you are looking to them for a support which they will never give. Your spiritual nature will be always dwarfed as long as you are with and depending upon them. Take the Bible as the man of your counsel and depend on the Holy Spirit for your sole guidance.

When you do this you must not think that all is to be smooth sailing into paths of peace. A child is born *in a moment*, but it does not grow to be a man in a moment. You will not grow to be strong in a moment. You have first to learn to go to God. Then God will commence to teach you His way. He has a way in this world. What-

ever may be bad in your path, go directly to God with it.
Take everything which you think is out of your power to do
or to overcome, to the throne.

Ask God in all of the affairs of your daily life to help and
guide you and your steps. Whatever is in your way to do,
and *to do good, do it*, but at the same time do not do anything without asking God to help you in the doing of that
thing, no matter how humble and how small it may appear.

Do not forget that it is all between you and the Spirit of
God whether you will become a child of God. You must go
to God. But when you once go to God he does not leave
you in the dark. His Spirit comes down and teaches you
what to do. You can not know all of God's purposes at
once. Little by little He will show you what is best for you
to do in His way. He will educate and guide you. Christ
said He would send the Comforter, and either the Comforter
has come or He has not. If Christ told the truth, then the
Comforter is here and waiting to help you. The Comforter
is come. All the ills of this life will appear very small in
this life if you are a child of God. And you may be assured
that if anything happens to you that there is some object in
the thing happening, and take it as from the Father. Do
not worry and fret about the spiritual part of existence if
you have done all in your power to help yourself. The salvation of the spiritual part is the work of God, and He is
not likely to make any mistake about the work which is especially His.

If you have taken all the care of the spirit you know how,
it is not worth while to be worried about the future of that
spirit. Your duty is to be sure you are right here and not
worry about being right hereafter. That future is the provision of God and you will find that He is alone the One who
will take care of that future. If the mind worries you after
you have done all in your power to keep the mind easy, ask
yourself if there is not something which is wrong with the
body. Your liver may be bad and in such a case it is natural that there should be some gloomy thoughts. We can
know when we are right mentally, because the mind is light

and buoyant.   And we can know when we are right bodily
when we feel that there is no pain or ache or weakness.

The object of this book is to aid you in preserving your
bodily health and to assist you in taking care of that body.
The knowledge which is in this book is of no value to you
until you have that knowledge in your head and can use the
knowledge for your own self.

You will know whether the knowledge is true or not by
the time you have tried it.   You can tell whether it is new
to you or not.   All the knowledge concerning your body
could not be put in this book, but if you desire to get
knowledge, there will be an opportunity to get that knowledge which is of use to you.   .

The spiritual nature is alone fed on spiritual things and
not on the food of the body.   The food of the body will not
feed or edify the needs of the spiritual nature, and when one
thinks or fancies that the affairs of this life can make the
spiritual nature satisfied, there is made one of the grandest
mistakes of life.   We can not do it.   The moment we are
satisfied with the things of this life and with the affairs of
this world, and we are satisfied with the goods of this earthly
existence, we are spiritually starved.   The spiritual nature is
in the condition of a hungry child.   It lacks food.   To feed
the spiritual nature there has to be food appropriate to the
nature.   This food is alone prepared by the One who made
us, and is as abundant as the bodily food is.   Everywhere
there is this spiritual food, if we can take it and assimilate it.
But we can never assimilate the food which is around us until we are in a condition to take this food from the rough
places where it may be found.   The person who thinks of
dinner as the main thing of the day will never see any beauty
in the clouds or the sunshine.   The person who is thinking
how the dress is trailing along the street is not one who can
contemplate the beauties of the stars.   One who is after a
dollar to buy bread is not the one who is contemplating the
source of the Northern Lights.

To have this spiritual life as perfect as it should be, we
should live as close to the great God who made us, as we

know how. The gossiping and the tattling of the common herd should not find an entrance to our minds. We should shun those people who are ready to carry any of this earthly and foul-mouthed gossip. Shun all and every kind of idle words. Shun the companionship of those who are in the habit of telling those stories or repeating the tales which will make any person unhappy.

We think the best way to get this spiritual food is to go to the Bible and read until the Lord and the Word are as one to us, and we can see what is meant in the Word of God.

The reading of the novels of the day is one of the methods by which we can starve the spiritual nature. The most of these stories are based on some love affair which is never true to life and which is always of the most material nature. It can not do us any good to read these things which are untrue and do not leave us as well fitted to battle against the world as we were before we read them. We have a false idea in our heads and this false idea is often what places us at a disadvantage in the battle for bread.

The mind should be trained to the exact truth, and with such training there will not be any trouble in looking at the things of life so as to make the exact case as it stands and as soon as we can see the exact condition and the exact relation and the manner in which we stand to the rest of mankind, we shall be able to select our place and give to ourselves the food that is needed, to our spiritual natures, as well as the food to our bodily natures. Why should we become servants to someone else who is not as good as we are? We can take care of this body and elevate the spirit and mind at the same time. Perhaps the best example of taking the eyes from this world's affairs is to be found when Moses lifted up the serpent of brass and bade the bitten people to look to this image. They had to take off their eyes from the place where they had received the bite and gaze on something else. They must cease to dwell on the snake bite; they had to take the eyes from this place where they had received the bite, and turn them *away from* their material bodies. The very fact that they had to take their minds from the bite and look to something else was enough to *change* their minds. As long as they were looking at the wound which they had received from the snake they could do nothing. But when they took their eyes *from* this wound and placed them on something which was placed there by someone else, then they were healed.

So in the desire for a spiritual elevation. We have to take our minds from the contemplation of these earthly things and go to the spiritual throne and to "One who was lifted up" before we can get any relief from this earthly torture which comes to every one in the world at some time.

While this work will deal with the bodily nature mostly, we say, at the outset, the spiritual nature is of far the most value and without the elevation of the spiritual above the material there will be no true happiness. Study how to have the spiritual nature in the best possible condition and we think the best way is to have a sound mind in a sound body. Do not neglect either of these natures as you value your peace of mind and your happiness.

CHAPTER II.

WHY AM I A WOMAN?

This question has been asked countless times, and we have never seen any satisfactory answer to it.

The differences in the sex are accounted for in the following manner. When there is union between the parents directly *after* the menstrual period, there will be a girl. If a period of six to fourteen days elapse, the offspring will be a male.

This rule is asserted to hold good in all the mammalia.

The body in its general make-up is precisely alike in both cases, except that, in the case of the male, the scrotum descends *outside* the body and carries the testes down (*or vice versa*), and the organs enlarge under the influence of increase of nutrition. While in the female, the organs are retained *in* the body, the scrotum becoming the uterus and the testes the ovaries. The organs of the female have each counterparts in the male. But this is the condition of sex only and it is evident that there is in the woman, a something that there is not in the male.

We have been told that the female is the "weaker vessel," but, in reality, if one examines the body and the habits, this should not be so.

In nearly all the animals the female is as strong, as enduring and as long or longer lived. There is no reason why it should not be so in the human race. The facts are visible that the girl who is treated correctly, dressed properly, and has proper exercise, is as strong, robust and vigorous as the male.

Still the equality of the attributes of the body does not prevent the fact that the woman possesses something different from the male, outside of the conditions of strength, vitality or long life. A something which renders her superior to the man as long as she has it, and inferior to the man when she has lost it, or when she has been robbed of it.

As I have never heard a name for this fact, and it is a fact that at once accounts for all the contrary things we see concerning the female sex, why at one time a woman is raised to the rank of a queen and a goddess, and at another time she is classed as a slave, we have decided to call it *feminine power.*

We think, we assert, that every woman has this power born in her, and that she is the possessor of the power as much as she is the possessor of the reproductive organs.

So long as she is in a certain state, the female is a queen, a ruler, a lovely being that controls the world and is favored directly from heaven. She has the power of heaven to create happiness around her.

When once this power is gone, she is no longer a queen, but a "weaker vessel," a plaything, a slave, seemingly a misfortune to herself, a source of trouble and unhappiness. Understand, please, that this is a *man* writing (whose mother was a woman), a father, lover, husband, counselor, and that with no outlines to go before, we are stating a fact as it appears to us and *new* to the world—a cause why *woman* as woman *exists.*

We say the cause is, that God designed a superior, higher, better, purer life than man could naturally possess, and for this reason he made that superior, higher, better, purer being and gave her the same body *reversed, retained, innate,* and called it woman.

A short space only will be taken up by the consideration of this fact, although it is of such vast importance and the proofs are so abundant that it would take a volume to do it justice, and to mention this series of facts as they are in history, and in the experience of every thoughtful person, man or woman.

Throughout all nations and ages we have these queens ana superior creatures, and we have also a corresponding class of slaves.

We read of the women of the Bible, the women of history, and we see the women of to-day in the same two great classes.

We assert that the same power, the same superior purity,

the same instinctive excellence exists in the woman of, to-day as has existed since the days of Eve. She is the center, the loved, the life, the dependence, the happiness, content, peace and comfort of the world.

Woman the queen; the mother; the controller of man's happiness.

At the same moment she becomes a slave—a cruel-hearted monster, "afflicted with devils," a "weaker vessel," a burden, a hindrance, and likened to a "dog."

Can such a series of facts exist (and they do exist and are easily recognized in any community) and yet we possess the key that tells us of the reason why?

We think so.

As long as a woman is pure and virtuous she is endowed direct from heaven with this queenly power. She is, in herself, the embodiment of some special aim and special grace; some gift that God endows her, making her from above, purer, better and more broadly powerful over the worker, man, than any other being living. Men worship her. She is truly a queen because she rules. She orders or wishes. Men obey.

At once, when she loses her virtue, or yields to passion or persuasion, arts or force, she loses this high estate and drops to be a beggar, a slave and a weaker body. The power is gone. The woman who yesterday was a queen is to-day "a body of death."

We say to every girl: No matter your station or your acquirements; your poverty, your looks, your surroundings or your ancestors; your color or your nationality; no matter your deformity, your dress, your dirt, your shoes or your bonnet, or whether you have any; no matter how low, how vile, how degraded, how meanly sprung you were, nor where you came from; no matter all these—are you a woman? God has created you a queen. You have power. The world is at your command. All that makes life enjoyable is yours to have, to take, to own, to keep, to enjoy. You are a queen and have only to make your wishes known to have the world yours. Yes, more. You rise above this world and take hold of hands in heaven, which bring you up out of all the low grovelings and heartaches of this world.   Angels wait upon you.   God looks upon you and smiles.   You are a King's daughter and you wear a royal robe that angels have woven.   Angels watch you and although ten thousands of devils—of poverty, illness, surroundings, relatives, weakness and want, cold and hunger, shall peck and taunt you, you shall overcome them all and breakfast with your Father, the King of Kings and the Lord of Lords;   The world is yours. What any one has you may have.   What any one enjoys is all yours.   Keep your powers.

You may say "Oh, I am only a poor girl and haven't any power."   But I tell you that is a mistake.   You are a woman.   *You have this power.*   God gave it to you at the moment of conception.   God never makes a mistake and as sure as He made you a woman, He put this power in you and only by your own act can you lose that power and reduce yourself to be a beggar and a slave.

You may say you are now a beggar and a slave.   Very well.   You are a King's daughter.   Run away from where you are—get away from bondage—put the ocean between you and that master, and become free, rich, and take charge of your own house.

All this may not be clear to you.

We will try to make it clear.   As long as a girl is virtuous, as long as she retains control of her body—so long as no one —not even herself—by thought or action—has control of the body, or can stimulate or pander to her passions—just so long does the woman hold the power of the world and the direct favor of God.   When the woman is married and is subject to her husband, she gives that power to the husband, in a measure.   She is no longer the queen of the world, but she is the queen, mistress and ruler of one man—the worker—and the controller of one household—a home.   Her home.   His home.   The woman owning, controlling, making, holding, keeping, building up the home.

But once let the woman *lose her virtue,* once let her become subject to passion, or the plaything of a man, or yield to her own passion, and *her power is gone.* She is the weak vessel. She is a slave and beggary follows. She can no more lift herself back into her place in the universe as a superior being than she can take hold of the moon or grasp the stars. It is impossible. The woman who has once lost her virtue has lost her power, and she is in comparison to what she was an hour ago, a weaker vessel, a slave.

With these assertions we now come to the answer of " *Why am I a woman?*"

Answer. Because God, in His wisdom, made me as a vessel of honor, to do his will.

If you do His will, you are a specially gifted servant of the Most High. If you do not do it, you are a dishonored servant and an outcast from heaven and despised on earth.

We think this is the answer to the question. A woman is superior if she is a true, virtuous woman. If she is not virtuous, she is fallen so low that nothing on the earth will do her reverence.

How shall she keep this power?

We reply that no woman is safe who does not have a companion stronger than earthly companions. And in our idea that daily and hourly companion is the Holy Spirit—the comforter.

This companion is to be brought to dwell in you by reading the Bible and by prayer for the Spirit of God. This is a matter that is to be thought of more than can be written. It is a matter full of facts which are at your hand. If you are a woman you are a superior being. If you have lost your virtue, you have lost your superiority and are beneath the men. It may not be *known*, but it can be *felt.* Your presence; your body; your whole body, tells the story of your superiority or your fall.

External appearance may assist to deceive the unthinking, but the *inner sense*, which is the true judgment, can not be misled by any outward show or any affected airs. Jewelry, clothes, accomplishments, relatives, can not weigh a hair for or against you. It is *in* and *of yourself.* If you are virtuous you are a power, a queen, a King's daughter and a companion for one who is to come for you. In you are the germs of a future nation. Power is yours. Angels smile on you. Circumstances may dishearten but they can not conquer or hurt you.

The very fact that you are a woman is the fact that God has a special work for you to do. You are blessed above all men. Only keep yourself a woman and do not allow yourself to become a piece of jewelry or a feather, a beggar or a slave. Remember that you are priceless. Money could not make you, and it should not buy you Let nothing tempt you to forget that fact for one second. "I am a woman." The grandest, most beautiful, most powerful and most perfect piece of workmanship in the world is a woman. Fashioned by the special thought of Deity—a woman, the mother of earth Made a woman because of the special command of God in her behalf.

CHAPTER III.

BEING A WOMAN, WHAT CAN I DO?

"Being a woman, what can I do?"

Being a woman.

We shall take a few observations before we tell you what are your possibilities.

When a ship leaves the port the captain or commander of that vessel takes a departure from all the landmarks which are in sight.

When he is leaving the port he will shape the course of his vessel towards the nearest place that he desires to go and that he will see (or sight), and then, if it has not been done before, he will set a watch. All the night there is someone at the wheel and someone on the lookout. Someone is awake constantly and someone is always guiding that ship by means of the helm.

The captain or commander has a sextant and compass, and also in the cabin there is a chart showing the depth of the water, all the reefs and all the quicksands, and all the distances to and from distant points.

Being a woman, you have a more priceless vessel than all the vessels and all the cargoes which ever floated on the ocean, and you are of more priceless value than all the commanders who ever strutted the decks of all the ships on the ocean.

Let us take our observation and see how you stand and how you are fitted with the things of this life.

Are you well?

Health is a most priceless blessing, but it is not the most valuable of all blessings.

Upon the condition of your health depends, in some manner, the choice of your pursuit.

Are you educated?

Education is of great value.

If you are without a good English education, you have a

23

much harder load to carry than if you could do all the sums in the arithmetic and write a neat hand. But the education can be acquired. It takes time and takes much trouble to get an education after one is twenty and over, but it can be done, and you need not fret about this lack.

About your disposition, there is something to be said, but these attributes are soon remedied if lacking, as we shall soon see.

Have you any money?

We hope not.

If you have any money you are liable to depend on that money and you will soon lose that little money to some sharper and so you will be worse off than you would have been if you had none.

Have you friends?

If you have, discard the idea that any of your earthly friends are to be leaned upon.

It is true you have a mother. She is truly your best friend. There is no one who would do more for you than your father. But on your going out into the world there are no friends who can help you but One.

And here at this point you will take a look at your ship and see just how you do stand and place it down for your future reference and for your future guidance and encouragement.

The first thing you need is a friend who can help you to a situation and give you wisdom enough to keep it and strength to hold it.

Being a woman, what can I do?

This depends upon what kind of a friend you have.

In one of the Arabian Nights' stories there is a tale of one of the heroes who, after spending all of his inheritance, found a friend in the guise of a genie, who, after leading him in a multitude of situations, gave him an abundance of money, and then gave him the ninth statue. When this hero goes into the cellar to find this ninth statue, he finds the form of the girl whom he loved.

And the genie says to him, in substance, that of all the

treasures he has, the ninth statue, or the person of the woman who is virtuous and loving, is of more value than all the wealth of the world.

Being a woman.

Being a woman was once thought to be a weaker vessel. But we know differently now.

A woman is really the strongest of the two, and is able to bear the greatest burdens without any fainting or repining. But above this we know that the God who has made us all has given a power into every woman's hands and into her keeping which is above the power of all the kings of the earth.

There is nothing that is not possible for her to gain and nothing that is beyond her reach. What is in this world is hers if she will only reach for it. She is a woman.

All the treasures of the world, which are won by severe toil and prolonged effort of the man, are brought to the feet of the woman that she may smile on the man.

Her smile repays all the toil and all the fatigue.

On the earth there is nothing of more value than a woman's love.

Being a woman, what can I do?

Being a woman, what can I NOT do?

The woman is the power and the woman is the ruler; let the man say what he may.

Next to Christ, WAS and IS the bride, and the bride was a woman.

But there is something which is of more importance than in determining the sex of the person.

Where do you start from?

Where are you going?

Who is your pilot?

If you have an idea that all the world is to run and fall at your feet as soon as you spread out your apron, you will wait until many a sun goes down and many a dewdrop falls, before that day comes to you.

There is something to do and you have to find out what is your part, and whose queen you are, and what world you are to conquer.

You are to get an observation and see where your voyage is to end, before you commence. If you are not the pilot of your voyage, and if you do not think you can pilot your own vessel, then you are to have a pilot who can tell you where you are going.

The first thing, in our mind, for you to do, is to find out what you are.

God made you.

Before you were fashioned in the womb God saw and loved you. Do not forget this for one moment. God saw and loved you.

And at this time you are the object of His solicitude, and He says to you, "Come to Me and buy gold" and all the precious things of this world.

"*You are my child.*"

While I have made man, I have made you to comfort, succor, uphold and guide him.

Next to the high God, the man worships the woman he loves.

The facts are, that, being a woman, you are a ship that is freighted with the most valuable of all cargoes in the world, and you are the embodiment of all the most valuable of all the possessions of the earth.

You are a woman.

The world centers in you and in your welfare.

You are the home.

You are the mother of all the children on the earth.

Without you there would be no real happiness on this earth and no abiding place.

You are the pillar and the hope of all of the men and of all the growing nations of the earth to-day.

The man who looks at you as a plaything is a fool. The man who does you an injury is the man whom God is going to punish. SURE.

The man who thinks he can live without the woman is one of the biggest fools in the world. He can not do it. The woman is the home-maker, and there is no such thing as the womanless home.

The home without the woman is simply a den where the wild beasts hide.

BEING A WOMAN.

God bless you, my daughter; the Lord has blessed you by making you a woman—the treasure of the earth.

But, with this responsibility, there is some account to be given to your Maker.

God made you. He demands of you a perfect obedience to His will, and he is determined that there shall be no mistakes at all. With so much power there shall be some responsibility and some accountability to Him.

This is the only rock your vessel can ever run on to that will wreck you,—the loss of the pilot and the loss of your charts and compass.

We commence then by saying to you that with the fact of your being a woman there is more accountability than in the man.

You have more at stake.

You have more serious enemies than the man. They are hidden by the wayside and they are of the beasts of the world who are possessed of the devil.

The storms which strike the man are worse to you, since you are the objective point with the devil.

All passions, all the hatreds, all the envies and all the animosities in this world are concentrated on you to break you up from any object in life. Your home, your children, your husband and your subjects are every moment being tampered with, and someone is trying at this moment to rob you of your rightful possessions.

Can you conquer these enemies?

That depends.

If God made you, and we do not doubt this for a second, then He must be looking at you and willing to help you in all of your undertakings. He is. He has said so.

He has said to you, "Come unto Me." And it is noticeable that all the writers of the world have acknowledged the fact that the women are more ready to go to God than are the men. The women are more ready to bow down to their Maker than the men.

We think this is because the woman stands nearer to God than the man does, and feels her nearness to her Maker more than the man, who is too apt to drift into the material part of the universe and allow the spiritual part to escape his notice.

But there is something for you to do, and that something is for you to make all the ways of your going and your coming depend on the Lord who has made you.

In short, if you have a proper sense of your position in this life, you will as soon as possible try to have the Lord to be your help in all your actions and your Mentor in all of your thoughts.

Let the good Lord be your pilot, and let God be your chart. Keep yourself in all cases subject to the will of the Maker of you and have the most perfect understanding with Him.

You need not fear one moment, if the Lord is your helper. Oh, the people who are called the world are of no more value to you in your guidance than so many chickens. Do not listen to them. Go to God and get your desires satisfied and feel that you are the King's daughter and that this earth will never hold anything half as precious as your own self. And this is easy. Take your own mind and go to God. Look at your book of instructions (always the Bible) and you will soon learn what are your possibilities. Do you want a situation? God will give you one.

And right here there is something which you should learn that is not laid down in the so-called associations of this world.

The world and the people whom you are liable to fall into contact with tell you that "the Lord helps those who help themselves."

This is one of the lies of the devil, and one that you must get rid of just as soon as you know how.

The Lord does no such thing.

The Lord succors those who are not able to help themselves, and if He was that kind of a God who helped them who helped themselves, I, for one, would despise Him.

That story is a lie born of the devil to take your mind off the actual facts of this life.

The facts are that the Lord loves and helps (don't forget this) those who are desirous to do His will and to learn of Him. You have one Book of instructions, and this Book of instructions is all that you can go by. This is your priceless chart, sextant, compass and chronometer.

God does not *need you to do* anything. If He did. He would not be the all-powerful God that He is.

He asks you to come to Him and He will satisfy you with all the gifts of the earth. The idea that you must do something to merit the favor of God, is an old idea born of the pagan idolaters. You simply have to look to God and desire Him and He appears to you and becomes your friend.

This shows you how absurd the idea is that "you must help your own self." Look at the condition of the Israelites when they came out of the land of Egypt. They could not help themselves. God helped them.

When they could not help themselves then God helped them.

When Daniel was in the lions' den, did anyone say "The Lord helps them who helps themselves"? Did Daniel say so?

Well, we do not think he said anything of the sort.

When Christ hung on the cross did anyone say "The Lord helps those who helps themselves"?

When the apostles were in the jail and manacled, did they sing "The Lord helps those who help themselves"?

We do not think they sang anything of the sort. *They sang*, all right enough. But they never had any such a fool thought that "the Lord helps those who help themselves."

Napoleon had that idea, and one of his famous sayings was that "Providence was on the side with the heaviest artillery."

Napoleon believed in the heavy-artillery business, and he kept on believing in it.

One day his artillery turned up missing; and Napoleon died at St. Helena with a cancer of the stomach.

But the hens of your set will tell you that you have to do something, or, as they will come at you, they will say, ·· Oh, well, then you can sit right down and the Lord will bring these things into your lap."

But that does not follow.

We do not mean anything of that kind.   That is a kind of razzle-dazzle that these people, who do not have any God, have over to frighten you and to shake your mind.   These old black crows try to keep you from believing anything at all.   We mean this: If you make a point of being right with God, we tell you in all confidence that God will come to you by means of His Spirit and guide you in the proper way and show you what to do, and you will not be mistaken in any of your goings or your comings.

We say, first, get down on your knees and ask God to go with you and to be your guide in this life.

And we will tell you that if you do this you will find that every day you will live nearer to God and every day you will have the Spirit of God to guide you in all of your undertakings.

We do not mean that you are to sit down.   But we say that if you are in doubt as to what to do, then we say to you stop and see what God will have you to do.

There is no such thing as any failure on the part of God in showing you what is the best thing for you to do in this life.

It is a sure thing, and the God who has promised this guidance is a God who does not lie.

Therefore, in all of your uncertainties, we tell you, first, go to God.

Do you want a situation?   Ask God.

Do you want a pair of shoes?   Ask God.

You need not hesitate a second.   God made you and He loves you.

Ask Him for your wants and do not be any ways backward.

He has bidden you to come to Him, and tells you that He will answer.

Are you weak? Ask God for that strength. He will give to you all that is needed. Whatever you may lack, do not hesitate to go to God and ask Him.

People will tell you if you do not work you will not get it, but do not listen to these worldly people who will try to keep you from being owned by the throne where you are a daughter. Just ask the Lord and He will bring it about that you will have all that you may need, and it will come, just as certain as you are reading this book.

I have heard some women wish that they had been born a man.

This sort of desire to change one's condition in life, which is impossible to be accomplished, is one of the foolish things of this life.

If one should be thankful for life, one should be thankful for being born one of the King's daughters.

There is nothing impossible with God and there is nothing one can ask of any earthly father that is not usually granted. With the heavenly Father there is yet more readiness to answer our petitions to Him. We should be the suppliants.

There is no promise of anything unless we go to Him and ask for what we may need. But if we do go, then there is abundant promise that we shall receive all that we may need and we may ask for.

To any one who has never been in the habit of asking God for anything, this may seem to be very foolish, but it is a fact that what a child of God asks that child is quite certain to receive.

Being a woman, what can I do?

If you are a woman, whom has the Lord put on your side? We tell you that the world is to be conquered by just such persons as you are. Go to God and find out what He desires you to do and the rest will be easy. Do not worry about the circumstances you may be in or the family you came from. Do not bother a minute whether you have any education or whether you have any sense. God can give you all of these earthly things in a minute, and the only thing which should occupy your attention one minute is, whether you are a child of God or not.

That is all the Master desires to have of you. He knows it. And if you are a child of God all the world is yours.

Being a woman, what can I do?

If you are one of the womankind that live near to God and one of those who desire to live near to God, we tell you that the angels have you in charge and you need not be discouraged at anything which may come before you. All will be well. You are a King's daughter.

No matter what may happen. God is seeing you and God is your Father who is going to take care of you, and you should not waste one minute nor one second in trying to know just what the Lord is determined to have you do.

Do what the Lord sets in your way to come before you, and the good Lord will see to all the rest.

No matter what misfortunes may happen to you, remember that the sparrows fall, but they have the Father's notice.

You are much greater than all the sparrows in the world.

You may have met misfortunes.

There was a story repeated in our hearing to the effect that in one of the companies belonging to the U. S. Army, the captain got mad at one of the inferior officers and degraded him and sent him to the rear to cook. The army moved on and the poor degraded officer, now a private, was still in the rear cooking for the company. The company bivouacked on a place from where they expected to make an attack. But in the early morning the enemy fired a mine directly under the place where the company were sleeping and all were blown up and killed. Not a soul was left from the company, who were all alive and in the best of health an hour before.

But the private who was degraded for no cause was alive and well.

And keep another thing in your mind. "The darkest day, live till to-morrow, will have passed away."

Don't feel that all is lost as long as you can get down on

your knees and pray. Do not repine a minute at things which are not your own fault.

You are a King's daughter. He smiles on you. Have courage becoming a daughter of a King.

Look up and think that the Father who made you is sitting on His throne and is watching you to see how you are going to win this battle.

Do not allow the spirits of evil to have any influence over you. Stick to truth, and that truth is, that, being a woman, you are the best and the grandest of all creatures who have been made by the Lord of heaven and earth.

Your Maker and your Father has made the sun and the heavens and all that in them is and now is waiting to give you all there is of the earth, if you will be faithful and patient.

Who can tell the lessons which your Father wishes you to learn?

The trials which may seem so hard to bear and so grievous to be borne are of the lessons which your Father wishes you to learn.

Will you not have patience and bear anything, if it be the will of the Father?

Yes.

That is a good daughter. Be brave and think that as God has made you, so you are here to do His will, and that will is your pleasure.

And when God lifts you up, as He surely will, do you remember your low estate and all of your trials, and thank the good Father for His mercies.

Whatever station you may be placed in, recall the fact that all your responsibilities are *to your Father* who is looking on you to see how you will bear prosperity. Not everyone can bear to be made prosperous and raised into an elevated position.

Think of this. It is true. Could you bear prosperity?

Do you think over all the paths you have been through and see that you are not proud nor forgetful of the fact that God is your father and there are also some other daughters in the world beside yourself.

C

Keep it constantly in your mind that as you are the daughter of a King, so you must behave in a manner becoming the King's daughter.

What can you do?

Being a King's daughter you can do anything that is to be done on the earth.

Being a woman, what can I do?

As a King's daughter I am a princess, and can do the will of God, my heavenly Father, the King of earth and heaven.

Being a woman.

Being a daughter of a King, I can do anything which is to be done on earth.

CHAPTER IV.

THE CARE OF THE BODY.

The first thing any young lady should learn is to take the best of care of her person. She will take a pride in this care as soon as she sees how much different one looks who takes good care of one's body, and the appearance of one who will not take care of the body. It is difficult to say which is the most important part to take care of, as the whole body is so evenly connected together, that any failure to take care of any one part of the body surely places more work on some other part of the body, and this extra work on any one organ always means a state of departure from the state of health. Thus, we see that if we take care of the skin and do not pay a proper attention to the condition of the bowels, there will be a state of constipation or a state of diarrhea, which will surely bring the body to the state of departure from the natural or healthy condition, and it is this departure from the natural which is called disease.

· We will commence with the bowels, as there is no doubt but what there is a tendency in everyone, who has never given the matter much thought, to allow the bowels to get out of order.

The bowels, from the mouth to the anus, are said to be as long as five times the height of the person. Thus, if the person was five feet high, there would be twenty-five feet of intestines. One can see how important it would be to keep this length of a hollow tube in the cleanest condition, and it is true that unless this tube or intestine is kept clean there will surely be a disease of the body.

The first point to remember is, that unless the food is thoroughly chewed up while in the mouth, there is no promise of any regularity of the intestinal discharges. Mastication is positively necessary to good health. In other words, there is no certain discharge of the bowels, and if the body

35

becomes constipated there is a positive source of injury to the body at the lower part of the bowels.

The law of nature is, that there should be an operation from the bowels daily. If this does not take place there will be some of the dejecta which should pass off from the body, remain to be absorbed and again pass into the blood.

Elimination of all of the effete materials from the body commences with the thorough mastication of the food. Unless the saliva is first mixed with the food there is sure to be constipation of the bowels.

If this proper chewing of food is done, there is good reason to think there will be a daily movement which will cleanse the lower bowels, and, in turn, cleanse and relieve the whole body from its effete materials. It is certain there can be no health while there is constipation. If this movement of the bowels does not take place each day, there should be some means used to have it take place, and this should be in the line of assisting nature and not for the purpose of punishing the body for its remissness. In other words, there should be some means taken to help the body to have this natural movement and not an artificial movement forced from the bowels. An artificial movement is one which is caused by the action of some article which is taken for the avowed and specific purpose of *moving the bowels*. These artificial substances are called "medicine" but they have no right to the name of medicine.

The most common of these substances is some form of quicksilver, or mercury. The form of mercury most commonly given, is in the form of calomel, or blue mass, and is given in the form of a pill. The immediate effect of mercury is to irritate the bowels, and then nature makes an effort to drive this poison out of the system and there is a copious discharge from the bowels. This is what is called physic. This is also called a "cathartic" action. The secondary effect of this and all other kinds of mercurial preparations, is to salivate the victim and loosen all the teeth.

Nearly all of the patent pills of the day are composed of mercury as one of the ingredients. There are other substances given, among which aloes has been one of the most common. Aloes causes the bowels to become irritated and the muscular coats to become contracted and there is an action from the bowels which is said to be beneficial. But with this contraction there is also a contraction of the muscles at the end of the passage, or the anus, and the veins are strangulated. Then, when these veins are strangulated, the portion of blood which is in those veins is coagulated and dies. In this condition at the next operation or movement of the bowels there is this dead blood to be passed back into the system, and this dead blood is of such a nature that it clogs up the finer capillaries of the liver and the skin and one can see these muddy complexions anywhere one goes and looks; in society or on the street. In nearly all instances of these muddy complexions the bearer of this complexion has piles.

To attribute all of the conditions known as piles to the use of aloes, or to any other cathartic, would be erroneous.

The use of any drink which is stimulating to the muscular portion of the body is apt to cause the conditions favorable to the piles. Thus coffee is one of the most certain provocatives of piles, and it may almost be asserted that every one who is a habitual drinker of coffee is certain to have the piles. So far as we can judge, there are none of the people who are subject to this distressing condition known as the piles who have not been coffee drinkers or have taken some of the common articles of so-called medicince, which are termed "*cathartics.*"

The first thing which should be learned is to thoroughly chew up the food in one's mouth. If this is done there will be good digestion and good peristaltic motion. (*Peristaltic motion* means intestinal motion.) And there will be, also, a good condition of the bowels to keep free from constipation.

But if the constipated habit has already been formed on any of the readers, we would say it is time to break up this habit, and the sooner one breaks up this habit of constipation the sooner there will be the condition of health. No person can be healthy who is constipated. To overcome the habit of constipation there have been thousands of remedies, and

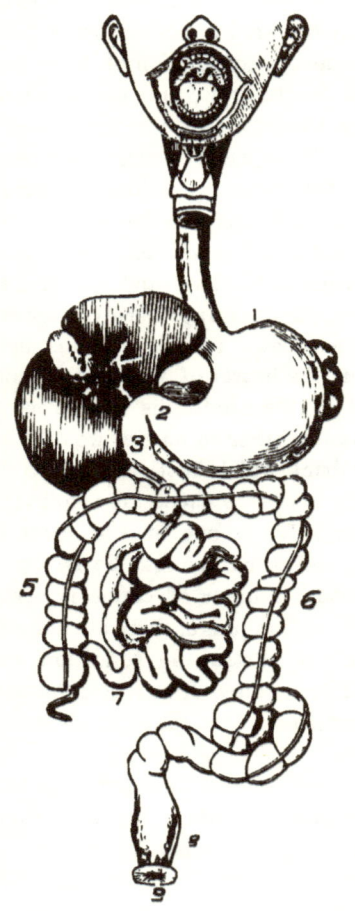

FIG. 1.

1. The Cardiac Portion of the Stomach. 2. Pylorus. 3. Duo-
denum or Second Stomach. 4. Transverse Colon. 5. Ascending Colon. 6. Descending Colon. 7. Small Intestines. 8. Rectum. 9. Anus.

there are few of them that have even the faintest grains of common sense to support them in their pretensions as aids to the body.

We will give some remedies for constipation, and while we do so let it be understood that there are some persons who can not take many of the good things, and there are others who seem to desire to have something entirely different from anyone else.

The first article which may be truly said to be the famous remedy for all ailments of the bowels is the use of water.

One can drink a glass of cold water in the morning and one before each of the other meals and then if there is not immediate help there can be two of these glasses of cold water drank which will, in the shortest possible time, bring on a regular movement of the bowels as well as the daily evacuation of all the materials which should pass off through the bowels.

We class water as the great remedy for all kinds of bowel troubles, and we can say that we have yet to see the first case where the continued use of water would not remedy these conditions quicker and better than anything else which has ever been invented. Some persons may have to drink three or even ten glasses of water early in the morning, but usually one or two glasses of water will overcome any ordinary case of constipation which has been acquired through ignorance or neglect.

But if the water, by a steady use, does not seem to carry off all of the materials, or does not act quick enough, then we may try to aid nature so that this effete material shall be removed out of the system.

To this end, a *daily use of an injection* should be made to the bowels. This injection may be made of warm water, or water which is not too warm to relax the tissues. Absolutely the cold bath and the cold injection will do more to eradicate the conditions which are known as constipation and piles, than any other remedy we know of.

The use of the injection has been deprecated and placed aside by many people as beneath their notice, but we think this is not wise.   There is nothing so bad as a constipated habit, and, although the use of the syringe is not a pleasant thing to contemplate, there is this to be said: It is far better and a thousand times safer than the use of anything that is commonly called a purgative, or a cathartic, in the shape of medicine.

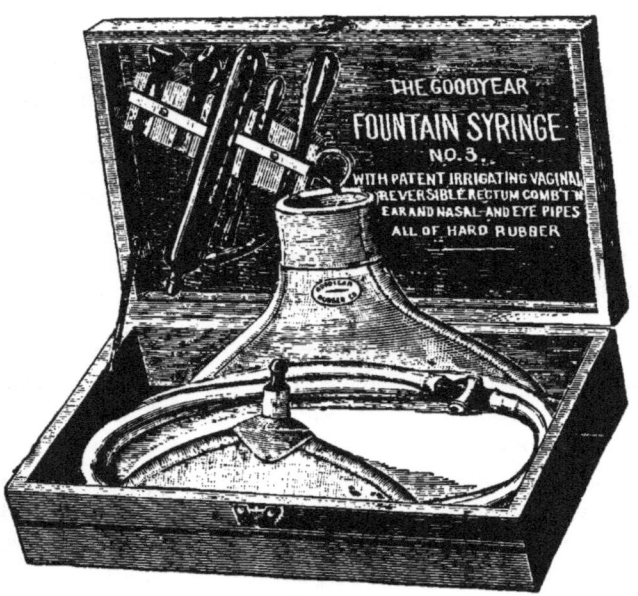

FIG. 2.

We think that the Fountain syringe is one of the best, and it can be purchased for about a dollar or for two dollars, and if this is not practicable there should be a common bulb syringe, which can be obtained for a dollar, and of these there are a number of good kinds that are reliable.   The Davidson (the No. 1) will cost about $2.   The No. 2 will cost $1.50.   The Goodyear Rubber Company manufacture a syringe which is called their " Union No. 3 " and is sold for about a dollar, and is as good as any in the market, and we think the best in the market for the money.   The lower grades of syringe are not worth carrying home.   The brands "Alpha" and " Omega " are also good syringes.

We do not advise the use of these articles unless there is and has been constipation, but if this habit is formed we think there is nothing of so much value as the syringe, and we are sure if every young lady would possess one of these useful articles to relieve the overburdened body when it is needed, there would be much less of what is called "female diseases."

After one has the syringe and is in earnest to regain health, there are some things which will assist in bringing about the habit of regularity of the bowels. These are the foods. The grains are best, as there is nothing which will so soon bring the bowels into a soluble condition as the use of grain and a vegetable diet and especially a free use of the coarser grains and the fruits. The use of meats as a food while the bowels are constipated, should be avoided. Milk is an article which often constipates the bowels and is a producer of pimples on the face. The use of milk should be guarded until its action is known, as it is not the same on all persons. Some persons can drink milk with impunity, and others can not touch it with any safety. Potatoes are unfit food and should be avoided as detrimental to the body. They do nothing in the body which is of benefit, and are of all the vegetables the worst for a young lady to eat. Squash, cabbage, turnips, beets and beans are of value as well as are all the grains, the grains being of far the most value as they contain the elements of nutrition in a far greater degree than the watery portions of some of the vegetables named, but these vegetables are useful in carrying off the wastes of the body (or more strictly speaking, they furnish a material which is of value to the vital force to aid in a carrying off of these effete matters), and the same may be said of the fruits.

If anyone has constipation and is able to have a good daily movement by eating raw apples, it is sometimes advisable. But there are many persons who are constipated who can not bear to have the raw apples in their stomach, for, as soon as the apples are in the stomach there will be a roughness come on the face. Many times there are a set of pimples which come on the face which are alone attributable to this raw-apple eating or to milk drinking. Baked apples do not have the same effect. The common buckwheat cakes are another detrimental article which should be avoided by any of the delicate organizations which are not out in the open air constantly. Cornstarch is an abomination, but corn meal bread is an excellent remedy for constipation. In all of these conditions there should be an absolute avoidance of all of the finer parts of the grains, as of buckwheat and of wheat, and a recourse to the parts that are called *coarse*, as of the graham and the whole grains. Fine-flour bread and the fineness of the buckwheat are causes of constipation. All fried things are usually causes of diseased skin and of constipation. These articles should not be taken as food until one is in the open air and has all the exercise which can be taken.

For the falling of the womb, for the leucorrhea and for constipation, we counsel every young lady to possess a syringe and use it daily, with an abundance of warm water, say four or six quarts, so as to wash out all the large bowels which are known as the rectum, the transverse colon and the ascending colon. Wash out this colon and this large intestine; fill this part of your bowels with warm water once a day and the time will soon come when you will be rid of your falling of the womb, the leucorrhea and every vestige of constipation. This habit of a large injection to the bowels to cleanse them out, so that you do not have any of the old matter to go into the internal organs by *absorption*, is of more absolute value in every female disease, than all the medicine which was ever dug up out of the earth.

For these large and copious injections, use the water as warm as you can comfortably bear and take the injection while you are lying down, and have patience until you have placed the quantity of four quarts in the bowels. Warm water can not hurt you, and it will do you good by cleansing out the most common sources of body poisoning viz., the refuse from the great colon.

After the syringe has been named there are yet some

other modes of overcoming the habit of constipation, which
are not injurious.

The eating of a ripe orange in the morning is one of
the good things, as well as the habit of eating a baked
apple as soon as one is risen and washed and dressed.
The glass of cold water should follow this fruit, and the
glass of cold water will be found as of the most benefit
just after rising.

There was an old prescription which at one time the author
was very partial to. Take an egg and beat it up in a pint of
cold water and drink it as soon as one is up in the morning.
But he found it was the water that did the acting and the egg
did not have much of any effect except as the water was in
excess of the egg. So we returned to the water.

After one is an invalid from many habits and much medicine and there does not seem to be any action to the bowels,
then it is advised to have a large spoonful of good sweet oil
and to have a lump of sugar, and dissolve the lump, or
scrape it up and take this oil as early in the morning as one
can after getting dressed. If it nauseates, lie down a few
minutes and wait until the oil passes downward through the
intestines.

The habit of chewing up a mouthful of the pulverized
slippery elm bark has been found to be of great use to some
of the hardest cases in constipation. This is of no value
except where the bowels seem to be dried up, and then it
seems to work like a charm. We think one of the reasons
why the elm acts so nicely on some of the constipated persons is because there are worms present and the elm is one of
the safe vermifuges.

Whatever you may think of doing, do not neglect to have
a passage of the bowels daily, and see to it that the bowels
are well cleared out at each evacuation. Do not allow any
of the material which should pass off to remain in the bowels,
to be absorbed again and to come out as bad breath and offensive secretions in some other parts of the body. Think
this over carefully as there is much more in it than appears
on the surface.

CHAPTER V.

THE SKIN.

We have a little study for you this morning which will be profitable for you and yours, if it is learned and kept in your head.

Do you see this figure?

FIG. 3.

c. Stratum Corneum. *l.* Stratum Lucidum. *g.* Stratum Granulosum. *m.* Stratum Malpighii. *n. b.* Nerve Fibrils.

It represents the epidermis of the human body.

The epidermis is the outer covering of the skin.

It is, in fact, the outer skin. Inside of this is the true skin.

You see the wavy lines which are opposite c. This is called the stratum corneum. This stratum corneum consists of many layers of horny, dry, non-nucleated scales—which means that there is no nucleus in these substances.

This layer is always thickest where pressure is applied, as on the soles of the feet and the palms of the hands.

Look carefully at this layer and you will see that the scales appear to be flat or flattish, so they can fit each other in a most accurate manner. This is called the horny layer, or the layer of scales.

You will notice on the feet of persons who walk much that there is a much greater thickness than on those who do not walk a great deal. So, too, on the working man's hand, the skin appears to be tough and hard. This is because the stratum corneum, or the horny layer, has been growing thicker to protect the inner skin.

Nature has a way to protect herself, if she is allowed to have her own way.

The next layer is called the stratum lucidum (seen at l), but the upper part of this layer is called the stratum granulosum, or the layer of granules. (See g.) Look at m and you will see what is called the stratum malpighii. These together constitute the layers of the outer skin and when together are called the epidermis, or the covering skin.

It is in this last named layer that all the coloring material is found which distinguishes the light from the dark races.

This layer of malpighii is not a straight layer like the rest of the layers, but is wavy and dips down to fill in the spaces between what are called the papillæ of the true skin. (See Fig. 3.)

When we remove the epidermis we find that these papillæ are all over the body, but are largest in the hand and in the foot. In the foot and the hand these papillæ are arranged in rows. These papillæ are surrounded by blood vessels and nerves.

Although this little engraving looks quite small there is a large amount of study in it.

You will notice in the cut showing the epidermis we had:

	1.	Stratum corneum.
Epidermis.	2.	Stratum lucidum.
	3.	Stratum granulosum.
	4.	Stratum malpighii.

Now notice that there is no sign of a blood vessel in the epidermis. But the moment you strike the papillæ there are blood vessels in great abundance found surrounding the papillæ, as well as a network of nerves.

It is into this true skin that the poison-dosing doctor pushes his hypodermic needle and discharges the poison narcotic that will narcotize the victim and possibly send the sick wretch into the next world without waking up. Or, if this is not done then it is certain that the body will not be in as good condition to resist the encroachments of the disease as before the poison hypodermic was put under the skin.

There are two kinds of glands in the skin: The sebaceous glands and the sudoriparous gland.

Figure 5 is a cut of a sebaceous gland.

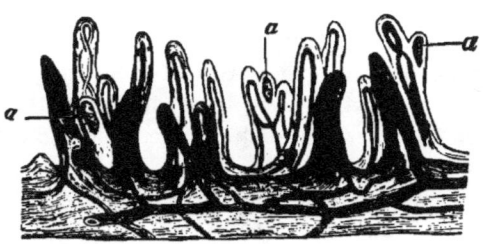

FIG 4

Papillæ of the skin. (The blood vessels injected) *a*. The touch corpuscles. Wagner's. Capillary loups are seen.

Usually this gland opens into a hair follicle, but not always. On the red margins of the lips and other places these sebaceous glands open directly on the surface.

The matter which is secreted by these sebaceous glands is

of a fatty nature and is fluid. But often this fatty fluid stagnates and becomes solid and forms the flesh worms so annoying to the growing youth of both sexes.

In some persons there are also minute, mite-like animals which are alive and in fine order to live, found in this sebaceous gland.

The physiologists call this animal the *demodex folliculorum.*

It does not require any great stretch of the imagination to say that people we have seen in large gatherings have these animals in their sebaceous glands and that we can not stomach them. They smell badly. People who do not wash every day are the most likely to have them. And those persons who do not wash oftener than once all winter are among those persons who are the most likely to have the animals as well as any of the fevers which arise from filth.

Of a certainty, the persons who do not wash are the ones who have the animals living in their sebaceous glands. You can not wonder that these non-washers have that "tough" appearance.

Oh, no! We do not say that you and your people have these bugs for sure, but we may suppose that if you belong to the haters-of-water class, those gland animals have a good hold in your sebaceous glands.

And the more you hate water the more you have these little bugs.

There is now a certain fact to which we wish to call your attention, and have you remember that we are talking to you for your own good and not for ours. This study is for your benefit.

We have tried to impress upon you the fact of there being four distinct layers of the epidermis.

Now note that there is not a blood vessel in the epidermis, but around the papillæ there is no point where a pin could be put down and not touch one of these blood vessels. There are some nerve fibrils in the epidermis, but no blood vessels.

Notice that each layer looks differently. The outside is a layer of *scales.* A clear layer. A layer of granules, and a

layer that dips down and surrounds the papillæ. The papillæ are all surrounded with blood vessels.

Notice, please, that the outside layer is being thrown off
at every move of the body. When you wash there are
some scales thrown off.

As fast as the horny layer is thrown off there is a fresh
supply goes up from the stratum lucidum or clear layer. And
in turn there is another fresh supply from the stratum granulosum, and the blood from the arteries surrounding or entering the papillæ, supplies new corpuscles for the stratum
malpighii.

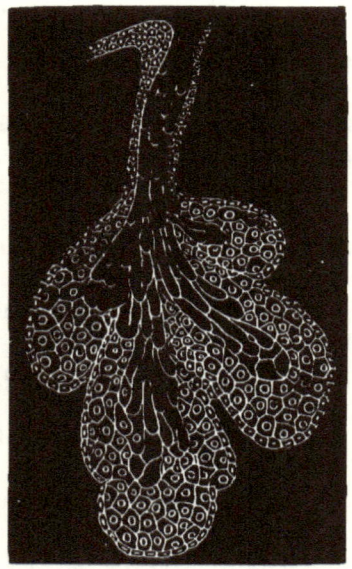

FIG. 5.

Sebaceous gland. These usually open into a hair follicle, but
sometimes open directly upon the surface.

Just think of this for a minute. When you wash the body
there are some of these scales thrown off and all the layers
move up to supply the loss of the outside layer.

When you rub the papillæ, this motion causes a good circulation of the blood and some of these scales of the outside layer are thrown off. Then the layers supply this loss and new skin is formed.

You know very well that when you wash the body you have what is called an increased circulation. The skin becomes red. The blood flows into the capillaries of the skin and fresh blood seems to fill the skin.

Consider still farther. When you wash the skin there is a new supply of scales formed for the outer layer, a new supply carried up from the layer beneath; a new supply all the way round. And the blood that surrounds or enters into the papillæ carries a new supply for all the layers in their turn.

Is not this a wonderful provision of nature?

The more one uses the skin, the fresher and the newer that skin becomes.

We begin to understand now how it is that when one washes the body frequently, that a new skin and a fresh look is on all of the body that we can see.

And we can see how it is that the people who do not wash every day have that peculiar "tough" appearance which we can not help but despise.

This not washing also explains why it is that many people, whom we may think all right in other respects, have that dreadful smell about them so hateful to others as well as to themselves. The sebaceous follicles are filled with the animals that are like mites in a cheese. Their armpits, their toes, in fact their breath and their entire body, have a smell which is execrable.

You begin to understand how important it is to have the body washed every day. We can see that if our body is not washed every day that it stands a chance to grow up a "tough."

Yes, indeed, our body is going to be washed every day.

We do not want any toughs in our family.

If we have any desire to see any toughs we can go on the street and see a thousand. These toughs have a greasy look which comes because the sebaceous glands are not cleaned out daily. And the little fat and dirt-loving skin bugs are held

D

in such love with these toughs that they will not wash them
out of the skin.

May we now call your attention to another point which
will be of great service to you one of these days.

The skin is washed.

By washing the skin you have rubbed off some of the
horny layer, or layer of scales.

Now the stratum lucidum has to come up and replace the
horny, scaly layer.   Then the other layers have to come and
supply the layers above them.   And then—then the arteries
around and in the papillæ have to supply fresh blood corpuscles to form the layer of malpighii.

You have a new supply of blood.   Where from?

Can you think ?

That fresh supply of blood is directly from the heart.

Do you get the idea ?

You have not only washed the skin.   You have called the
blood from the heart to supply the demand made upon the
outside layer of the skin.

You have actually made a fresh circulation or a better circulation than there was before you washed the skin.

Yes.   And that circulation is not alone to the skin, but
you have made the circulation of the whole body better and
fresher than it was before, because you have washed off the
older layers of the skin and brought up a new supply from
the blood of the heart and allowed the old, worn-out, effete
materials to pass through the pores of the skin.

Do you see something else ?

Do you see that if the blood has been brought up from the
heart, that it must be fresh, arterial blood that comes from
the heart ?

You have washed out the sebaceous glands and so you
have given them a chance to secrete more material.

This material comes from the blood.   It is said that the
old and worn-out and effete material is passed off from the
blood and goes out through the sebaceous glands and the
sudoriparous glands.

Your washing has had this effect on the blood.   It has had the effect of cleaning the blood that was surrounding the papillæ as well as cleaning the skin. So that the blood that was washed out is going back to the heart really better than it came away from the heart.

That is, some of the materials which were effete were passed off in the washing and the blood was better when it went back to the heart than it was when it came out of the heart, in some of its constituents or waste material being passed off.

Consider this a moment.

You have cleansed the skin by your washing.

Made a better circulation.

Washed out a portion of the blood.

Cleansed the body.

Anything else ?

As the pure blood goes back to the different parts of the body and carries the cleansed blood, it must be true that the inside of these organs, the liver, the kidneys, the heart, the spleen and the lungs, have all received a supply of blood which has been purified by this washing of the skin. In other words, although we can not take out the organs we have named, yet we can wash the blood that passes through them, and so we may say that we are able to wash all of those organs by washing the blood that passes through them.

Do you think that what we have been talking about is all true ?

Do you ask how often one should wash the body all over ?

Are you really interested in the care of your body ?

Let us ask the question.

How often do you have a passage of the bowels ? Once in twenty-four hours ?

If you do not, you should have.

And this answers your question as to how often one should wash the body.

Once in twenty-four hours.

Consider that the glands of the skin secrete and throw off, every twenty-four hours, the amount of twenty to forty ounces of insensible perspiration. If you do not have these glands in a clean condition you can not pass off that amount of material, and if you do not pass off that amount, or the amount necessary to your bodily health, you may be sure that your body is sure to suffer sooner or later.

Unless you wash every twenty-four hours it is a certain fact that you have not a clean skin.

Have not a good circulation of the blood.

Do not keep your internal organs in good shape.

Have an extra supply of the scaly layer of the skin, and you are in a condition to become acquainted with disease.

Won't you make this a little study?

Don't you think that this little study can be made to benefit your body?

Are you so well that you can keep perfectly well under all circumstances?

CHAPTER VI.

THE TEETH.

Some years ago while on a journey on the cars, a professor of a medical college got on the train and came and sat in the seat beside us.

The conversation turned on the teeth and digestion. Among other assertions this medical professor told us that "it did not matter so much what a person ate, as digestion was a physiological act, and not a chemical act." "Moreover," said this professor of a medical college, "if you think about chemistry, you are not fit to practice medicine."

In those days the writer of this book was not very well dressed. Did not have money to do much dressing and feed a family of little children. And although we felt that he was not right, yet we also felt that we had no right to antagonize his assertions to his face.

(Perhaps it was because this professor had on a span new suit of blue and we were wearing an old suit taken from a son of the Emerald Isle as a payment for the catching of a tape worm. And this countryman of ours had the suit from a Hebrew who was in the ready-made-clothing business. Oh, there is a wonderful sight of difference in the way one is dressed, about having confidence in one's self. But it is an erroneous saying that "being well dressed gives one a tranquillity of mind that religion is powerless to bestow." That is not so. If one has a true dependence in an overruling power and a constant faith in God and His Son, there is no more care for what one wears than there is for the thought of one of Armour's dead hogs. The being illy dressed makes one feel badly until, *in our minds*, we rise above dress.)

If we should meet this quondam professor of medicine to-day, we should not bother our head to talk with him. We now know that his knowledge did not get up into his head, but was passed off before it ascended.

In short, if one should ask us our opinion of this professor we should say he was unthinking. He was like the wreckers of Barnegat, bobbing his light up and down to catch the ignorant.

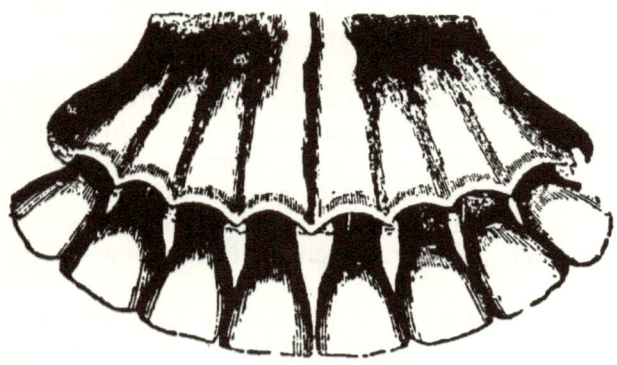

FIG. 6.

Showing cow's teeth fed on grass and grain.

Does it make any difference what we eat?

We desire you to give this matter a little thought.

Here is a cut showing the teeth of a cow fed on healthy and sound grass and grain. You see that the teeth are all even and of a proportionate size without any blemishes in them. These teeth are smooth and nice and one can almost smell the fresh breath as the teeth are seen.

This engraving was taken for John Burdell, who died long ago, in the city of New York. Burdell was a scholar, and his works live after him. His profession was dentistry.

Here is another cut showing the condition of a cow which was fed on the "still slops" of the city. How do you like these teeth? You see the enamel of the teeth is all destroyed and there is one tooth gone. The bones have also suffered, and the alveolar process is decaying.

Wonder who ate the meat of that dead cow. Where the teeth were decayed, the flesh was also in an inferior condition.

The black spots which you see, are spots showing the decay as it had commenced and would soon have been more rotten than it was, if the butcher had not stepped in and prevented.

Mr. Burdell found that all of the cows fed on these slops were diseased in the teeth.

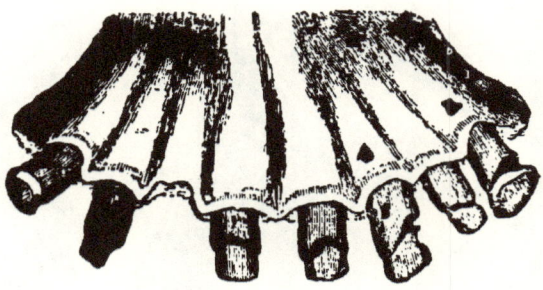

FIG. 7.

Showing condition of teeth of cows fed on "still slops."

Let us ask you a question. Do you think it makes any difference what you eat?

Do you think you can digest all the swill that any of the boarding-house keepers may get up for you and yet you may remain perfectly healthy? We tell you it is impossible for you to do this thing.

The food you eat has an influence on you. You may be a saint. If you eat the hog you may be sure that the natural law will give you a return for that eating of the hog and you will be diseased.

If you drink coffee you will suffer as sure as you live.

Figure 8 is another cut showing the various stages of decay.

We see the teeth as they are in the jaw.

At 2 we see the decay on the outside of the tooth and we can see an internal ulcer at the root of the tooth. There are also ulcers at the roots of 5, 6, 8 and 9. 2 and 9 are the worst. 3 is a healthy tooth. 7 is just commencing to decay; so is 4. 5 is on the way to become a bad tooth.

Kindly note that this is not a fancy picture. It is made

from life, and the person died from some other disease than the toothache.

But it is a condition that is prevalent in thousands of people to-day.

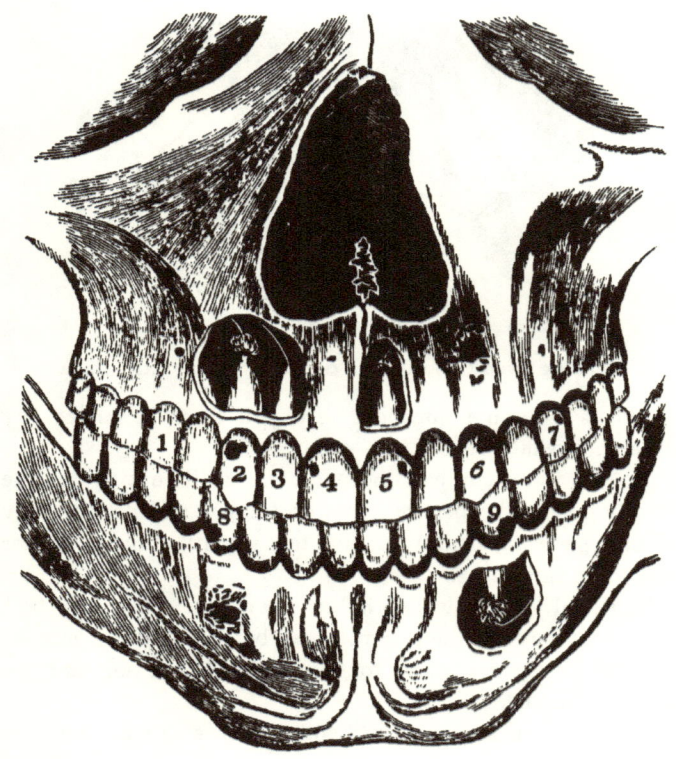

FIG. 8.

Figure 8 shows the condition of teeth in their various stages of decay. In 1 there is a small cavity and also a spot to show where there is a corresponding commencing congestion at the root of the tooth. The ulceration of the roots (or the fangs of the teeth, as they are sometimes called) is well shown in 2, 5, 6, 8 and 9. This figure also shows the conditions which we have often asserted to be the fact, viz.: that the teeth decay at the roots before they show their decay on the outside of the teeth.

There is more unhappiness, more anguish and more solid agony than one can estimate.

There are more dentists and things called dentists than anything else except doctors.

Do they do any good ?

Well, that depends on what you call good.

Why should one get in this condition?

Our idea is that you ought to study some for yourself and for your children and not allow the common laws of nature to be so illy understood.

Why should you not understand the laws of your being ?

And what is the use of your allowing these laws to be in obscurity, when by a little exertion you could find them out and have these laws serve to give you a happy and contented old age ?

Think of this for a moment.

This medical professor said it did not matter what we ate, as digestion was a "physiological law." Thousands of doctors will tell you the same nonsense to-day.

But the cow that had to eat the "still slops" said by her teeth that this medical professor was a liar.

The teeth do not decay for nothing. There is a cause for that decay.

You have thirty-two teeth in your head (or you will have when you get them all. The four wisdom teeth do not always come through at the age of twenty-one), and do you not think it would be better for you take care of those teeth to-day than to wait until they have begun to decay ? Now you are a young lady with your future before you. Do you not think there is much more sense in your learning about those teeth than in crochetting or in playing euchre ?

Oh, the anguish and the wretchedness you can prevent by understanding these laws of eating.

Take a moment to think why these teeth decay.

The cow's teeth decayed, (1) because there was not suffi-cient tooth nourishment, and (2) because the teeth of the cow had come in contact with dead blood corpuscles.

Very well. You have been to school and you can see

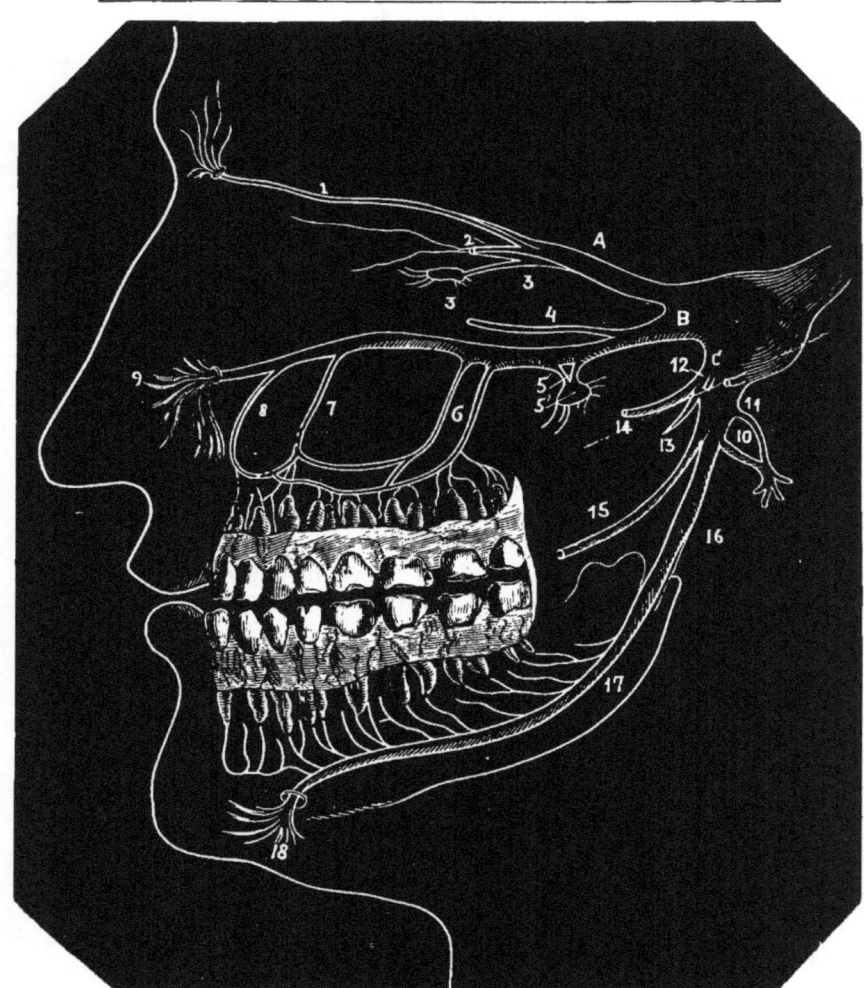

FIG. 9.
"Keep Your Teeth Clean."
BRANCHES OF FIFTH NERVE.

A. Ophthalmic division.—1. Frontal. 2. Nasal and long ciliary. 3. Branches to ciliary ganglion.

B. Superior maxillary division.—4. Orbital. 5. Sphenopalatine (Meckel's) ganglion. 6. Posterior dental. 7-8. Anterior dental. 9. Infra-orbital.

C. Inferior maxillary division.—10. Auriculo-temporal. 11. Masseteric. 12. Deep temporal. 13. Pterygoid. 14. Buccal to buccinator, etc. 15. Gustatory. 16. Mylo-hyoid branch. 17. Inferior dental. 18. Mental.

This cut shows the connections with the various nerves which are connected with the teeth. By a little reflection you will see that any battery which would commence in the teeth would affect all the brain in general as well as the eyes, the ears and the face in particular. It also shows how the amalgam filling, when it gets to working as a battery, will cause the twitching and the jerking of the muscles of the face and the eyes. This is seen in various ways and has been experienced by thousands of victims. When the dentist assures you that the quicksilver filling is all right, you can retain your presence of mind and say nothing. But you will know, if you think and take the testimony of other victims who have been duped and are the sufferers, that when the dentist utters this assertion he is guilty of one of the meanest of falsehoods which he could utter.

what is the reason why we have the condition of the teeth shown in figure 8.

First, there is not sufficient tooth material.

Second, there are particles of blood made from a food which is of the same nature as the still slops of the city-fed cow. And this slop makes blood clots in the arteries, and produces ulceration.

Do you desire to have good blood? To continue to have good teeth?

The blood must continually be in good order.

To eat good food, such as will nourish the body, is one of the essentials of good teeth.

Are you careless about your personal appearance and do not care whether you have good teeth or not? Then eat everything that is in your way, and suck the sweet candies, the cakes, the tea and the coffee, and we will promise you that with all the care you may take of the teeth and all the "Sozodont" and the other fraudulent tooth powders you may squander money for, you will have the condition of teeth shown in cut 8 or worse. One other idea that the writer desires to impress upon you is the fact that *all the baking powders*, without any exception, are destroyers of tooth material.

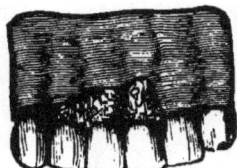

FIG. 10.

Tartar on teeth.

FIG. 11.

Tartar removed.

Consider the condition of the teeth shown at 2, 5 and 9, and, also, think of the corresponding condition of the blood of the body.

What do you think caused that condition of the roots of the teeth?

We can tell you.

Filth.

Internal filth.

The blood was not in good order, and, in some portions of the body, blood corpuscles died and became burdens to the living corpuscles.

At the roots of the teeth some of these blood corpuscles clogged and prevented the good or living blood from having a complete circulation. Dead blood corpuscles. Obstruction. Putrefaction followed and the condition which is shown to you came on, and the teeth decay and the jaw is affected while the entire alveolar process is aching because of this stagnation of the blood. It does not matter where that filth may be. You may take a glass of soda water.

What is that soda water made of ?

Filth.

All the pop, ginger ale, "cool drinks," coffee, tea, chocolate, cocoa shells and the whole category of stuff that is swilled down one's throat in summer, are simply vile.

They make degraded blood. This material can not, by any possible change, make good blood.

If there is not good blood there will be no sound tooth material, and it is only a question of time when these teeth go to decay.

Take another very common occurrence. Tartar on the teeth. What makes it ?

The food one eats has as much to do with this condition as any one thing, although the medicine which is commonly given has a great deal of effect on the teeth.

Eating candy, drinking warm drinks, especially sweetened coffee and tea, are direct producers of the tartar.

The saliva is vitiated and tartar is deposited.

When you go to the dentist he will very glibly talk to you of "salivary calculus," for when one gets into a conversation with one of these professional people they have a technical name and the technical name for tartar is "salivary calculus," and he will tell you that it is "composed of earthy salts and animal matter." But there are quite a number of differing kinds of tartar and none of the kinds are alike in composition and none of them are to be desired.

One of the causes may arise from keeping the mouth open. But the main reason comes from the fact that the food eaten is not digested and the saliva is not used up in chewing the food properly.

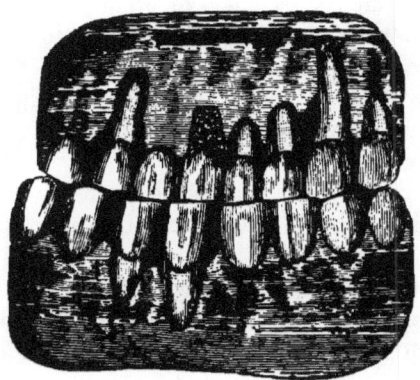

FIG. 12.

Showing roots being gradually uncovered from various causes, *i. e.: hot coffee* and *tea*, candy, sweets, and "*cool drinks.*"

The saliva joins with the remains of a meal and tartar is formed and sticks to the teeth. When once there is a lodgment of tartar it soon accumulates.

Some kinds of tartar are not so bad as some others, but there is no kind of tartar beneficial to the teeth.

The sweets of the candies are one of the causes of the formation of tartar. These sweets soften the enamel of the tooth and leave it in an enfeebled condition which is favorable to the formation of tartar.

We sincerely believe that breathing through the mouth has a deleterious effect on the teeth, but we do not think it is of so much real injury to the teeth as the substances eaten. And you will notice that in all cases of tartar the saliva is affected before there is any deposition of tartar. In other words, the *saliva being vitiated* by improper food is the *first cause of the tartar.*

While you are young this tartar may be removed and the teeth not suffer much, but as you get older this tartar is of more detriment and is more pernicious to the teeth.

It should be taken off carefully and the teeth taken care of until the hardness is again restored.

If, at this time you care less of what you eat, you may be sure this condition of tartar will reappear to show you the results of certain kinds of food.

We think what you eat to be of more importance than what you may wear.

Consider a moment.

If what you may eat affects the teeth, do you not think what you may eat will also affect the other parts of the body ?

We assure you that every particle that is put into your mouth is of more real importance to you in your life on this earth than anything that may be said about you or yours.

When the selected grains, the fruits and vegetables which are grown from the soil, are eaten, you are quite sure you have the basis of a sound body.

The moment the meats and fats of dead animals are mixed up in the pastries which may taste good, but are really hurtful, and you change the vegetables for these uncertain compounds, you are not sure of what your body is composed.

If your body is diseased, you may rest assured your mind is likely to be impaired.

If you have a diseased body and an impaired mind, are you going to be of much value to yourself or to anyone else ?

Do not take this as a scolding, but think it over for your own good.

We desire you to be benefited and to be perfectly healthy and happy.

From what we have already written it will be seen that the teeth commence to decay *from the inside*, and the cause of that inside decay lies in the lack of sufficient nourishment for the tooth.

This tooth nourishment should come from oatmeal, cracked wheat, graham bread, nuts of all kinds, acorns; and a thorough and total avoidance of candies, sugar, pastries, coffee, tea, and cocoa or chocolate.

But if this does not reach you in time to save your teeth, and the cavities are already in your teeth, the best method of preserving is to fill them.

If the shell only is left and the decay is extended through *chemically*, that is, if the chemical effect of food, drink, and the acids of the mouth has supplemented the decay *from the inside*, then it is best to have the tooth extracted. Have courage to have it cut around carefully and have it pulled.

If only a little decayed, have it filled as early as practicable.

The fillings which are most common are gold and the amalgam.

Gold is the best filling. "Soft fillings," so called, are soon out and have to be replaced.

The amalgam filling is composed of mercury (commonly known as quicksilver), and is mixed with tin, copper, cadmium, and other metals, which, when mixed, form the basis of a galvanic battery, which is always in order as long as there are any fluids in the mouth.

The dentist commonly calls this a "silver filling," but when he calls this a silver filling, he knows very well that he is presuming on your ignorance and is going to swindle you in the matter of your tooth filling.

We should understand by the term "silver," that it is a metal which is like our silver dollar. But such is not the fact, and the dentist knows you will be deceived by this, for there will not be one particle of the silver in this filling which he calls silver, but there will be *quicksilver*, which is of a different nature, and a different mineral altogether.

This filling of this common amalgam is of the most dangerous character to the mouth and to the whole body.

It destroys the eyes; destroys the ears; destroys the intellect and renders the one who has, this unfortunate filling in the teeth a victim to the action of a slow decay, which has to be seen to be appreciated.

It is one of the common causes of loss of memory, loss of the faculty of thinking clearly on any subject, and of the feeling of despair or downheartedness, that has ever been invented by any person on the earth. We assure you that we have seen suicides made from the presence of this filling.

We have seen, while this book is in preparation, a man, a physician, having these fillings in the teeth, have a swelling in the throat, and the doctors did not know what was the matter, and an old woman of a doctor called it a cancer, and the man died from the effect of this amalgam filling which he had worn some eight or ten years.

It does not do its work in a moment. The filling will get settled and then the system may resist the encroachments of this battery for many years, but the end will come and then the brain will be ruined.

There is no doubt but the great majority of dentists know of these facts in the main, but the desire to make a dollar is too strong for their honesty, and they are in the habit of uttering these deceitful lies so that it comes out of their mouth before they can think of the effect of their falsehoods.

This battery is made in the teeth, but the effect is not confined to the teeth by any means. The current is sent to all parts of the body and often the young lady will think there is a slight deafness coming on, which is the result of this current from the teeth.

The eyes become weak and there is such a feeling of despondency that it is hard to overcome it. And we think we know of a lovely girl who threw herself in a well for no other cause than the melancholy which came from the presence of this poison and electrical filling in her teeth. She was not killed by her attempt to commit suicide, and afterwards as her consulting physician we had these amalgam fillings removed, and then she slowly recovered.

The current begins in the teeth but it is sent into all parts of the brain. From the brain this current affects the spinal cord, and there is often a weakness which the doctor who does not look at the cause of things, attributes to what he has been taught in his school to think is "female disease," and the young lady is subjected to a brutal treatment for a disease which there was no sign of and which the doctor should have learned the nature of before he left school.

Unfortunately, the age is one of dishonesty, and thus the young lady should learn of these facts for herself and shun the dictates and the pompous assertions of the doctors and the dentists. Be at once aware that when the dentist is telling you of the "silver filling," he is trying to deceive you, and when he is allowed to place this filling in your mouth, he will place something in the mouth which will ruin the rest of the teeth while it may stop up a cavity at the present.

But, even as a filling for the cavity in the tooth, it is not really of benefit. The amalgam slowly hardens after it is mixed, and while it cools, it shrinks, then this will leave a hollow place around the amalgam filling and the tooth will not be filled. The places which will be left around the filling and between the tooth and the filling, will fill up with the food and the acids of the mouth, and there will be a horrible breath arising from this tooth filling which will often make the young lady to wish she had no teeth whatever. And the worst of it will be when she tries this and that and there will nothing do her any good for her bad breath, and finally, she will lose all the teeth on that side of her jaw.

We assure you this is a part of the fact, but we could not tell you all of the mischief which these fillings do nor all of the injury which are resulting from these fillings, if we should attempt to place this book full of statements.

Should you have been so unfortunate as to have lost some of your teeth and be obliged to wear a plate of some kind, we caution you against wearing the plate which is said to be of the common red rubber.

It is also called "Vulcanite," but goes by the name of "red rubber" almost wholly. This so-called "red rubber" is not red rubber at all. This compound is composed of: quicksilver, 24 parts; sulphur, 36 parts; rubber, 40 parts. The quicksilver and the sulphur form the bi-sulphuret of mercury,

E

and this poisonous compound is at once ruinous to the mouth, the teeth and the general health.

How many, many women we have seen killed and how many invalids we have known who were invalids from the wearing of this villainous plate which looks so harmless.

Do not, under any circumstances, allow yourself to have a red rubber plate. Be content to go without any plate until you can get to an honest dentist who can make you a gold plate. Or have a black rubber, which is not so totally offensive to your health and so ruinous to the brain as this bi-sulphurous mixture which is so common and so filthy.

You may rest assured of one thing which you will find of much advantage in all of your dealings with the dentists. That is, that owing to their education, to their habits of training to get a dollar from their patrons, they will not tell you the exact truth in relation to the matters which concern their profession. They take you for game, to get and to hold, and the fine honor which prompts one "to do to another as one would that others should do unto them" is almost unknown among the dental fraternity. There are some exceptions, but they are few, and when you find one that will tell you the truth, he should be prized.

This reminds us that there is no profession which is so lucrative and so readily open to the young ladies at the present, as the dental profession. When you enter this branch, do it with the understanding that you are going to do good as well as to earn a livelihood.

A lady dentist is not uncommon, but we think the men are usually afraid of her, and if they can get her to join their society and keep up her prices so that they can cut under her in the way of work, they will do it every time.

Get your diploma and then start out for your own self and do not allow any one to dominate over you.

It demands some skill, but is essentially a lady's profession. There is room at the present for, at the least, five thousand dentists to take the place of these villains who are robbing the people with their amalgam fillings and these villainous bi-sulphurous plates which they style red rubber.

We hope this will set you to thinking there is something for you to do in this world and to fill your niche with credit to yourself and good to the poor, ignorant young persons who may intrust themselves to your care.

So shall you be blessed.

The teeth should be cleaned after every meal and upon rising, as well as when going to bed.

Do not use a wooden toothpick under any circumstances, as the splinters from this wood will get into the flesh and cause inflammation of the gums. Use a quill toothpick, if you need to use any. But if the teeth are far enough apart to get a stout floss thread between the teeth and draw this thread between the teeth to clean out anything left there from the meals, it will be better than any toothpick whatever.

The common tooth washes are destructive to the teeth and should be avoided. Even charcoal, which is said to be the best of all the powders for the teeth, is an abomination to the enamel and should only be used when absolutely necessary.

We think a brush, which has a trifle of soap on it, and clean soft water, are enough to take out all of the bacteria from the mouth, as well as to take off all the outside covering which should be taken off at one time. If there is care taken as to what is eaten there will soon come the whitest of teeth which are tough and solid. Keep the teeth and the body well supplied with *tooth nourishment* in the shape of coarse food and nuts, and keep the teeth clean by a soft brush and we can assure you that you will have sound teeth for all of your natural life.

CHAPTER VII.

THE MENSES.

About the age of twelve or fourteen, according to the precocity and condition of the girl, there comes a discharge which is commonly called the "menses," or the courses, or the flow.

This is also called a "show," "regular," and among some of the people who make a great effort to be chary of speech, they designate it by the name of "company."

Briefly. this discharge is a provision of nature to carry off the excess of blood which, possibly, will be used up by and by in the sustenance of a growing child.

It is certain this discharge will not and does not occur if there is no surplus of blood or of something which should be discharged from the system.

We may compare this discharge to an overflow of the animal economy, which occurs at regular intervals and leaves the woman clean and pure in her body.

This should be the case. But. unfortunately for the woman. there have been so many theories, that no girl who does not have this discharge in some prescribed quantity, is safe from the meddling effects of the fond mother and the malicious, ignorant doctor, that it is seldom a girl is safe during the commencing period of the menses. We say "malicious." because there is usually no need of any interference. But the doctor, to earn his fee, and because he does not know any better, will give a parcel of drugs, and advise some poison stuff to be taken into the body which is detrimental to the body, when there should be none of these things placed in the stomach to force or to drive out a discharge which, possibly, is not there.

In other words, there should be no forcing medicines given to any girl to force this discharge when it is possible there is no excess of blood in the system.

Take for example. If you have a glass which is half full

it would not run over if there was quite a little more poured into it. But if the glass were filled with water and only a very small quantity were poured into it there would be a running over. So we may explain the discharge which comes on with a great degree of regularity, if the woman is in good health, but which is stopped if there are any obstructions which prevent the excess of blood in the body.

For instance: If there are worms in the body there will not be as much discharge into the vagina as there would be if there were no worms.

This is also seen; if there is any open sore on the surface of the body. While this sore lasts, there will be not so much of his menstrual discharge as if there were no open sore on the body.

So, if the young lady takes cold at this time of the discharge, the discharge is liable to be obstructed by this cold condition of the system and the discharge will be scanty. It is at this critical period where so many young ladies are ruined by taking medicine to regulate a function of nature which nature knows better how to regulate and to manage than the doctors or the persons who are always minding other people's business.

This may be said to be so literally true that we assert that any young lady who is in her sound mind should never have any medicine for the stoppage of this discharge. Never.

If this discharge stops at some time, there is some reason for this discharge, there will be some reason for its stopping. Ascertain this cause of its cessation.

If there is a cold in the system, clear out the cold.

If there are worms, send the worms out of the body. If there is too much exercise or too much mental exertion, it is quite certain there will be a scanty discharge; while if there has been some heavy lifting, it is also quite possible there will be an excess or an overflow from some strain, or, possibly, from some actual rupture of some tender blood vessel in the uterus. These excessive flows are called "flooding"; also called "menorrhagia." When there is no discharge from any cause, it is called "amenorrhea."

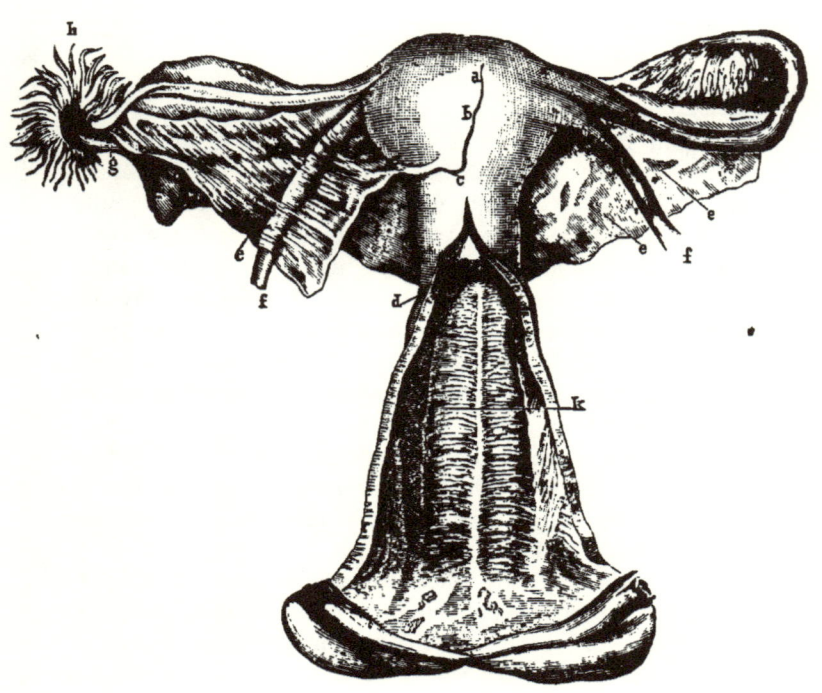

FIG. 13.

Reproductive Organs of Female. Unimpregnated Uterus and Appendages. *a.* Inner membrane. *d.* Os uteri. *c.* Upper part of vagina. *f.* Round ligament. *g.* Fallopian tube. *h.* Fimbriated extremity. *k.* Lining of vagina.

Perhaps there has been no state which has been so prolific of evil to the growing girl as this state of non-menstruation. The mother thinking this "flow" must be brought about at any hazard, goes to the doctor and gets some forcing medicine, and thus she poisons the child she tries to help. She thinks if this discharge is once started all the wheels of life will go smoothly. But the fact is, that this is not the proper way to look at the condition of menstruation. Menstruation is not the act of a motor; it is the result of an excess in the system, and if there is no excess there, there would not be any discharge to be expelled.

There are, at present, two theories to account for the menstrual discharge. The first one is by Pfluger, who asserts that the uterus is being prepared for the reception of the ovum (or egg), and when this egg is brought from the ovary to the uterus there will be a fresh surface and a membrane which will be ready to have sustenance to the egg, in case there is any pregnancy. This view would receive confirmation from the fact that there is always the discharge before the ovum is ready to leave the ovary. When the menses are over then the egg comes into the uterus and stays there for some six to twelve days.

The other theory is that of Reichert who thinks there is a sympathetic condition of the lining of the uterus and that when the ovum is ready to be discharged there is a corresponding change in the mucous membrane of the uterus and when the ovum comes into the uterus and is not impregnated there is a degeneracy of this lining membrance of the uterus, and this degenerate lining of the mucous membrane is discharged with the amount of blood which is called the menstrual discharge.

There are cases of women in perfect health who never menstruated and yet have borne children. Instances of this kind are rare, but are of sufficient frequency to show that such a state can exist with perfect health. If a girl is in perfect health and does not menstruate, there is no call for medicine. The body is well. Let it alone.

Painful menstruation is often caused by the mouth of the

womb being contracted, and sometimes from the congested and contracted state of the fallopian tubes.

This may be brought about by cold; by corsets; by improper food, and from lack of proper exercise. The corset is the most frequent cause of painful menstruation. This steel prison holds the bowels in such a shape that there is constipation, and then the watery parts of the feces are carried into the general circulation. The womb absorbs this material which should pass off out of the bowels, and the retained material causes the menses to be painful, and also of a dark color, and very offensive. The womb is congested with these dead materials. It is in a cold state. The habit of retaining the urine is also another reason of there being foul materials in the womb. When the menstrual discharge takes place, nature, or the vital force, endeavors to expel these foul elements which are to be passed off from the body, and this effort causes the contraction of the uterus and the consequent pain as well as the villainous smell which accompanies the discharge.

This condition of things will soon be changed if the young lady who is now a victim to ignorance, will wear low-heeled shoes, dress warmly and take a walk each day as soon as it is light enough to see. We have seen this tried and we can say it is better than all the medicine which the doctors have in their drug stores. The habit of wearing tight and too small shoes which do not fit the foot is another reason why there is painful menstruation. All the blood goes from the heart to the extremities. When this blood from the heart reaches the feet and finds the feet and the capillaries so that it can not get through into the veins, there is some of the blood corpuscles which die and then there are some of these corpuscles which must be carried off out of the system. These dead and now cold blood corpuscles are carried back into the kidneys or into the general circulation and find themselves in the kidneys and thus the kidneys are clogged; there is some obstruction and the back aches with an ache that is almost unbearable. If, in this condition, the young lady is so unfortunate as to take some preparation of opium or laudanum, she will have a serious case of heart trouble, or some derangement of the digestive tract which is liable to last her as long as she lives.

If this condition is present with the young miss we will stop and tell her how to get out of it and not hurt the body.

The feet have been cramped and as these dead corpuscles are from the feet and the feet are the outposts of the body, so to speak, the blood corpuscles have been killed in the feet and passed up as dead blood corpuscles and are detained in the uterus. The habit of soaking the feet in warm water is one of the best things to do in such cases, since it sets these dead blood corpuscles free again, and restores the circulation. Then take some of the warming and stimulating infusions which are well known and commonly used among the well-informed mothers, as pennyroyal, mayweed, motherwort, or spearmint with ginger. These bland remedies will produce a perspiration and so induce the flow of the amount which should be expelled. In any ordinary amount these infusions can not hurt the body of the young lady. A rest in a warm place should be considered one of the most imperative of conditions. Keep the entire body warm and allow no chill as long as there is any flow. If any constipation use copious injections of warm water to the bowels. Make them large. Say two to four quarts and repeat them every six hours if the parts are not relaxed. Resume the daily quick cold bath when the flow is over, and we can soon promise immunity from all this unnecessary pain during the menstrual period. One of the methods by which the doctor has to obviate what is called "painful menstruation," is to examine the girl with a speculum and to force the mouth of the womb open with the end of a steel which he calls a "sound." This is a steel instrument about a foot long and smooth and rather pointed and it is quite effectual in opening the mouth of the womb so there is no more pain, but it also, in many cases, destroys the ability of having children and also destroys much of the powers of life. Nature will open the womb all right if you will give her an opportunity to have

some assistance or to keep her from being clogged up with
dead blood corpuscles.

Another great cause of so much painful menstruation, is
from the fact that the food is wrong and causes constipation ;
and also from the fact of these little shoes with high heels being
worn which cramp the feet into a mass of non-circulating
medium, and throw the body forward out of its proper erect
position. This will be plainer to you when you consider that
the feet are the farthest away from the heart, and the warm
blood comes from the heart and goes to all parts of the body
and then returns to the heart and to the lungs again for what
is called oxygenation and purification. Now, if on the way
to the heart in any place that blood is stopped, some of this
stopped and delayed blood will die, and instead of their being live blood corpuscles, there will be dead blood corpuscles.
These dead blood corpuscles are really enemies to the live
body and must be carried off out of the body before the
body can be in good order again to do anything as it should
be done. So there is an effort to carry off these dead particles, and there is some effort on the part of the vital
force which is in the body to carry off these dead blood corpuscles. This effort is called a fever. While this effort,
which is called a fever, is taking place, there are some of the
other corpuscles which are used up in the endeavor to carry off
these dead corpuscles, and so there are two sets of dead blood
corpuscles, one set which has been killed by the cold, or com-
pression, and the others which are dead through exhaustion.
These dead blood corpuscles are some of the things and
some of the material which are carried off out of the system
by what is called the menstrual discharge. And it is this
theory which makes the mother so anxious when her daughter
is not regular with the monthly discharge.

This is the correct view to take of the importance of the
discharge when this discharge is solely for the purpose of
carrying off all filthy and dead material in the body.

But it is *not* the correct thing to think of in some other
cases where there is some delay in producing this discharge,
when nature is using up this discharge in some other locality

of the body. In other words, if the girl is exhausted by her studies, she will use up all the surplus blood and there will be none of this surplus to be carried off out of the body.

But when there is an excess there will be some way for nature to be rid of it. And it is likely at that time to be carried off through the uterus. This will be, when there is much of a flow, called a "profuse discharge." It is one of the conditions which certainly does not need so much medicine as it does the regulating of the system so as to see that the body is to be free from any of the dead blood corpuscles which we have spoken of. We think these dead blood corpuscles are, in a great measure, produced by the conditions which we have just mentioned,—cold, and cramped feet.

The feet are pinched by the common-senseless shoes and so the blood corpuscles die and remain in the system.

They go to the heart, and nature, or the vital force, sends them to some place to be thrown out of the body. Then, when the time comes for the menstrual discharge there will be some obstruction and the flow will not progress and the womb will be congested or cooled from the presence of these dead blood corpuscles and while nature is making this effort to carry off this effete matter there will come some message from the uterus to the effect that the womb will not open and there is what is called a *pain*.

A pain is a telegraph message from some part to the effect that there is some obstruction in that place.

It is at this point where so many of the young ladies of the present day receive their death blow to all hopes of a future health and a career of future happiness.

The doctor is seen for this "painful menstruation," which comes from the presence of dead blood corpuscles, and this doctor gives something to lull the pain; but he does not give you any idea of what makes this condition of painful menstruation and he does not really do any good for the next time; in fact this doctor really makes the next time worse.

With his poisons he will make the condition of the body worse by killing more of these important blood corpuscles.

In the first place there was a pain which was a message

from the parts to the effect that there was some obstruction to the flow, because there were dead blood corpuscles at the mouth of the womb and in fact in all the womb, and these dead blood corpuscles were obstructing the flow.

These dead blood corpuscles were once alive and were killed in the presence of the too-tight shoe which did not give the blood a chance to circulate in the foot and so it died in the foot. Then it was dead. The feet were cold and so the blood corpuscles were unable to go back to the heart of themselves and had to be carried back. Then there was an effort on the part of nature to carry them back and this effort was called a fever, and the doctor did not know what a fever was and so killed down the vital force with aconite or with belladonna, and when the discharge came on there would be an amount of pain which was unbearable.

The doctor, instead of thinking out this matter and realizing the exact cause of this painful menstruation, gives a poison which makes more of these dead blood corpuscles and so makes the body in a worse condition than it was in the first place. The next time there would be more of these dead blood corpuscles and the womb would be in a more congested state than it was before and so there would be more pain.

The proper way is to relax the parts, and, as we have seen, this is best done by soaking the feet and by the use of warm infusions which will tend to keep the blood in good circulation. When this discharge is over, the time is come to prepare for the next period, and this is best done by having wide, comfortable shoes, and by warm stockings, and by all the dress that is necessary to keep all the parts thoroughly warm and from any changes of atmosphere. For this reason we say, in the winter have all the clothes, especially the underwear, closed up so there will be no chance to have any cold air strike the lower part of the bowels while out of doors. The great cause of what are called "growths" and conditions of the womb by which there is so much of misery and there is so much sickness among women, and there is so prevalent a form of what is called "female disease" is produced from this cause of dead blood corpuscles. And these dead blood corpuscles come in a large majority of cases from tight shoes, because these tight shoes do not allow the free circulation of blood. Also from cold to the bowels, from insufficient clothing to the lower parts of the bowels. And while this cold is supposed to affect especially the womb, there will be some of this cold which will be detrimental to the intestines as well as to the womb.

There will be likely to be some trouble with the urine and this affection can in many instances be dated from some cold to the lower part of the bowels and some dead blood corpuscles which are killed by the action of cold.

It will be said that in some countries there is none of this trouble. This is true. But in all of these nations where there is very little of this painful menstruation there is a better class of food and there are none of the things which are detrimental to the body as are the articles of food and drink as we have them in America. These articles which are the most useless and the most clogging to the system, and which do as much harm to the body as anything else are the baking powders, the potatoes, the pork, the tea, the coffee and pastry. These articles are truly blood destroyers and they are the real prime causes of so much trouble among the female part of our nation.

These mentioned articles of diet can not by any means make good blood, and the corpuscles of blood which are made from these articles, if the corpuscles can be made from these articles (we deny that tea, coffee, baking powders can make any blood corpuscles, as there is nothing in them to make anything like a blood corpuscle; they are killers), and, as a consequence, when there is any chill these corpuscles which come from these articles are weak and are more readily killed by the cold than the corpuscles which are made from bread and from fruits. In other words, we say that there is certainly some difference in blood which is made from the different kinds of food. And the food which is made from the biscuit, the hot bread, the cake and the stuff which is on the modern table as food (ham and eggs, for instance) can not by any means make as good food as that which is made from good wheat and good oatmeal and rye and cornmeal. These grains are the natural food of this country, and oysters, pork and the tuberculosis cow are unfit food to have when the body is growing up into the shape where one wishes to live for a hundred years.

If this body of ours is to be kept free from pain and from all of its aches and distresses there must be some attention given to the first beginnings of the life, and not wait until the head is ready to drop into the grave with consumption before this attention is given. So we return and say, if there is to be any opening of the womb, do it by natural methods, and the great method of nature is to have exercise. The daily walk is much better to open any obstructed part of the body than any of the operations of cold steel which are just now in vogue. Take the daily walk in the morning and keep yourself properly clad and there will soon be a cessation of all painful menstruation. The womb will soon be in its place that is daily exercised and kept warm and comfortable. But not alone the womb, but all the other organs of the body will be out of place and in a miserable condition where they are not taken care of and are chilled so that there are more dead blood corpuscles in these organs than there are live corpuscles.

There is no need of iron or wine to force the menses if the body is kept in good order. There is no need of any doctor to experiment on you if you will only pay attention to the natural laws. If you have not already learned of these laws, the sooner you pay some attention to them the better for your body, and the better for your mind.

The basis of a good body is good food and correct habits. The next thing in order is to have the body properly clad. Tight shoes, corsets, constipation, tea and coffee, meats, pastry, candies and exposure of the lower parts of the body to all the changes of the atmosphere will surely ruin any constitution, no matter how well that constitution was put up in the first place. The habit of allowing the skirts to drag on the lower part of the hips is another of the follies of this day. Have all of the weight that is possible over the shoulders and see that the bowels have good room to do their important work. These are important points. They are only touched. You are to some extent the chooser whether you desire to be well or ill. And upon your own conduct will your body depend. God has given you the body which He saw proper for you to have and which will be the best for your mind to dwell in. You are the one who will decide whether there will be a good body or a body which will be diseased and filled with pain. We tell you that if you obey the natural laws of life there is much of happiness in this world. But if you think all the fashion and all the things which society and the stare of fools can give, are compensations for the pain which your body can be made to feel, then stick to society and throw this book in the fire. If you desire to be free from all of this common pain and these delusions which are unhappiness, then we say to you, study out the laws of your own being and see where the One who has seen and fashioned you before you were born, has shown you the right way to live without any pain and without any of this misery which is so freely bestowed on those who will not obey the laws of nature. Do not think of any single rule to go by. Study out these laws and have a clear understanding with nature,* so that when anything comes up which is foreign to your present knowledge there will be law to go by, and you will have the law of being in your head, and so you will have something to go by and not have to go to a doctor whose business it is to make money at your expense.

Think of these things and ask the God who made you to so open the eyes that you can see better than anyone else what is good for your body and what you shall do to get rid of all the impurities of the body. If you do this, the mind will be better and the body will be the house wherein you can worship God and feel as if there would never come a time when you could not depend on that body to make the bread needed for you and the children to eat.

If you have a good body there is every likelihood there

will be a sound mind. If your body is diseased there will be every probability that the mind will become so weakened that you will be a slave to someone else, and so drop into a slave's grave. You will never commence any earlier than to-day to commence this new life. You know all of your failings as well as any one in the world and if you are to commence there will be never any better time when you can commence to improve this body than the time which is called *right now*.

CHAPTER VIII.

YOUR INNER SELF.

Any day you may choose, you may go along the street and see some face which has all the symptoms of disease and the peculiar sallow cast which is so disagreeable to the eye of one who understands what that sallow look indicates.

You may also, at the same time, see some face which to you is beautiful. The forehead will be broad, large, smooth and clear, and the eyes are clear, limpid, full of expression and intelligence.

If you have some thought about you it will naturally occur to you to ask yourself why there can be so great a difference in the complexions and the countenances of the different people.

To explain these differences is the work of this chapter.

Up to the time of eight or ten years of age there is usually a smooth, clear countenance in almost every child. After that age there is a muddying of some countenances and a further clearing up and a gain of intelligence in the faces of some others.

The muddy countenance denotes, in brief, that the blood corpuscles are in a disordered condition.

The clear countenance denotes that there are certain things about the blood that keep everything in the body in the best of order. Or, in other words, the blood, which is the life, is in the condition which is able to do the best by the body, by keeping it in good order. The countenance is simply an index which God has made so that anyone should never be mistaken about the persons one meets. It is an index of health and it is also an index of the character. An index of the thought as well as of the habits of the possessor of the body that carries such a face.

The body, then, is the real cause of the style of face which meets one on the street. As one keeps the body so is

F

the face to be. To look nice, is to have this body in the best condition. To have the looks of disease, is to have some taint of body which the body will impress on the surface, in spite of all the powders and paints in existence.

The great thing which tells on the face of early womanhood, or of an adult, sooner than any one thing in life, is the lack of perfect sexual control.

This is said as deliberately as one can say it. We tell you that upon your thorough control of the sexual organs your face and your intelligence will largely depend. May we say almost *wholly depend*. Unless one is married, and even then, except at the times of desiring children, there should be no loss of sexual power. This is emphatically true of both sexes. But, as this fact is not understood, and, as these people who are engaged in so many good works have never allowed their daughters to look at any book bearing on this subject, the daughters grow up in ignorance, and so these sexual wastes occur, and occur far more often than any one can readily understand who is not constantly in the medical practice and daily witnessing the dire effects of this sexual abuse of the body.

To bring this to your notice is one thing and to tell you how to have this perfect control is another thing. We shall feel happy if we can aid you to understand this and to have the best control of all the different portions of the body.

It is said that there is much more virtue among the females than among the males. We do not think this is true. But the girl learns sooner how to control herself from the nature of her being, and sooner comes to an understanding of the general laws of nature, so that she is sooner emancipated from the passions which in some men are only eradicated by death. We are sure these passions can be and should be under perfect mental control.

In girls this passion is followed by a sexual loss and is called a loss of *nervous force* and is accompanied by an ejection of fluid which is passed under the name of *mucous*. But this is not the only loss which occurs. There is a descent of the womb each time there is any sexual feeling, and each time the womb descends it makes it easier for the descent the next time.

The habit of gratifying this passion is called self abuse. This self abuse consists in having some passion until this ejection occurs and this loss has taken place. Not alone a loss of fluid, which is the best of all fluids of the body, but a loss of force which directly draws on the general system, and weakens all the body. Where there is the perfect intercourse which may take place between the husband and wife there is something of a compensation to both parties for their respective losses, and there is no show of such devastating shocks to the nervous system as are seen in the self abuse of the unmated. In the perfectly mated parties, the female gets the semen of the male on the mouth of the womb, and this being absorbed, furnishes a share of needed fluids to lubricate the uterus so that the great loss, which would be simply destructive if yielded to alone, is not so much felt. In the single person there is no compensation and the loss is felt directly, and the body, and especially the nervous system, suffers in a manner which is frightful to witness, although there are very few who know of the reasons that cause this destruction of nerve force and its attendant mental and bodily weakness. We desire to help the reader to overcome the beginnings of this loss and so we desire you to look at the plate (Fig. 14) and pay attention to the arterial system which supplies the organs of generation in the female. The arteries are fed or come from the arteries in the interior of the body, but when they are to supply this part of the body there are special valves which open and allow the blood to pour into this system and at once there is a filling up of this system (which should be unused until marriage) and that condition which is known as a "passionate condition" is present, in which there is the utmost self-control demanded to overcome this "passionate condition" without any loss of nervous force or any of this fluid which is used by nature to lubricate the parts and to keep them from chafing. If this is seen in its simplicity, that is, if one can see this as it is, there will never be any case where the woman, who desires to be virtuous, needs to be ever overcome by anything which is called "passion," or her feelings. If this fact were known and understood, seduction would be impossible. The act of passion is only present while this system of arteries is filling these parts full of blood, and while these parts are full of blood there is passion. There can be no passion unless these parts are filled with blood. When there is no blood in these arteries, or while there is only very little blood in these parts there is no passion and one has a perfect control over all the body. When these parts are filled with blood there is the passion present, and the more the blood is poured into these parts the harder and more turgid they become and the more intensely passionate one becomes, and the sooner this loss of nervous force takes place. At the same time, the womb descends and there is a corresponding weakness that follows each act of sexual orgasm or sexual passion. The person therefore who is addicted to the habit of self abuse has a daily and constant loss of force which is dependent on the supply of blood to these arteries which supply these parts, viz.:—vaginal walls, the clitoris and the labia, etc.

More than this, the oftener this act is performed the more readily the blood flows into these arteries, and thus one act paves the way for another until the body is one mass of living waste and heated corpuscles, destructive because of the want of compensation from anywhere. The blood is heated and the tissues are weak. The mentality becomes daily weaker and more imbecile. There is also the lack of any permanent satisfaction to the body, and it follows there is such a constant sexual unrest that there is something lacking in the life of one of these persons who are abusers of their own bodies. Their life is one dreamy scene of burning passion and destructive waste which shows itself on all the body. It would be well if we could think that our own children were free from this vice, and that it is only the children of the vile and the vicious who are the parties connected with these habits so pernicious and so destructive to the human race. But alas! the fact that comes to our everyday knowledge is one which does not admit of any fond idea that our own children are guiltless of this error.

The wisest and the best, the most carefully nurtured as well as the street gamins are just as likely to have these feelings, and to yield to these feelings is only the yielding of the mental to the natural instincts of the animal.

As long as these arteries are daily filled with blood there will be the daily "passion." And to gratify this passion is only the natural propensity of the animal nature which God has implanted within each body, to be controlled by mentality. However this gratification comes, except with the most full companionship of love, reverence, sanctity, affection and law, and we may add also, the complete mateship of the opposite sex, we assert there can be no health in the body, and at each gratification there are some particles of material which are in themselves dead, and as dead materials they are passed off or passed into other portions of the body ; and as dead and inert particles they are offensive in the highest degree to the rest of the body, and while the body is in the state of driving off, or of carrying off, these dead particles, there is what is known as a fever.

The kidneys participate in this effort to get rid of these effete atoms and so the urine becomes high-colored and thicker than natural. The face assumes a muddy hue and thus the condition of the girl who abuses her body is well known to any one who can read these symptoms.

It would be naturally supposed that when one was married, or mated, there would be a stop to all of these practices. But we have known of women, it would be a misnomer to call them ladies, although they often pass for ladies where they are not known, who have been so addicted to the habit of self abuse that upon their wedding night they coaxed their husband to use his fingers upon them for an hour before the orgasm could be produced, and this passion was followed by a hysterical spasm. The fact also remains to all who can read the faces on the street, that there are too many of these dead countenances among the married to allow of all being at rest among them. We know this by their faces if not from their own confessions. But their own confessions are not wanting. When we hear a couple saying that they do not want any children, we may know, as reasonably as if we saw their daily acts, that they do something to prevent the children from appearing.

This something is not to have perfect sexual intercourse, which criminal act is done in many ways, or else they are abusers of themselves, which is the same thing. The body is cheated and destruction follows. If the married woman does not have the intercourse perfect, she will lack the needed moisture on the womb, and when the orgasm takes place without this semen on the womb, there is a direct loss of power to her without any compensation, which in the shortest space of time kills her body for sexual enjoyment. She becomes absolutely filled with dead and offensive material which nature tries to send out of the body. She is as bad as when she abused herself and the punishment comes as swiftly, in the shape of "female weakness" and of "womb disease" which are so common all over the civilized world. As for the man who is guilty of this practice, we can learn what God thought of it by reading the history of "Onan." God cursed him and placed him among the dead at once.

To-day God places these Onanites among the dead, and we have an abundance of evidence to this effect when we look around us and see the persons who are dead in mind and still apparently exist in the flesh of some rotten body. Of course it is a shame to speak of these things; but what shall we do?

Not so long ago we saw a minister who declared he did not want any more children and that when his wife did not "come around" he gave her an injection of warm water so as to bring her "around." The woman was, no doubt, "brought around," as they had no children. This minister, a regular priest in the Episcopal church, was sore eyed and his throat was continually sore. But when this writer, in the humility of reverence to the powers that be and full of personal respect to this particular man, asked him if that was not murder, this priest said there was "no life there."

After a time this man saw his error, but it was too late, and he went down to death in his prime of life. The woman narrowly escaped with her life. We mention this fact, and might bring up a thousand like it from our own personal observation, to show that the loss of this nervous force is one of the things which is ruining the civilized world to-day. It may be said that this passion is natural and should be gratified, and as all the animals are gratified so should the human animal. This is an assertion which is sometimes made among the persons who are unacquainted with the habits of animals and are perfectly ignorant of the physiological effects of this sexual loss to the body. The animal allows the habit of the mate at certain times, and after that there is no approach allowed by the female. The human being, from causes which are attributed to the usages of society, is far more addicted to the sexual passions than are the dumb animals. And in this particular the human race could take a truthful and beneficial lesson from the dumb brutes. These animals which we call brutes, but who are infinitely superior to many of the so-called human race, do not allow any mating until the female is old enough to understand what she is about, and, then, not until the female is perfectly willing. But society has made some marriage customs and placed the woman in the nature of a slave, so that she seems to be obliged to submit to the husband whether she will or will not.

This is a matter to be thought over by every young lady before she has given herself up to these bestial usages of society, and thinks out and determines to obey the laws of her own being. But this will appear more fully when we speak of the marriage relation.

At the present there is room to know more with all parties.

We desire to assist you to know how to overcome all of this passion and to have it under your most thorough control.

How can you do this? We think we can make this so plain that it will be a wonder that it was never put in print before.

We have seen that there is to be no passion where there is no blood, or very little blood, in the arteries which are carrying the blood to the walls of the vagina and to the parts of the sexual organism. This is a correct assertion and one which is not generally known. It is this flow of blood to the parts which exerts such an influence on what is called the passionate nature of the woman. In other words, there will be no passion if there is no blood to the parts of the feminine organism. If there is any way by which a person can prevent this blood from going into these parts, it follows that while there is no blood there the passion can not be present. Think this over very carefully, as it is the secret of all self and sexual control. Or, in other words, if there is no blood to flow to these parts, there will be no passion, and the woman or the man who can do this will be free from all sexual passion. This is of great importance to know. If one can do this (that is, restrain the blood from entering these arteries), then there is most assuredly no need to say that any passion ever overcame them.

On the other hand, we know that if the sexual organism is filled with blood, and the parts are filled with blood, there is nothing but a burning passion, and the persons can with difficulty control themselves. They have a beast to torture them, for this passion is an ungovernable brute. And we also know if there are oysters eaten, wine drank, or the habits of coffee, tea, or chocolate taken, as the beverages at the meal time, there are going to be excesses of blood carried to the parts and there will be the greatest sexual passion. We venture to assert there is no sexual crime which can be named which has not been committed by persons who have been under the influence of this heat and arterial excess in these arteries, which are called the "passions" or "amorousness."

We are aware that the diet of eggs, oysters, fish, and all kinds of meats, are direct producers of this sexual passion, because these foods are stimulants of the blood and they excite the passions by having these arteries in a condition where they will be rapidly filled with blood. When these parts are filled with blood there will be passion and it is only when the person is too old to have any flow of blood to these parts that there is anything like cessation from these spasms of heat and turgescence of the reproductive organs which are called the "sexual passions."

Wine is a direct stimulant to all the blood flow, and it is a fact which is easy of proof, that the great majority of girls who are ruined by the promise of some man, are under the influence of wine at the time of the occurrence. This is why we object to the use of wine, and it is one of the things which every girl should know, viz. :—that under the influence of wine there is no safety for any woman. We may go yet a step farther and assert in all truthfulness that while any person is under the influence of coffee, tea, oysters, eggs, and pastry there is no such thing as becoming free from the sexual passions. And when we see these youth drink these and other articles and eat these heating, stimulating foods, we can say to ourselves that there is no such a thing as being free from the sexual passion.

So, we may assert that with all of the ideas which are correct as to the perfect control, we have the fact before us that there is no such thing as control, where these foods are eaten and these stimulating beverages drank. But where these articles are abstained from, there is no need to be a moment without full and perfect sexual control and this control means the control of our situation on this earth, the control of body and mind. We would not say there will be an opportunity for us to be in the greatest scale of what is known as society, or that we shall have an exalted place in the world does not follow the fact that we are wholly virtuous. But it follows that we shall be greater than if we were not virtuous. And it also follows that whoever is strictly virtuous, will have all there is of this world in point of enjoyment. This will occur because it is the mind that gives the enjoyment, and not the position and the rank or station of the person. Nor do we say that with the knowledge of this perfect control of all sexual passion one will at once become able to control a passion which has been let

run riot for some years past. The body which has borne
the habit of self abuse will have some decided effort to re-
cover from its downward grade. But we are quite sure that
the natural elasticity of youth will soon bring out the best of
the body, and there will not much time elapse before we
shall see the greatest improvement in the body.

Let us come to this sexual control. We have seen that it
is the flow of blood to the parts which causes the passion.
If we can control this flow of blood we can surely control
the passion, or rather we can prevent this passion. Not
that we may prevent this passion if the body is in the state
of heat already. That would almost be an impossibility in
case there was already some powerful passion at once taking
place in the body. But in any ordinary case, and especially
in all of those cases where there is the least desire to become
better, we are sure there can be an immediate control regained, which will grow stronger as the time goes on. And
this control, once so gained, will grow to be perfect as one
keeps the control of the body.

In every case of passion where the blood is carried to
the parts, almost without control of the mind, place the
parts at once in the coldest of water, and sit in that water
until all the blood is carried away from the arteries which
carry the blood to all of these organs. If one can not sit in
the water long enough to make sure the parts are measurably
free from blood, then wash as quickly as may be possible,
and repeat this washing in cold water as long as there is any
particle of passion left in the body.

If, from any cause, there seems to be a passion which can
not be overcome, and one can not wash, then the best thing
to do is to walk as far and as fast as the person can go, and
walk as long as the strength will hold out. Walk until the
body is entirely exhausted, and follow by a quick, cold bath
and a thorough rubbing of the skin. The washing is undoubtedly the best antidote to all passion, as the moment
there is cold applied to the parts there must be a contraction
of all the arteries there and as soon as the arteries contract,
there is an end to all the passion.

More than this. As soon as the arteries are once contracted they will be more ready to be contracted the next time. Or, in other words, when the parts are no longer supplied with blood there will be no passion. This is sure. When once there commences to be a control of the parts to get this passion under control by contracting the arteries, there will be a readiness to contract these arteries which was not there before. The commencement, which is always the worst and needs the most will power, will have been something, and the next step will be easier, and so on until the parts are in absolute control of the person and there can be absolutely no loss or waste when some object comes up which in other persons would create the fire to burn them.

By a reference to the plate we shall see that the moment we are in control of the blood supply to the parts we are in control of all the passion of any person.

The idea is not only feasible but has been in use by persons whom the writer is acquainted with, and has been told to many without any single failure, so far as the writer knows.

If, from any cause (menstruation, for instance), there is no opportunity to wash, there is still the walking, which will always prove beneficial Washing alone will prove the safeguard and the antidote to all kinds of sexual passion which are now on the earth if one has the diet properly regulated.

We think there is no doubt of this, and we feel sure that at this age of the world there has never been anything given to humanity which is of such real benefit as this simple but efficacious remedy for all passions in every stage.

But there will always remain other things to foment passion which are not under the control of the washing, for the reason that these other stimulants are not in the surface of the body, but are deeper seated and will not go down at the first washing.

We allude more particularly to the food, or such stimulants which are so common in every household.

The custard of eggs and milk. The beefsteak smothered in onions. The tea and coffee which are at once direct stimulants to the sexual organs, and we have no hesitation in saying the person who eats of these articles will have a passion which the water cold and effective though it is and always will be, yet this water will not put out this internal fire until there is a change in the constituents of the blood.

Nor do we think the fact of washing when one has been sitting on the lap of some young man, will *at once* cool off this passion. These habits should not be thought of. The washing is the greatest of help and if persevered in will overcome any passion in the world. But we can not think that when the blood is all on fire there is anything which will at once change all the parts of the blood and make all the blood cool. But it will help. The will will accomplish the rest. If the young lady who has been subject to temptation, and has been the victim to passion, is desirous to at once become perfect mistress of her own body, and if there is any widow who is desirous or under the absolute necessity of becoming at once strictly chaste, there is no remedy which we have ever heard of so easy and so effective as the sitting in the bath of cold water for the continued washing of the parts on the surface as much as can be placed in contact with the cold water.

As soon as the water toucnes the parts there is contraction, and the passion is abated. The next time (as it is sure that one washing is not sufficient to overcome this flow of blood to all the deeper arteries), the act of contraction will be easier and it is also certain that the effort will not have to be so great to overcome this second sexual passion as it was in the first place. So the next time the parts are washed or bathed in cold water there will be an easier task than in the first place and so on each time the task is easier and the arteries are really and permanently contracted. As soon as these arteries are contracted, there will be no more passion in the body. Glory be to God, whose grace is sufficient to overcome the beasts of the world. But shall we say there can be an immediate control while there is the mental *idea* of the causes of passion in the system ? No. We think not. The *desire* of the person must be for control and then these aids are effective. But if there is any condition where the person is yet desirous of going on in this road of passion, we do not think anything will have any permanent effect on them, or their passions. As long as the diet is wrong there will be passion. As long as there is the desire to have passion there will be passion until the passions are burned out and gone for all time. Mental desire must precede the bodily fact. This is for you to decide. So, that to assert there is a sure remedy to control all passion is one thing (and we think we have that sure remedy. Indeed we *know* we have a sure remedy for all passion to those who desire to live better), and to control that passion which has been blazing along for a length of time is another thing which is not so sure.

We think we may say as follows:

First (and this is of the utmost importance), one must possess this desire to do right and to be obedient to the law of God. To the law of a perfectly virtuous body. Second, there is the inexorable law of food which is of so much importance that we do not think there can be any virtue among the classes of people who do not pay the strictest attention to the diet line. We say it with all desire to utter the truth, when we assert there can be no effort effectually made towards a virtuous life, where the parties eat the unclean things and are addicted to the intoxicants of the day. It is simply an impossibility. We may add a third condition which will be apparent to any one who thinks of the difference of a life of strict virtue and one of the opposite character, and this is the fact that when the person who is desirous of living a good life is in a place where there is constant temptation and constant thoughts of the opposite sex placed before her; we say with these thoughts in the head there is not much chance of a virtuous life. But with the fact of a desire to live aright, a determination to have the body aright and virtuous, and the dependence on God which should always come first, there is no person but what can break off all of these vile habits and at once become a better woman, and every one will be surprised at her advancement in what is termed the knowledge of the world, and the immediate superior condition of the body which is strictly virtuous. She will in a short time be looking at others and as she sees the others she will see the effect of the folly of this loss and this waste of life. Her eyes will be opened.

She will also have the eyes opened sufficiently to see the difference between the persons who are obeying the laws of virtue and those who do not know how to live. Virtue is knowledge. Knowledge is power.

How often should this washing be taken ? We think this depends in a great measure on the condition of the one who has it to do. If one has been in the habit of self abuse and the passion comes up there should be the washing or soaking in cold water as often as the passion comes up, and not allow any thought of any one person or any body to get into the mind or overcome the determination to get the control of your body. Wash fifty time a day if the passion comes up fifty times a day. And if this does not do, go without the food until there is no food for the blood to have any surplus to flow into those arteries.

As you get control of this set of arteries there will be no need of washing save at the morning bath. This will keep you all right.

Recapitulation. 1. If there is any desire to live a strictly virtuous life, make the first dependence on God and then get hold of His laws. Keep these laws and these laws will keep you in all cases. 2. The food is of the first importance. There is no possibility of any one being virtuous who eats eggs, oysters, pastry, fish, flesh, drinks tea, coffee, or chocolate. Wherever you know of one who drinks wine, beer, or any spirituous liquors, you may be sure there is no strict virtue in the person. No matter if this is the habit of the greatest person you ever knew, you may put it down as an absolute fact that there can not be any virtue while there is this food and drink in the body to cause a condition of blood which is directly opposite to virtue.

Sleeping in a room which has bad air will destroy the lungs.

Bad air and warm beds will cause a flow of blood to the parts and this excess of blood causes passion and loss of force. It is better to sleep in a cold or cool room than to sleep in a room which has air so bad as to cause the blood to be degraded and dead. Degraded blood corpuscles are liable to produce gusts of passion in the growing body which can not be controlled. Sleep in a well ventilated room. Better, without the dust from a carpet.

The mind has always a good or a bad effect on the body. Keep your mind from any of the incentives to passion which are already in the hands of your associates. Do not read them and do not think of anything which will have a tendency to keep your mind on these thoughts of passion or of the other sex. Wait until the Lord will provide you a mate who is worthy of you, and then this so-called enjoyment will be all your own. There can not be any pleasure where there is no perfect love. Mind this and do not think of what might be, but think of controlling all of your powers to become better and stronger, to do more good and to serve the Master better. The washing in cold water is the most important thing which one has in the world to control the passions of the body, because the cold and the water are at once contracting to the blood current, and thus if there is no blood there it will be impossible to have any passion.

After one has washed and the passion does not seem to be conquered, the next thing is to make a prolonged fast of from twelve to forty-eight hours, during which time neither water nor food should pass the lips. This is another of the aids which the Lord has provided to all of earth's willing and anxious souls, to overcome the body and to gain perfect control of the animal nature. Fast persistently and you will never have any passion for anything of the sexual nature. You can as surely overcome this passion as you may be sure that water will overcome fire if placed in contact with the fire.

And you can be just as certain that if there is no food and no drink placed in the body that there will be no passion, as you may be sure there will be no fire where there is nothing to burn.

Food makes the blood, and when this blood is in excess in the body there will be some of this blood go into these arteries. But the fasting stops the supply of blood and thus you have another certain method of destroying all the fuel which is burning you up.

Some of the no-God doctors will tell you that to go without your food for one or two days will destroy the vitality, but you need not be afraid of this, as, if there is too much sexual passion and you can not control it, you may be reasonably sure you have an excess of vitality, which is better to be starved out from the body rather than to have it left in the body to burn the body into a cinder.

We have accomplished many days of this fasting, and we know what we say when we tell you that fasting is one of the aids to a strictly virtuous life. Go without the water as well as the food, for the water increases the size of the blood corpuscles and this is what is not wanted. Try this fasting for any of the passions. These are two of the greatest helps in the world.

Laborious exercise of any kind will do you good if these passionate thoughts are in your head. Walking is one of the best modes of getting rid of this surplus of blood. But if you have other work to do, do not hesitate to do it and keep the mind from anything which will bring on these thoughts which you are trying to get from your mind. Shun all persons who tell stories which are of a double nature or have any tendency to excite you. If you are in such a place, get out at any cost and get into some better place. But remember that if you will take all these passions with you there is no better place to conquer all of your passions than in the place you know, and the place you now are. Your own mind is first. The body will follow the mind. In your own home and in company with your own mother—there is no one who can do any more for you. It is not in the convent nor in the cloister that these passions are overcome. Remember this. The priest is one who has never overcome his passion, and to-day there is not one of the great classes of earth's toilers who is not more free from those sexual passions than the priests in the church.

You must conquer your own passion without any reference to what any one else may be doing. It is in you and all the world can not help you unless you take hold of the aids which are held out to you. The fight you will make to become strictly virtuous, is the fight which is between a diseased body and a body of health and long life. It is a fight which is between the early death of a consumptive, and the long life of those who are respected and happy up to the time of death. Virtue sweetens every task and makes it seem light and easy. The wastes of life are the things which are burdens and which are the drags down to death and worse. If you are a virtuous woman, you are a queen and a daughter of the most high God who looks and smiles upon you all the day and is waiting to have you come up higher in all the scales of this and the next life. No matter the trials and troubles of life, so that God your Father smiles on you. His smile is for the virtuous. He loves your inner self.

CHAPTER IX.

THE SUPREMACY.

In all the animal creation, there is a time of age when both the female and male comes to the period which is called "maturity." There are other names for this period, as, for instance, in some of the animals this period is called "rutting," and in others it is called "heat." During this period the female will permit the approach of the male and (perhaps with the exception of a few days after) then there will not be allowed any approach from the male until the next period of rutting or of heat. The commencing of this period in the man is called "puberty." At this time, the man is able to beget offspring, and this ability, in the male, may reach almost any age, while in the female, this child-bearing age will only reach as long as the menses are in regular recurrence.

When the menses cease, this period is called the "menopause." After the menopause there is no possibility of having any more children. (Sarah, who bore Isaac at the age of one hundred was an exception.) The time of the appearance of the menses has something to do with the continuance of the menses. For, if the menses appear at the fourteenth year, there is a likelihood of there being a cessation of the menses at the age of forty-two. In the latitudes where the menses first appear at the age of eight, the menses are said to cease at the age of twenty-four. Any young lady may be quite sure at what age the menopause will occur, if she can .date the commencement of the appearance of the menses. There is no doubt but what at the time of the commencement of the menses there is the same animal heat in the human race, and it is at this time that the young lady is in the greatest danger of losing the control of the body and finding herself in the control of animal passion, which she should never allow to have any control of her body.

93

This is the natural condition, to have sexual heat in the body and to have the passions which were ordained by the Architect of the world to coerce the race into bearing children. But there is also another law which enjoins us to have all of these passions in the most severe subjection. It is therefore a matter of the greatest consideration to all the race that both the male and the female shall be in the best order and have the most perfect control of themselves at the time of this passion or heat which comes on after or during the time of the menstruation in the female and puberty in the male. And this should be considered a period when the slightest approach to anything of a stimulating nature should be sedulously avoided.

Anything which is stimulating to the nervous system at this time should not be used as food or as drink. Tea, coffee, all kinds of alcoholic drinks and all the meats (unless the female is at the most laborious work) should be totally abstained from. Eggs, oysters (which are the vomit of a later aged immorality), wines, seasoned food, as of spiced cake, all the peppers, onions and garlic, should be abstained from, if one desires the perfect control of the body during this passionate period of existence.

Those foods which are in themselves heating, as the potato, pastry, lobster and crab, chocolates, cocoa shells, ice cream, clams, all the kinds of fish, are those which should be kept away from the stomach. The habit of eating cream on all kinds of fruit, and the habit of filling the stomach with milk is another menace to the body which should be avoided. We say these classes of food should not be eaten and that all kinds of drinks which are stimulating must be kept out of the stomach, if there is desire for the supremacy of the body by the mind. One of these natures will now assert itself, and it is at this time that the mastery is gained by the one or the other of these natures, and when this mastery is once gained it is usually kept by the one which is dominant at this threshold of life.

We are assured that it is best for the mind to have control

of the body and for this purpose we have devoted a short chapter to this subject of supremacy.

If the mind is to have control of the body, and all of this passion is to be under the most absolute subjection, there should be a full recognizance of the spiritual part of the being, and this spiritual should have the utmost control. Appetites and desires for anything on the earth should be the second thought, and this fight for the supremacy should be the first thing in order. Which shall rule? The mind or the animal part of the body? We think we hear the answer. The desire for the mind to rule and to have this body in the most perfect subjection.

We will group the aids to this subjection in the shortest possible space to be made available to those for whom this is written, and to those who are alone struggling for the supremacy of mind over matter. We say "alone." For happy is the girl who has a mother to tell her of this critical period of life and to warn her of the dangers which are ready to beset her. Fortunate is the girl who has a judicious friend who can point out the beasts of life and warn the young lady of the enemies which lie in wait to devour her and her substance. We think the following are the best means to obtain the supremacy of the mind over the passions of the body. Valuable in their respective order.

1. Prayer to God.
2. Fasting.
3. Washing.
4. Labor. Exercise.

By the term prayer, we do not mean the ordinary repetition of a certain formula of words, even of the form set by our Lord; because this repetition will eventually lose its effect on the mind unless there is the innate dependence on God which comes from a contemplation of God as He is. There must be that inner desire to live a near life to God and to do His will before this form of prayer becomes available. We think, by prayer, to indicate a sincere contemplation of the bright and glorious Being who has made the world and all the things therein, and a constant desire to see

Him, to be His child, to feel as if your entire existence were in the hands of your Father, and whatever happened were the work of Him who knew all things from the beginning.

This prayer is one thought for the throne of God, where we are seen as we really are and not any of our imperfections are hid. A throne from where the angels see us and from where all our aspirations for a better life are known and appreciated. From where the Lord Jesus looks down and sees the children who are desirous of becoming nearer. This is a prayer and contemplation which is of the utmost importance in that struggle to have control of the body. While we are in the state of contemplation of this Father, we shall not be likely to commit any sin by thought or yield to anything which is of the earth.

This is one of the hardest places to find one's self in the existence of this life. To drop all of this earth's annoyances and to give up all to the guidance of God. To look to God and forget our present troubles. To drop all the cares of life so as to think that the good Father will manage them better than we can. This is a prayer and a frame of mind which is hard to obtain. It can be obtained by any one. By the desire to live a pure and devoted life. By a desire to be more serviceable to the Master. By a desire to overcome all these "fleshly lusts." Because God in this instance, sends the Spirit down and shows us the existence of himself. We can contemplate the throne and the Son on that throne.

The writer of this was at one time an infidel. During that lonely time there was nothing but unhappiness. When he commenced to pray, there was much of the time when the prayers seemed to be no more than vaporings of the mind; everything which was of earthly life came in front of the desire to do better and then all aspirations would vanish and everything would come into the mind instead of the prayer which should have been uppermost. But with each failure to find peace of mind and to be able to pray, there came a desire•to persevere in this prayer. And every day the power to pray became clearer. The more the distance from all passion the clearer the prayer became; just as the road becomes clear as one travels over it towards the end.   Finally, in one of the great trials of life there came a time when it was certain, that nothing but the intervention of something beside the natural law would save the writer from degradation; there was one prolonged effort to have the Father look upon his child.   This effort brought peace and the Spirit of prayer came and assisted the writer to gaze steadily at the throne of God and see the Son.   Not with the natural eyes.   None may do this.   But with the spiritual eyes which are opened by the power of God to *His* children. It does not require a faith which is almost impossible.   It requires a constant desire, and this desire will be fulfilled.   A constant looking towards the throne which is only just in front of all of us.   This is the prayer which will overcome all passion and leave the body in that condition which is purity.   If one has never prayed, this is hard to commence. But if there is a desire, and one can repeat the Lord's prayer in earnest, the time will soon come when this earnest prayer will avail against all things and against all earthly natures. The throne will always be in sight and the appeal to the throne will always be heard.

Although we use this prayer in this place for the purpose of overcoming all this earthly passion and bodily nature, yet this prayer is available for any purposes of life and is one of the best methods of obtaining the entire guidance of the Holy Spirit in all our ways through life.

There is a class who do not believe in the existence of the Holy Spirit.   At one period of life this writer was very doubtful of the fact of there being any Spirit of God in the world during this present age.   But there is no warrant to prove that there ever was the Spirit taken out of the world after the Lord sent it into the world at Pentecost.   And if Jesus said "I will be with you unto the end of the age," surely He is with us, or in His person and guiding us ; or, He is with us by presence of His Holy Spirit.   We think one of these facts must be true.   We think this is the very Spirit of God who listens to our feeble cries and we are sure it is the "Spirit who helpeth our infirmities."

2. Fasting. The value of fasting as a means of obtaining the perfect control of all sexual passions and all the grosser elements of life, has been known for ages. But in this age which is certainly a gluttonous age, this habit of fasting has.gone into disrepute. Very few except the Roman church have a habit of fasting, and this apostate human organization has only the semblance of fasting and the reality is gone. The fasting which is essential is the total abstinence from food or drink for some stated time which may be longer or shorter. The moment one can fast, the control of the body is assured. The more that any one will yield to demands of the appetite, the more they will yield to the demands of passion.

In order to obtain control of the body the celibates of all ages have fasted. The nuns and the monks in the Roman church have made this fasting a basis for the absurd statement that the Roman Catholic church held more virtuous women than any other church. This statement is without any foundation, in fact, and on the contrary, the church which is so largely dominated by celibate priests could not under any circumstances, become a virtuous body of people. It is not in the nature of things, nor in the law which governs the world. The fact that there are hundreds of instances where the bones and skeletons of infants have been found near or under the convents, are enough to prove that all the arrogance of a superior virtue by the so-called Roman Catholic church is all false. But there is a better proof than in digging away at the rotten records of a corrupt and anti-Christian church. The fact which states and proves its assertions false at the outset is that in all the houses of prostitution of this nation and of Great Britain, there is a very large majority of Roman Catholic prostitutes, and this fact which is easily proved in any large city shows conclusively that their boast that they have anything which will prove a safeguard to the virtue of their women, is totally false and purely imaginary.

We have no hesitation in saying that there is not one in a thousand of the Roman Catholic priests who have lived and do now live virtuous lives.   This is not a slander.   The very faces of these priests show that they are sensuous and devilish in their sexual passions.   The fat neck and the sensuous mouth all betray their sexual passions which are too well developed to be held in subjection to their spiritual nature. Their faces prove this fact so well that any one who can read may run as they read the amorous and sexual appetites developed and satisfied.   There can be no doubt in any intelligent reader's mind as soon as the face of a priest can be seen. The stories which are daily retailed about these so-called "reverend gentleman," are not devoid of truth.   So that the more quiet these Roman Catholics can keep about their superior virtue the better will they appear.   Fasting among the churches is really gone out of date.   Among private individuals this habit is observed but rarely.   Fasting and prayer seem to be unknown.   It will not be long, when one tries this habit, to show that of all the acts which are of use in the mastery of the body, there is nothing which approaches the act of fasting.

We do not think any explicit directions are needed, as there will be no two who are alike in their body and in their mental and bodily needs.

But this may be given as a general rule :   Go without the supper.   If this does not help, go without the breakfast also.   If this does not leave the body free from all desire and the mind free from all fancy, go without all food and water for one entire day and then eat the next morning.   I am quite sure this fasting will take away all sexual desire, and as sure that there is no other act on earth by which so thorough a control may be gained of the entire body in so short a space of time.

When this act of fasting is added to the act of prayer there is a bond which appeals to the Father and is not denied. It is an act of sincerity in desire which no formalist ever obtains.   It is an act which is of spiritual origin and is freed from all this earth and its desires.   The Roman Catholic does not have this fasting, because there is in that church no necessity for this absolute fast.   The Romanist, by his belief, is saved *by his baptism into the church.* The duties of the church being over, there is nothing for him to do except penance. And as they pray to the dead bodies of men and women like themselves, they do not have their prayers answered. Their ideas of virtue are not correct or rigid, because if they make any lapse in their path, they can go at once to their priest and make confession and gain absolution.

There is another point which is well to be looked at in this connection. There are two kinds of Protestants, a good class and a bad class. Those who are after a higher and a purer life and a better, purer existence while they are on this earth, who desire to serve the Father in spirit and in truth. The other class are hypocrites who are bad and desire nothing good in this world, and care nothing for anything to come afterwards. But there is only one class of the Roman Catholics, and that is the class who believe that all the Protestants will be damned and eternally burned up and still being burned. These are the Roman Catholics as they are and as they desire to have the Protestants under their dominion, and are likely to have them if there is not some educating accomplished more than is being done at this time.

The class has no compunction of conscience in lying to or cheating a Protestant any more than one would take the life of a chicken. This is the fact, as any one can tell who has ever had anything to do with these Roman descendants of a barbarous empire.

Nor can it be wondered at. These people (the Roman Catholics) believe in a materialist church, the work of men's hands. They hold and teach that there is no salvation outside of this church. To join this Roman Catholic church one must be *baptized* into that church, and it does not matter whether one has any change of heart or not. So that they are baptized into the church they are safe here and for eternity. But the Word of God teaches that we must be "*born again*" to enter into the kingdom, and if we have not that "new birth" we are not of Christ.

The Protestants may be divided into two classes—those who are born again and those who are not. The Roman

Catholics are in one class; the class that has never been born again. They are of the earth, earthy. They are to be shunned in this fight for the supremacy of the spiritual. All their habits of thought are to be shunned. All of their Jesuitical ideas are to be avoided. When we speak of fasting, we do not allude to any Roman idea of fasting, but we mean the total denial of the body to all water and all food for some space of time. Make your space of time to suit your body and your needs. It is your body that is to be controlled, and not the body of something which is an appanage of some human society. And it is your mind that is desirous of having that body under its control, and not under the control of some fat-necked priest of Baal. You need to go to God, but to the priest you do not need to stir one step. You do not need any advice in this matter, unless you take the advice of the Book. "Ask and you shall receive." Some space has been given to this fasting, because the Roman church makes a false claim of knowing all about this fasting, and we are convinced they know nothing about it. Also, because at one time we were in the error of supposing that some Roman Catholics might be pure. We now know better. None of them are ever "born again," and this leaves them in their true light: a class of people who are the advocates and followers of the great beast. *

3. Washing. The daily bath and the continued washing

---

*It may be thought an expression of prejudice to assert that all the Roman Catholics are advocates and followers of the great beast of the Bible. But such is the fact. In the XIII. chapter of Revelation is found our authority, eighteenth verse.

The solution to this is in "the number of the man."

The pope of Rome wears on his tiara the words, worked in diamonds, *Vicarius Filii Dei.* The first word (as the letter "u" is unknown in the Latin language and is a "v"), will count up 112, as follows:

								TOTALS.
V	5	U (V)	5	F	0	D	500	
I	1	S	0	I	1	E	000	
C	100			L	50	I	1	112
A	0	Total	112	I	1			53
R	0			I	1	Total	501	501
I	1			Total	53			**666**

Verily there is nothing like the word of God. It is a lamp to the feet and a path to the children who are travelling home.

for the subjection of the body are among those subjects which are treated of in another part of this work. We will not allude to them here farther than by saying that everybody who is not daily bathed is not and can not be clean. The daily bath is one of the means which is given to us to take care of the body. If this is neglected there can be no such a submission of the body as there would be when the body was daily washed. The outlet of the body after the bowels and the kidneys, is from the skin. When this outlet is clogged there will be disease. Disease of the body means disease of the brain, and there can not be a clean mind in a dirty body. Pay especial attention to this washing and the time will come when that care will come back to you a hundred fold.

4. Labor. Although it seems hard to be obliged to labor for a living, yet there is an abundance of evidence to prove that all labor by the hands and the body is of the utmost benefit, and without any of this labor the world would be a mass of wild animals.

Hard labor will more readily dissipate any passion than all the sermons in the world. This fact accounts for the greater virtue among the laboring classes than there is among those who do not have to labor for a living. It also accounts for the cause of so much sexual passion among the priests and ministers who do not have enough labor to keep their animal passions in subjection. There can be no supremacy of the mind over the body until that body is fitted to control its own passions. The body must be taught proper subjection, and this subjection will never be reached until there is some muscular development of the body. This development of the body is found in those who are in the habit of using the body and not otherwise. A body that is not used, is a body not worth anything in the battle of life.

One of the causes of the decay and fall of the Roman empire was the decay and degeneracy of the human bodies which were the rulers of Rome. If you do not have labor enough, see to it that the body gets a proper amount of exercise and give each muscle something to do which will be

exercise and allow the blood to flow to all parts of the body
and carry the life stream of blood so that it shall be clear
and running, instead of stagnating and dead. Keep your
body sweet and free by exercise, and so shall you keep the
evil thought out of your head. This is so true that there
will be a greater consideration than at first sight seems to be
on the surface. Consider—that all the blood flowing towards the sexual organs can be drawn away and kept away
by any work which will occupy the body in drawing away
those supplies from the parts. Consider—that when you
labor, you increase the part which does the labor. For instance, the blacksmith's arm, and the penman's and the
piano player's fingers. Consider the legs and extremities of
those who have to march during the campaign of some army.
Also the bodies of those who are obliged to labor during the
early part of their lives. Do not allow yourself to loll on
the bed or the lounge and dream away the hours. Think of
the poor who are awaiting something to come to them from
some unknown source, and think if you can not do some
good and win some special smile from God, who has made
you as well as the rest of mankind, and those who are poor
as well as those who are rich. Be up and active, and do not
rest until you have conquered every vestige of passion in the
body; and do not stop this exercise, if you have no work,
until all the animal passions are burned out and you are
completely master of the body which God has given to you
for a covering to your soul.

Labor is a benefit to anybody. If there can be no labor
and no exercise, there will be a decay of the body as sure as
there are any natural laws to be obeyed. If you have gained
the mastery of your body there is no hesitation in saying you
are the child of the King and that you can look up and say
God is your Father. But if this matter has been delayed,
see to it that there is no time to be lost in the future. You
can redeem the time and become the mistress of your body,
and your mind shall have the supremacy of all the
actions of the body. Then no appetites nor any passion
shall ever cause you to do an act which will cause a blush of

shame to mantle your check. The Father, Son and Holy Spirit will help you to reach this glorious place where there can not be any anxiety as to what is coming next.

Supremacy of the mind over the body means purity of the heart, intelligence of the mind, and an entire consecration to the laws of God. You can have it. Commence at once and do not stop short of this entire control of this body of death which is yours to use, but not to abuse. God has given this trust to you and it is your mind which should have the supremacy, and not the body. Allow no appetite, no passion, nor gross desire to ensnare you for one second. Commence at once, and if there is the least trouble, or if there is any doubt in your mind, do not hesitate to pray, to fast, to labor, and to have every habit of such strict cleanliness that there can be no possible chance to fail in your gaining the entire control of the only house you have to live in on this earth.

Consider that this supremacy of the mind over the body does not consist in having a continual quarrel every day and night. Your mind can not stand any quarrel like this. You must have an absolute control of these passions and there should not be a second of time for these passions of the body or its appetites to have a say about anything in their nature. Control them absolutely. See that no obscene thought is allowed in the region of your mind. Have no book or picture which will allow the body to have even a semblance of independence. Keep your body as much under control as if it were a machine and liable to run away from you. You are to have no more sexual passion than if you were a post. Time enough for this passion when you yield that body to the husband of your choice. 'Then, and not until then, will the time come when you can yield up the supremacy of the mind over the body, when love and law are both yours and own you mistress of the world.

CHAPTER X.

THE PERSON.

If I were to say the best thing I could wish a young lady to have, I would say, the proper idea of taking care of her person. I mean by this, I would have her versed in everything which would pertain to the good care of the body. As she would wish to be virtuous in herself, so I would have her careful of the feelings of all the rest of the world, and especially the other sex. I would have her keep her person as sacred as if the very touch of a male hand polluted it, as it surely does,—if that touch is not the touch of a brother or a father or a wedded husband. There is no doubt of this, as the very touch of a woman is, at times, enough to set many men into the wildest passion, and there are many of them who do not know what the matter with them is and so they become crazy on this point of personal magnetism which should have been guarded against by the young lady, who should never have allowed the least approach of the man. The very touch of some females is of so much power as to be the most dangerous of fires to a young man of ardent passions.

Look at the many lovers who have thought they had lost their love, or became jealous, and they have killed the girl and shot themselves. True, they were foolish. Crazy, if you please ; but there should have been no familiarity in the first place to have brought about so great a passion. This passion grows by the feeding, and if there is not the least encouragement in the first place there will never be any of this crazy love which is all on one side. The girl is always to be blamed at the *first*, as there can not be any love at the heart of a man unless it has received some sort of encouragement from the girl. I say, do not allow the slightest familiarity from any man until you are wedded. No handshaking even. I have heard it said by men who were versed in the ways of the world and had an abundance of personal magnetism, that if they could hold a girl's hand a moment all the rest of their conquest was easy. I do not say they were always correct. But it is unfortunately true that there are some men who have that magnetism which will allow them to persuade a girl against her own will, and the first time she yields to that persuasion she is lost. There is no such thing as any safe self confidence. There may be confidence in the good God. And he may keep you if you are in a position of danger and allow one to take hold of your person to aid you from a fire or from drowning, but in no other way should you allow the body to come in contact with the male, nor should you allow any one to have any touch of your person; not for any excuse whatever. Let no one *touch you*. It is too bad to say it, but it is the truth that all men are not in the habit of controlling their bodies, and when their passion is their master they have no thought of what they are doing. And there are others who have no idea of any right or virtue any more than dogs, and if they could ruin you, they would feel that something was gained for them, and, having accomplished that ruin of your person, they would go about and tell their young acquaintances of it.

This may seem cruel and harsh, unneeded language, but it is more than true, and there are thousands of unfortunate and sorrowful girls who have unthinkingly allowed their body to be touched by some acquaintance and dated their downfall from that first thoughtlessly permitted touch.

It is a certain fact, one which there are thousands of men and women who will testify to its correctness, that the first liberty of *touch*, holding the hand, or the arm, or merely standing in close proximity to the other sex; or a look is enough to convert a man (and this is always the fact in the case of a libertine) from a sane person to a wild beast who will not become satisfied until he has accomplished your total ruin. To obtain your body he will lie to you, in all the languages he may possess. His arts, his tears, his protestations of love and eternal friendship, his oaths and assertions may be, in his *own mind*, all true at the time. But, we say to you, fly from his touch, his looks, as you would from a mad dog.

Consider the fact, that no man who is so passionate that he can not control himself, can possibly make a virtuous, faithful husband. Also, that a man who loves you as a husband should will be as careful of your virtue, and your person will be as sacred in his eyes, as if you were his mother or his sister. The least familiarity on his part should be checked, repulsed, and rebuked by you on the instant, even if the *engagement ring is on your finger*. Keep your body sacred from the touch of a man until the law has pronounced you man and wife.

This care of the person is always to be considered if by any chance you are called upon to travel alone. Our advice is to sit in your seat and allow no one of the male sex to draw you into a conversation. If a question is asked you, answer it without anything more than a quick glance to see the person who asks the question. If he is old, infirm and crippled, you may assist him; but no young man needs assistance—mind that. His idea in his talk is to make you a victim, or a plaything, or a fly for his poisoned net of webbing, which possibly ensnared another victim a day or two since.

Either do not answer the young man, or do so quickly in *yes* or *no*, and refuse to look at him. Remember that the glance you make *towards him* is allowing yourself to be drawn into his personal magnetism and *yielding yourself a willing prey*, from which it is almost impossible to return. Keep your body chaste. Keep your thoughts chaste. Keep your very looks from anything which can pollute them. Do not allow a man to pollute you by his touch.

This advice may sound pedantic and old, and it is old and sound from all the bitter experience which could be crowded into two lives. Do not allow any man to pollute you with his touch, is the burden of the cry, and which you will one day appreciate, if you are not in a condition to do this at present. As long as you have the free and desirable graces of a virgin you can have your choice of the world. The moment this is yielded up to some one who may have a *desire*, but has no affinity for you and your nature, you are as much robbed as if the party had stolen a treasure from you, which indeed he has. The very touch robs you of something which is indescribable and which for want of a better name may be called the touch of a *personal magnetism.* When once this touch is gone from you, you are something which is hard to be described, but which is to the person you were before the touch, as a piece of iron, rusty and black, is to the polished steel magnet.

This is our text : Do not allow anyone to touch your person under any circumstances any more than you would have one steal your clothes. But it would be a comparatively small loss to lose all the clothes you have, for you could get new ones. But the fresh and pure touch of virginity will never come back, although you may sigh for it never so long and look for it never so bitterly.

Keep your person as sacred as if that was the choicest of gold, which it is. And remember this :—That the man who desires to fondle you or to embrace your person is not the one who will prove to be faithful to your memory when you are absent from him,

There are creatures I (would call them men, but I do not think they have a manly attribute about them), who will appear well dressed, easy in manners, suave, polished, ready to be your friend in your distress, and quite ready to give you some advice and money too if that is needed, who, when the opportunity comes, will seize your person and accomplish their desires while you are wondering whether you should cry out or no. Beasts who are already cursed of God and have neither care for man nor the God that made them. For these animals there is only one safe way to do and that is to have a sure and safe distance from them, which will result in their keeping their distance from and allowing you to own your person in peace.

These creatures are met anywhere. They are of no church. Of no denomination. Of all denominations. They have no mark on them that will tell you of their dangerous and mur-

H

derous proclivities. They are the politest of the polite. The best dressed of your acquaintance. We can tell you of only one thing by which they may be known most certainly, and that is that they will and do desire to rob you of your treasures by nearing your person. This is the only sign I can tell you, but it is good and unfailing. When a young man desires to come near to your person and to caress you, then is the time that all acquaintance should terminate.

There are snakes which will utter a little noise or get their victim to look at them, and then fasten their eyes on the unsuspecting bird, and when the bird sees this stare, there does not appear any power of the bird to take the eyes from the snake and the snake crawls slowly up until the foot of the bird is seized in the mouth of the snake and the whole body is speedily devoured. I have seen this act myself. It is called the charming of the snake. Meanwhile the bird will make the most piteous of cries. But, alas, there will be no escape from the horrible fate which awaits the unhappy bird which caught the eye of the snake before it had the power to fly.

Do you pity that unfortunate bird ? Pity your own fate of the future if you can not at once resolve and break off from all and any acquaintance which has any desire on your person, and from any and all acquaintance of the male sex who is in the habit of fondling your person, or of allowing his hand or foot to touch you anywhere. Shun the first approach. Shun the man. Avoid the public places where he will be met. Avoid all private places, and give him to understand that you are aware of his wiles and that you are not to be charmed.

Remember that the difference between one that loves you for your own self and this creature who will rob you of the greatest treasure and the only treasue of this earth is this: The one who loves you is silent and reserved in your presence. He does not influence you to become charmed. He is under your magnetism, possibly, but it is not for this he cares. He is seeking you as a partner for life and desires to rob you of nothing. The man who loves you will be satisfied to take you in any condition and in any place and from any walk of life and does not hesitate to tell you of this at the first opportunity. But your snake charmer is never ready with his love, but his passion is always ready to eat you up.

Have this in your mind, that your *person is sacred*, and that of all the earth there will be but one who can have that person, and that one is he who will make you a wife before he has the audacity to attempt to rob you of your birthright. The snake is the one who is never so ready with his love as he is ready with his protestations of friendship and fidelity. Shun the snake as you would shun one who is to devour you. Beware of the snaky eye which sparkles to pick your bones and leave you among all the victims of the shore.

We can not help you. Only God can aid you to defend yourself. Flee to Him while there is time and beseech him to keep you in His arms until this life is over.

To this we will add:—Do not laugh or giggle at any place or allow your mouth to be open.

When you are going anywhere it is best to be your own self and not try to be anyone else. Have a book and read. Keep to your own self. There will be acquaintances enough. There will be all you will wish to have. If you are a child of God you are in His hands and he will find you the partner which is to be your mate and you will not have to hunt for him.

That is one of the laws of God, that He provides us all that is needed for us and our happiness. But he demands of you that your person be kept sacred, and if you will not keep your person sacred you will be allowed to fight for your own self and in this choice there is a liability of your making some mistake.

If the God of Hosts picks you out a husband, as he surely will if you appeal to Him, there will be no divorce and no sorrow in the match. He does all things well, and if God picks you out a man there will not be any need to pick out a second one. Keep your person as sacred as if the God of

Hosts had told you of the great value you are to him and as if that *person* is to have the germs of some of the children of God within you. Think of this before you are waylaid and shot by some one with whom you could never mate. Think of this and keep all your glances for the one whom the Lord will choose for you.

Keep all of your person sacred and there will come such a happiness as is not often felt in this age of deceit and craft. Do not allow any snake to have the least eye of you. Keep all of the person as far away from these creatures as it is possible. Walk alone and as one to whom the Lord talked and loved.

CHAPTER XI.

PAINFUL MENSTRUATION.

We are sure there is no more necessity of having pain during menstruation than there is of having pain during defecation.

Yet there are thousands of young ladies who suffer the agonies of death and who do not know what to do to obtain relief. This chapter is for them. The well and happy persons can skip it.

We shall ask, in the first place, *what is pain?* It will not make any difference where the pain comes from and what the primal cause of that pain—*what is pain?*

We reply, pain is a message from some place, to inform the brain that there is some obstruction, which is in the way of a good circulation of fluids in the body, and that there is something that the vital force wishes to have removed from the body. Pain is a *message* and nothing else. A message of something unpleasant from the place where the pain arises.

Unless the pain is of an excruciating character so that the one who is having that pain is unconscious, there is a knowledge of the place from where the pain starts. This place is called the seat of the pain.

Of itself, pain is *not* an entity, as people and the falsely educated doctors think of it. It is no dog, eating the vitals. It is not a person or a living animal of any kind. It is not a germ or a parasite to be, as the doctors assert, "overcome" and "relieved" by something that kills the living matter. Pain is a message of intelligence from one intelligence to another intelligence.

Mark this fact, as there is nothing of any more importance in the subject that is before us, than to know of this fact, that pain is a message and something that arises from something which is intelligent in the body and without this intel-

117

ligence there is no such thing as pain. You must unlearn all the doctor teaches about the ideas of pain being an entity and something that is alive and ready to eat you up if it is not killed or destroyed in some manner.

Take an example of pain that is truly analogous. Suppose a young lady at one of the telegraph stations should telegraph to her father at the other end of the line that there is a fire in her town and the wind is sweeping towards her station. The father at the other end of the line will naturally feel uneasy at the danger of his daughter and will send repeated messages until he knows that his daughter is out of all danger.

But note. Did that message have any body? No. Did that message have any life? No. All the life was in the intelligence that was at both ends of the telegraph line and in the line which carries the message. There was no life in the message, and to a person who heard the signals that the message made, they would be as unintelligible as if there were no messages sent.

What we call your attention to, is the fact that there is no life in the message nor any being in this telegraph message, and therefore, if there is no life, there is one of the lies of the allopaths (and all the schools who use poisons as the base of the medication), nailed as a fraud on all the victims who have entrusted themselves to their skill.

The allopaths treat pain as an entity, and they go to work to poison that entity so that it can not have any more existence, according to their teaching. But, as there is no life in the message and no sentient thing in pain, except that the parts that are at the ends of the telegraph line are intelligent, so there is no entity to be killed or poisoned when there is a pain from any part of the body. The idea of destroying or killing pain is an idea that means the killing of the intelligences at both ends of the nerves, or the destruction of the nerves themselves.

Why should a poison doctor be so fond of relieving pain? Because he knows no better, and being ignorant of the laws of life, God, from his throne, has cursed him.

The people, ignorant of their bodies, in their blind grop-
ings after something to shield them from the consequences
of their disobedience of the laws of God, accept these emis-
saries of darkness, the doctors, as their guides. So, when
they relieve pain, they kill the intelligences that convey the
friendly, urgent messages.

It is of no consequence which of the conditions may cause
the message to be sent to the brain, announcing that there
is some obstruction in the body that should at once be removed. It is not the obstruction that causes the pain. It
is not the bullet that has passed through the chest that has
caused the pain. It is not the splinter in the toe that causes
the pain. It is not the toe that is the cause of the pain from
the splinter. Neither the toe nor the splinter are the causes
of the pain. It is not the fact that the young lady has a
uterus that causes the pain. Nor is it because she is at fault
concerning any make-up of the body; but the pain arises because there is some obstruction and some effete material in
in that body, or in some special part of the body (fallopian
tubes or mouth of the uterus), which does not permit the
menstrual discharge to pass out, and so there is a message
from the uterus to the brain to this effect, and this is a painful sensation and this is called a *pain*. If the discharge
passes out freely and there is no obstruction, there will be no
pain and the young lady will only know of its passing out by
the sensation of moisture. This is as it should be and as it
is in many latitudes, and as it will be in any young lady
who learns to take care of her body properly.

What then is it that produces this pain ?

In the case of the splinter in the toe, the vital force that is
in the toe sends a message from the parts surrounding the
splinter and telegraphs a message to the brain, and that message is one of anxiety and distress, and that message you
call pain. Place your feet, after they have been fatigued by
long walking and are sweaty and dusty, in a bath tub of
warm, nice soft water, and you will find there are soothing
messages come from those feet to tell you that those feet are
enjoying themselves.

But take them out and attempt to walk over some places where there are broken glass bottles, and you will not have the same soothing messages from your feet as you did while they were in the nice and soft warm water.

Why ?

Because they are in a different place and they can not tell you the same things as they did when they were in the warm water.

The feet are the same.

And the nerves are the same.

The same intelligence is in the brain and the same nerves are between the feet and the brain. But the conditions of the feet are different, and thus you have, in one case a soothing message, and in the other a message of pain.

In the case of painful menstruation the message is from the uterus or from the fallopian tubes, or from the nerves surrounding the organs of generation. But the vital force sends the message, and that vital force is the life power in the body.

Have you entered into this idea of having pain ?

Do you think you can define pain so that you will know the next time you have some pain, what that pain is ? Pain is a message, a telegram from some place, for some purpose, to the brain.

Let us repeat this lesson, for, while young, it is best for us to learn about ourselves and about our bodies so as to keep them "Temples of the Holy Ghost."

Let us have this idea that pain is a message, and if we can understand that message we can go to work with the laws of God to aid us and do valiantly for God and the elevation of our race.

That is about pain.

What is pain ?

Pain is not disease. Note that again. It is not needed to have disease to have a pain.

But there must be a condition that is unnatural in the body before one can feel a pain, because what is called a pain is a message that is unpleasant.

An unpleasant message is a pain.   As long as there is no message there is no pain.

But when the message comes to tell you of some condition that is wrong in the estimation of the vital force, then there will come what is termed a painful sensation.

The condition of pain is a condition where the body is departed from its natural state by reason of illness, or by reason of an accident, or by reason of its condition, or because of some obstruction that the vital force can not get out of the body without aid.

If we are now fairly able to understand about pain, we may take up the condition of painful menstruation.

If there is any pain it is because there is an obstruction that should be hastened out of the body.

The natural outlets are obstructed.   There is some cause for the obstruction.

And with that obstruction to the natural flow, there is something that telegraphs to the brain that this flow is obstructed by this obstacle and must be removed.

Then follow waves of messages that the vital force is constantly sending up to the brain and which make the young lady wish there was no world to live in, and wonder why we could not have grown on trees and fallen off when we were ripe.

But we will look after that obstruction and see from where it comes and what to do so as to be clear of this pain.

First.   The feet being cold will produce a condition of dead blood corpuscles that are not able (because, being *dead* they can do nothing) to go through the capillaries, and, as they do not go through these fine tubes so as to return to the heart, they clog up the fine arteries, and there is a condition that is called congestion.

The uterus is filled with dead blood corpuscles that can not get out, and as the vital force can not get them out, so the vital force telegraphs to the brain that there is some condition that is needing attention in that part of the body.

Tight shoes produce this condition and so also the tight stockings that are in these tight shoes.

Second. Constipation will produce a condition of dead blood corpuscles that will fill up the elastic womb and thus produce a condition of stuffing these capillaries, thus bringing the condition of stoppage of these blood vessels, and when these blood vessels are stopped from having a free flow, there is another message to the brain of this condition, and this message is unpleasant, and is called a pain.

Third. The garter around the leg just below the knee will cause a faulty flow of blood, and these faulty conditions will show themselves on the circulation of the uterus, and thus we will have some more unpleasant messages that are called painful.

Fourth. The food we eat will have an effect on the circulation, and if that food is largely composed of starch and materials that can not make stout corpuscles, and the blood corpuscles are weakly and can not stand any degree of cold, when the cold air strikes the lower part of the abdomen, there will be a quantity of dead corpuscles, and then we shall have this congestion and more painful messages.

Pastries, eggs, coffee, tea, pork, clams, oysters, candies, fried cakes, and all kinds of fried things that are cooked in grease, baking powder biscuit or cake, butter and milk (unless the milk is thoroughly digested), will all have an effect on the blood. And if this blood is not good there will be a weakness that can not be overcome by any artificial means (as of anything in the shape of medicines), and the corpuscles will die, and then we will have some more of these messages that are unpleasant, and we say there is a pain.

Fifth. The corset that impedes the circulation of the bowels, which should be free and equal, is often one of the causes of the condition that brings about the messages that we do not wish to have, and thus the corset is one of the frequent producing causes of a congested uterus and its appendages. In fact, the corset is one of the most frequent of all these conditions and is one of the causes of so much death from what is called consumption, but it is often overlooked by the things which go around under hats and are named doctors. The mother who allows the daughter to wear a corset, under any condition, is just as bad as the fool mother of the Fiji Islands, who files the teeth to a point, and places a big ring in the nose. A small waist and a painful menstruation go together, hand in hand.

Sixth. Cold food, that is bolted down in a hurry, is another cause of congestion. This cold food, which may be of raw apples, not properly chewed up, and the skins, are frequent causes of clogging of the intestines, and are some of the things that are the base of this condition of congestion. So, too, the custards that slip down the throat so easily. They are not digested, and when they are in the small intestines they will not pass any farther, and thus become cold, clammy masses of dead swill, and prevent the circulation from being as rapid as it should be through the intestines, and we have some more of these messages that are unpleasant, and we cry for some morphine to relieve us from these pains.

Seventh. The young lady does not take in a sufficient quantity of water to have the blood corpuscles in a good condition, and because this water is not in the system, the blood corpuscles are laden with materials which should have been passed off, and so there are some disagreeable messages which are known by the name of pain.

The books tell us that painful menstruation may arise from a "contracted os," or a "contracted uterus," or a "contracted state of the fallopian tubes." Or, there may be some "congestion."

These books advise the young practitioner to have an examination of the young lady and insert a "sound "(which is a crooked piece of steel) into the os (mouth of the uterus), and then give this young lady with the unpleasant messages, some "wine of steel " and some "iron " and some "morphia " to relieve the distress.

And these old professors who graduate these young men to "alleviate the sorrows of life" go ahead with their devilish crooked steel and their poisons, and thus they ruin thousands of young ladies who should never have had any examination, nor any "pain" if they would only have taken hold of the natural laws and obeyed them.

We have no patience with these doctors who are always advising these unnatural ideas, and we do not think it is for the best interests of this world that every young student shall have an opportunity to experiment on the daughter who will be the comfort in our old age if she is well, and if she is sick she will be a care and a burden and a solicitude which is beyond description.

We love our dear gir and there shall nothing be allowed to come between them and health if we know how to prevent it. Much more will we struggle to have them understand the laws of life so as to keep from these latter day antichrists, the regular allopathic physicians.

Now for the first.

Wear wide shoes and loose woolen stockings in the winter, and if the feet are yet cold, see that you have a pair of boots to go out in the snow with. Change the foot wear every day and have as comfortable feet as if you thought your entire brains were in your feet.

Wash those feet daily and see that every crack and every crevice is thoroughly cleaned between the toes with an old toothbrush and soap, and wiped thoroughly dry. If you get wet while you are out, change the foot wear at once when you come in and wash the feet in cold water unless at the time you are unwell.

Have the shoes made to order, and do not purchase the miserable articles known as high heeled shoes, nor any of the paper things which are sold for the articles of fashion. You will live longer to let these fashionable shoes remain in the shops and you go to some shoemaker and have a good pair made which will fit your feet. Have them made wide and sensible with low heels, and you will have more comfort with them than with all the fashionable things that every one in the world will see you wear all the year. without liking you a particle better.

Do you wear any slippers in the fall and early winter?

Do not wear slippers when you are about the house work and liable to take cold.

Then if your feet are cold after you have paid attention to all of these things, we advise you to have a walk every day, and take as much of a walk as will make you nice and and warm when you come back to the house. Do not be afraid of a three-mile walk. Do not be afraid of a ten-mile walk. This walking is all the better if you are weakly and puny, for it will bring the roses into your cheeks quicker than all of the tonics which the doctors and the evil spirits have ever concocted.

Don't forget it. Walking is one of the good things for your body and is one of the best things to remove the lack of circulation which is the cause of cold feet. But you can not walk in the fashionable shoes of the day nor walk with the high heels which have been so much the fashion during the past few years and sold under the names of the " French heels."

Let the French and the demi-monde wear the high-heeled shoes if they wish, but do you allow your feet to have a good circulation and we surely will have one of the causes of cold and congested uterus out of the way.

Second. Constipation. One of the reasons of so much and so persistent constipation lies in the food which is eaten. Fine flour bread is one of these causes. Graham is best and should be eaten to the exclusion of all of the fine flour which is made. But the graham which is too often sold by the grocers, is not graham, but a mixture of fine flour and bran. Good graham is made by grinding whole wheat and leaving it unbolted. This takes in all the elements of nutrition and is much better for sustenance than the fine flour.

If food does not regulate the bowels, do not hesitate for a day, but take a syringe and pump up into the bowels at the least from three to five quarts of warm water every night before you go to bed.

If you are bad and think that there is no relief from constipation, then let this water stay up in the bowels as long as you can hold it and rub the bowels gently so as to get rid of cakes which are liable to be on the inside of the intestines and which are one of the causes of this constipated habit. This injection should be used before you have any bad time with the menses. It should be used every day until you are rid of all pains and the bowels are in the best of order.

While the pain is on, that is, while there is pain during menstruation, it is a great benefit to take an injection of a weak pennyroyal infusion, and you can use as much as five quarts so as to thoroughly cleanse the bowels, and this will also relax the uterus and the appendages so that there will be no contraction and the pain will disappear as if by magic.

The cause of these unpleasant telegrams is in the nerves. But mark, if there is no obstruction the nerves will not telegraph a lie, and you will be free and easy. Not a pain.

We say, in the use of these large injections to the bowels, you will find more relief than from any courses of medicine which can be given. And mark: These injections are to be made *large* enough to not alone relieve the bowels and pro-cure a good passage of the bowels, but they are to be made large for the purpose of washing out and cleansing the small intestines of their refuse stuff and thus of relieving the uterus of any pressure from these stuffed small intestines; and also for the purpose of relaxing all the capillaries and allowing the obstructions to be forced out of the body. Because, when these intestines are filled and stuffed with the feces which should have been passed off long ago, then the uterus is pressed out of shape and out of place, and thus there are many of the messages from these parts which tell, in the language of the vital force, there is some obstruction which should be removed. And this large injection will remove it as certainly as the obstruction is there. You need not be afraid of using too much, as we have frequently used three and four quarts, and sometimes we have had an injection given into the bowels which would cause the water to run from the mouth. This does not sound reasonable. But we have seen it and the lady recovered of her very distressing disease.

We repeat that in the second place, you need to use large

injections of warm water and to have the food correct to cure constipation, and it will surely do it. And, finally, for this constipated habit, we tell you to go without the supper, and also to fast as often as three nights in the week. Do not be afraid to go without your supper and to go without any water to drink at the time you are fasting. Water is all right as a drink, and we do not know of any better thing to use and to take into the body in that state which we call constipation, than cold water; but when fasting, we advise you not to touch any water.

At the times you are not fasting, it is the best thing to do to drink plenty of water so as to give the 25,000,000,000 of red blood corpuscles a drink and allow them to have liquid sufficient to cleanse their little economies.

Think this over, for there is much more in it than appears on the surface. Drink all the water you desire while you are not fasting, and take some that you may not have any desire for, if you are of a constipated habit. It will not hurt you to take from three to seven, or even sixteen glasses of cool soft water in the morning when the body is out of order and needs to have this life-giving liquid to assuage the conditions of the body which are called by the name of fever.

The blood needs to have water and can not be run in good health without water and an abundance of it. We advise you to take a drink of water every morning and every night, if you are not in good health, but in the case of painful menstruation you may be doubly assured that there is not liquid enough in the system, and the more water that is drank before the menstrual period is on, the better you will go through this cleansing process, *menstruating.*

Recapitulation for this constipation: Food, habits, drink, large injections to the bowels daily and fasting at the least from three to five meals a week, or to live on two meals a day. Occasionally, we advise you to go without all food for an entire day or even three days, if you can stand it. Do not eat anything while there is any pain during the menstrual period. *Never eat while in any pain.*

Fasting is one of the greatest remedies for pain which has

ever been divulged to mankind. Why? Because fasting reduces the size of the blood corpuscles and allows them to flow more readily through the capillaries and so *reduces the congestions and all swellings.* Fasting thins the blood and reduces the spleen and liver in size. Make it a habit to fast two to five meals a week, or else eat two meals a day.

Third. The garter. Have all your stockings held up by some straps over your shoulder. Don't fool away another penny until you have these articles in the best of shape, and have three or four pairs of these straps to fit your shoulders while you are at it.

Fourth. Food. We have given you some hints as to food, and we just stop here to say that the natural food of man is bread and fruit. Eat this fruit in any manner you choose, but eat it at the meal times and do not make a pig of yourself by gormandizing this fruit between meals and then say it does you no good. While you have bread for dinner, pare a good ripe apple and eat this apple *with your bread.* But do not eat ripe or unripe or raw apples at any time unless you have a piece of bread to be eaten with them. Never eat the skins under any consideration, nor the core, nor anything that might be a nest for the eggs of worms.

Fifth. The corset. Have the dresses fitted over an under-waist and you will have a nicer form than is possible to have with anything on earth in the shape of a corset. Have an under-waist and do not have this under-waist too tight. If it is possible, have all the skirts hang from straps over the shoulder. Keep the waist and the lungs free and ready at all times to be filled with the best tonic in the world —pure air.

Sixth. Food should never be eaten in a hurry; and if you can not have time to eat your food, we advise you to wait until night and eat slowly, and chew up what you do eat, so as not to have a mass of this undigested food in the stomach. There are plenty of people who have only one meal a day, and they live and are well.

The habit of eating three meals is a habit of gluttony. We would all be better if there would be less eaten

Whatever food you eat should not contain too much starch, as the excess of starch is undigested and goes into the blood as starch, which is not good for the body. This is one of the reasons so much of the disease called "whites" or "leucorrhea," and a falling of the womb, are so common diseases—almost universal.

There is another thing about the food that is not known. It is this: When there is not too much eaten nature has a chance to use up all the *best* of what is eaten. But if there is too much eaten, it makes one really poor to carry this around. This is a fact, and accounts for the other fact that some of those who have encountered what are termed "hardships" during this life, are among those who live the longest. And those who have a good time in this world are those who are soonest sent out of this world and into the graveyard. Think this over a little.

Do not let the popular idea of eating for strength pester you for a moment. It is not true that one can eat so much as to force the strength by eating an abundance of food.

It is what is eaten and digested that gives the strength. Not what is placed in one's stomach.

We come to the seventh proposition, and we say in this seventh is all the rest included.

If the blood corpuscles are in good order and are in good trim, with a sufficient quantity of liquid to clean themselves, there will be no trouble in having all the rest of the body in the best of condition. We say this in the most emphatic language that we can command. If the blood corpuscles are in good order then the body will be in good health. And there is no scheme of medication that is of any value that does not include *all the systems* of keeping the entire body *clean* and clear from the seeds of disease. So that when a young lady does not daily take in water enough to run her body and give the 25,000,000,000 red blood corpuscles a daily drink, she will surely have some trouble somewhere.

And so we come back to our original proposition, to have enough of this water in the system; drink from one to three glasses every morning unless there is some reason to prevent

I

you from drinking enough to wash out all of the body, and to have all of the outlets of the body flushed out daily.

Take some clean water, my daughter, and give your army of red blood corpuscles a happy drink, and enough to wash their little faces.

We call to mind a case that had baffled all the physicians of a certain city, and the young lady was nearly wild every period. We advised the attending lady physician to place her in a full warm bath and keep her there as long as she could stand it. Say a full hour, if she would stay lying down in the bath, covered with hot water, and at the same time to give her freely of the infusion of Virginia snake root. The young lady was better right away, and entirely recovered on this treatment.

If there is anything that could be called a *specific* for any and all kinds of painful menstruation, it is a mild infusion of this article, Virginia snake root. Usually, this infusion which is made from the root bought at the corner drug store, is a nasty, bitter dose. But if the root is at all fresh, and it is not made too strong, it is not so bad to take, and it is of the greatest benefit to at once relax the tissues and promote the flow.

Place a pinch in a cup and turn full of boiling water. Sweeten a little, if nauseating, and drink as the stomach will bear, and after a little drink another cupful. The warm water may have as much to do with the speedy relief as the virtues of the snake root. But it is sure that there will not be much of any relief from the use of the fluid extract. If there is a home-made tincture it might answer, but we have found the warm infusion to be by far the best to allay the excruciating pains that arise from contraction and congestion.

As it is not every one who has the full bath tub to lie down in, it is well to know that the injection to the bowels, the hot foot bath and the infusion will answer the purpose in a very short time, without the necessity for any of the poison narcotics that the doctors give to destroy the nerves and poison the intelligence.

Shall we tell you anything else? Just a word. If the dear mothers and the overburdened fathers would take a little time and shoo the story papers out of the house, and fling all the novels and lies into the cook stove, and then sit down and have a real good loving talk with the daughter about herself, so that she understands her own being and the objects of her own body, and knows how to take care of herself, the doctors would have less to do and there would be fewer ruined women to be suffering the agonies of death, without relief, and a large increase of happiness all round.

CHAPTER XII.

THE BEGINNINGS OF ERROR.

According to the age of a girl, there comes a time when she knows what passion is. At one time or another, the valves from certain arteries are open and there follows a thrill which, though faint, is tremulously delicious and painfully sweet.

This passion, or the first appearance of this passion, is deferred in some to past the age of twenty. To others it is a fact at the age of four. Whenever this feeling appears, or wherever it appears (boy or girl), there is a desire to renew the feeling, which, although of a swift, fleeting passage, is a play and a vibration on every nerve in the system. This thrill of passion results in a loss of nervous force. When this nervous force is over, the passion is gone. The thrill has departed. The body can not be aroused again (for a short time is this true) to renew this passionate thrill.

Now, although it is true that the prime seat of this passion (in the girl) lies in the clitoris or in the intense filling of all the blood vessels in the genito-urinary organs, or in the vulva, yet it happens that there are points on the body that seem to open these floodgates of passion, and to these points we call your especial attention at this time. It is often that error and destruction commence at these points.

First, the breasts. Why it is that simply handling or rubbing the breasts provokes the flow of blood to the vulva and arouses sexual passion can not be satisfactorily explained. But it is a fact that we desire you to note.

Second. There is a spot on each side of the neck, that when kissed or fondled provokes the same sexual passion.

Third. The kissing of the lips.

Outside of the absolute *contact* of warmth, friction, moisture, animal magnetism and passions embrace with the genito-urinary organs, we have three points of attack, by which the members of the other sex endeavor to gain the control of your body, and to arouse and fire your passions, or array the animal against the spiritual or mental. These passions are based upon one fact, and if you understand the cause of them you can never be approached at any disadvantage. The causes of passion may be stated:

1. The blood must fill up the clitoris, the vulva and possibly the arterial system surrounding the uterus.

2. If you have a system of arteries that are rapidly filled so as to make the parts full, turgid and stagnant. If this occurs, *you are already filled with passion.*

The ignorance of these two points has lost many a girl her virtue and her honor. She is already assailed *in her own person* with these passions. Added to these fires, she allows *contact* with the hands or the person in one of the three "*points of attack*" which we have previously called your attention to, viz. : the breasts, the neck and the lips ; and if the pressure or animal magnetism is sustained at any of these points, *there comes a time when bodily passion overcomes all mental resolves and you yield your body to passion.* You are lost.

It is true that many have yielded to the embraces of a man and yet stopped short of sexual intercourse.

This is true, because some men are afraid, and some are conscientious. But we lay it down as a rule, and one that you will never regret having followed, that the man who caresses you, the man who desires to fondle your breasts, rub your neck or kiss you on the lips is the one who is doing his level best to have intercourse with you, and who is *trying to ruin you,* no matter all his protestations to the contrary.

We should make a concession to ignorance at this place and acknowledge that in cases of lovers there are cases where the man kisses and fondles a woman because he loves her, and as he confidently expects to be married, he thinks he has a right to caress the woman who is to be his wife.

We have given our opinion of that folly in another chapter. It is a folly and a mistake for the woman to allow the beginning of this fondling and caressing.

But every girl is liable to be so approached, and as this approach is subtle and gradual we will state our ideas of preventing these *beginnings of error.*

First. We do not think it possible for any one to be strictly pure and virtuous unless helped from the outside. Passion is too strong. Flesh too weak. Education of these matters is so limited that there is really nothing for a girl to go by except native modesty and common sense, and the devil can always find some way to overcome these where he desires to ruin a girl.

We say then,—get help.

You ask, "How?"

The reply is : God made you for a purpose. He desires you to be strong. He desires not only your body to be pure, but also the mind, soul or spirit.

For this purpose God sent His Son. And the Son on his departure sent the Comforter. (This word, *Comforter*, in the Greek is *Paraclete*, which word signifies an advocate and a strengthener.)

This is the Holy Ghost, the Holy Spirit and the Spirit of Truth. Christ sends this Spirit to all who believe on Him. You, therefore, have two great helps to aid and strength. The Comforter and your book of instructions—the Bible.

We urge you to get this help before any temptation or evil comes on you. Prepare for these trials as one should prepare for the winter or for a rain storm. The Holy Spirit is sent to all who believe that Jesus was the Christ. We hope you believe it. If you do not already, the belief of this is of the first importance. Our advice is this. Read the Bible daily and pray for help and strength and the assistance of the Holy Spirit.

Having done this you should not neglect any of the earthly laws which God has placed before you.

You should keep perfectly clean.

By clean we mean that upon your person there should be no stain, spot or discharge. Everything which makes an obstruction to the skin or remains to clog up the skin in any manner will render you the more passionate and your passions more ungovernable at the time of trial.

Cleanliness is therefore of the first importance.

Second. At once, as soon as you have resolved that you desire to be a perfect woman, fight down, conquer and stamp out every bit of passion that you may have in your body.

As we have said, the cause of this passion is the filling of certain places with blood. Certain arteries and places that do not habitually and should not have any quantity of blood —or an excess of blood in them.

We say keep that blood away from them, and control that passion. Do not allow a particle of the nervous force to be lost. Shut up those arteries and contract them. Keep the blood out of those parts and you can control the passion so that you need not allow any unforeseen accident or design to have any control over you.

If there is heat, wash in cold water. It is all right for you to bathe all your body in cold water at any period when the the menses are not on. And, if you have begun to fight down these passions, you will find that, from one cause or another, you are *more* passionate directly *after* the menstrual period.

For cleanliness. if more agreeable, use warm water and soap, if according to your ideas. But to fight *passion* sit down or continue to bathe in cold water until the excess of blood is returned to the general circulation and the passion is entirely gone. All this can be done if the mind is kept from the opposite sex. If you can not banish the images of passionate desire from your brain you *need work*—active, hard labor.

Walking, digging, washing, lifting, gymnastics, or, in fact, anything that will call away the blood from the generative organs and place the brain on a healthy, equable plane.

You may rest assured that until you have conquered every atom of passion and every feather of desire for sexual gratification, that you are liable to become the victim of some man's lust or desire. And you may depend upon it that if you are not the mistress and controller of your own body, that the time comes when some one else will control you to your intense despair and to your eternal sorrow and agonizing shame.

The moment you feel any passion, fight it. Bathe in cold water. Walk, ride, get up and get out of your surroundings. In the night—in the day—fight the passion until you are absolutely the controller of that system of arteries.

Third. To assist you to control yourself let us repeat that eggs, oysters, wine, potatoes, coffee, tea, and meats of all kinds, especially anything from the hog, pork, ham, lard and grease, taken into the body as food are, in a manner, irritating to the blood and are provocative of passion. Let all these things alone as food.

Oysters are direct passion producers, and thousands of virtuous girls have been seduced while assailed by the fried oysters and wine within and a smooth villain of a man on the outside.

Never touch wine, under any consideration.

Coffee clogs the liver and so thickens the blood. One can not be virtuous and chaste and drink coffee. Coffee is a virtue destroyer.

Tea is a filthy, scabby drink. It weakens the kidneys and makes the whites. It causes wrinkles and softens the brain. It weakens virtuous resolves and destroys will power. While one pours tea into the body, the body becomes rotten and unfit as a dwelling place for the Holy Ghost.

Keep the body clean and the Holy Ghost shall dwell in you. But if the body is filled with these abominations you can not expect to control it by the operations of the mind.

Heavy suppers are another destructive element in the body. Do not allow yourself to indulge in them. Eat a crust and take a cup of cold water if you are faint, but if you can, while you are fighting down this passion, go without your supper.

Bear in mind that there is always a *worst* time. Conquer that worst time and you are the victor. If the passion conquers you once, try again with renewed courage in God. Do not think that one resolve, nor one action is to render you

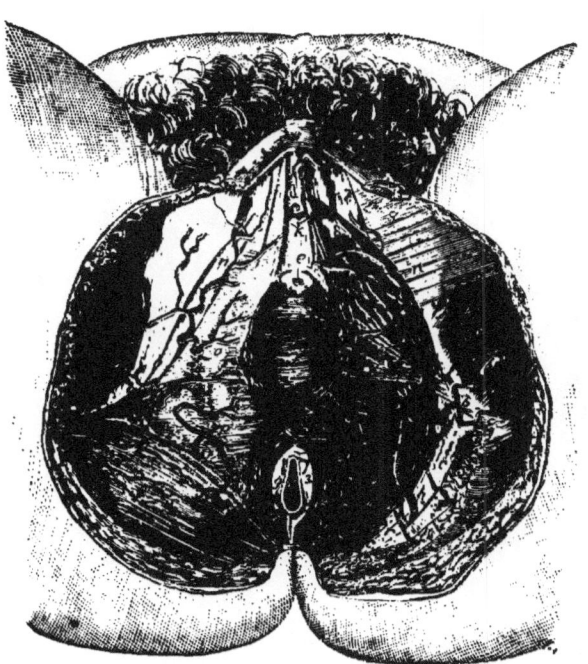

The Arteries of the Female Genito-urinary System.

The object of this figure is to show the network of arteries which surround the labia and the clitoris, and impress this fact upon the reader: that if this blood is kept from these parts there can be no passion, and if the blood is allowed to flow into these arteries there will be passion. To keep the arteries small, and not to have any, or, at the least, the smallest amount of blood in these arteries is of the first importance in a life of purity. Fasting, washing, purity of thought, and the most absolute cleanliness is the only method by which this can be successfully accomplished.

impenetrable and faultless. It takes time. You may fail in your mind once or a hundred times, and yet you will and must succeed if you persevere. Do not yield to passion an atom. Fast if needed. Keep the body actively employed. Keep the mind from the thoughts which bring up the least approach to heat or passion.

We know this perfect control of the body and the passions can be gained by any girl or any woman who is determined to do it. But on the other hand, if one allows this sexual passion to once gain the mastery over them, there is an end of all intellectual or physical development.

When one of these women is married who has yielded to passion or tried to gratify herself by the unfortunate habits of youth, heat and lustful ideas, the marks are carried on the body and shown upon the face. But this would not be so bad if it were not for the fact that all the body suffers in direct proportion to this miserable gratification of passion. The throat becomes dry and husky, and the voice for singing is gone. The eyes become heavy, dull, and sometimes the eyelashes are covered with whitish scales. The teeth become covered with slime and are rotten, from this gratification of the sexual organs.

The habit of self abuse becomes a second nature, and when marriage takes place there is not a particle of gratification with the husband. A patient of mine who married one of these women who had yielded to these secret gratifications of passion, told me that during the first months of his unhappy married life he had to rub this unfortunate victim of self lust *with his hands* for an hour after retiring. The result was a divorce. Perfect sexual intercourse is never known where one or both parties have abused their bodies before marriage.

Keep your body pure and clean. Fight down any passion *now, this minute*, and while you take all the precautions to have the body pure, read that book of instructions, the Bible, and beseech God to aid you by His Spirit. With these helps, you can not fail.

LOUISIANA.

CHAPTER XIII.

THE WEARING APPAREL.

In regard to the wearing apparel, wear that on the outside which is not conspicuous or showy. You will soon learn what colors are good for you and suitable for your complexion, your hair and your eyes. Keep away from red, yellow, crimson or bright blue. Have your clothes so that no one can positively describe you by one thing you wear, as, "the girl with the red ribbon," or "the one with bangs," or "the girl with the yellow skirt," and all that. Keep away from all efforts at eccentricity.

In regard to your underwear, we advise, *have enough.* By that, we suggest that you have at least six changes of undergarments, and not less than six pairs of stockings for summer and six pairs for winter, not less than three nightgowns, and if possible, have six. There is always some needy woman that has none, and you can make an odd nightdress from twenty-five cents' worth of cotton cloth, and the value of a clean nightdress *when it is needed,* is invaluable.

We do not believe in indiscriminate charity, but a nightdress is of more actual service to a sick neighbor, or some sick, weakly mother who has been cramped for means to supply herself, than any other article of wearing apparel. While the prime cost is little, you will do a world of good. Have enough for yourself and one or two to do good with. Don't think of yourself all the time. Be prepared to help those who are weaker and poorer than you.

Undershirts, stockings, drawers, bands, or anything which comes next the skin, should never be red, crimson, yellow, blue, or any color which contains any material liable to poison the skin.

Crimson and red are colors which have been known to cause a vicious humor of the skin, and you do not want an intractable skin disease. White is the safest, cleanest and

138

best color, and after the white, the natural grey, a very light buff or a cream color. Scottish greys are a fair color, but are more liable to be poisonous to the skin than the clear white.

Colored stockings are a special abomination. Wear white as much as possible, and if you have to wear black, have them thoroughly washed before they go on your feet. The blood from the heart goes to the feet direct, and in the case of red stockings, when the feet are poisoned with red stockings, the entire blood becomes poisoned. Pimples come to the face from red or analine-colored hosiery.

Have the shoes made to order. Save enough to have good rubbers, good shoes and high slippers. But see to it that you do not wear the slippers out of doors or on the porch. It creates a feeling of slouchiness to see a girl on the street in slippers. And to wear a Mother Hubbard dress on the street with the slippers, is sufficient to give you a reputation not enviable.

Whatever you have, do not be in debt for it a penny. Your body will be far better in the oldest and cheapest dress you can keep whole and clean than in anything which is unpaid for.

The same thing is to be said about cloaks and wraps. Do not owe a penny. Do not have a thing on you that is not fully paid for and paid for honestly. Keep account of your expenditures, and make it an endeavor of your life to have the wearing apparel good, clean, whole and becoming. But before you think of anything, be sure it is all paid for, and paid the last penny.

We urge this upon you with all the force we can command. Do not go into debt for a penny's worth of wearing apparel, under any circumstances. Keep debt from your back and your head, and you shall have a beauty and peace in your face which will outweigh all the advantages of dress a thousand times.

In the matter of economy, it is the best to purchase the best at once. But, as it is almost impossible at once to have access to the best grades of fabrics, we advise you to select those

goods of gray, black, or a very dark shade of blue or
brown, which will make up sober, and become you when
you wear them.

There is nothing that will ever make you feel as if you were
wholly independent until you earn all your own living. To
earn this living honestly you will do some good hard thinking, and when you do earn it, you will find that there are a
good many ways of earning the money but there are a thousand more ways to spend it. We desire to help you to
save that money.

You need good clothes and clothes which will look well in
the house and on the street. We repeat that which is already written : Whatever may be your complexion you may
be sure that any dress of red or any color of purple will
never become you, nor become any other honest, virtuous
girl. But nothing can become you which you owe for at the
store.

Some one may tell you red is the right thing, and that the
color is not red but cardinal, or some other name. What
they may tell you will not weigh an atom if you have good
sense. No fool color which is the color devoted to the
women of the town, as are the colors of red and of crimson
and of purple, will ever be becoming to the girl who intends
to be straight, honest and upright in herself. If you are a
blonde, we think that a shade of grey will suit your complexion. If you are a brunette, we think soft drab or black, or
if it is in summer you can wear white, if you are sure about
the expense of the washing. But avoid all pronounced
colors as you would avoid having your name in the daily
prints as a street-walker.

It is *your* dress, of course. But people will think and
fools will talk. And if you have a knack of picking out a
dress of calico or of gingham which you can wear on the
street and not have the gossips of the town wonder who
picked it out for you, and if you can be dressed so that
these street gossips will keep their tongues off you, there is
a great point gained in the happiness of your daily life.

We think if you have some relation who is a friend, or

some one who can tell you of the things you need and who can assist you in picking out your dresses and who will give you honest advice, it will be well to take the advice. But in the case of your being without friends, we think you will see that your best way is to do your own thinking and to feel as if you were the one to be consulted in the matter. Never hurry in your selection of your garments, or be influenced by the salesman. If you are earning your clothes, or the money for those clothes, there will be some thought needed to make your wages pay for the best when you start out in the world. The habit of thinking for yourself will bring greater results to you than if you had a friend who could carry you on her shoulders and do everything for you while you allow your brain to be stagnant.

These are matters which you will slowly decide for yourself. If you have beauty, strength and power, the clothes really do not matter. If you lack these attributes, the wearing apparel only makes you conspicuous.

CHAPTER XIV.

UNLAWFUL PLEASURES.

When there is something sought to be enjoyed, which does not belong to the one who tries to enjoy the fruits of some one's labor besides his own, then this enjoyment is said to be *unlawful*.

We will take up one phase of this unlawful enjoyment and look at the result. The young lady who thinks she can enjoy some habit all to herself, and in due time she will enjoy some one else as a husband, is the one who is going to be the greatest deceived person in this world.

Are there any such ?

Do we think any young lady will be foolish enough to use her own body for such pleasures as should only be allowed when children are desired ?

Can it be possible that any one would be so foolish and so stupid as to take away from the one she will love, the pleasures which rightly belong to him and to no one else ?

Is there any girl who is so devoid of understanding as to allow the habit of self abuse to overcome her best judgment and waste her body in a vain endeavor to feel what can never be experienced except with utmost love and with the utmost freedom ?

Are there any so foolish as to imagine that there is something which they can do and it will never be found out by some one ?

Can it be possible that any one will have the habit day after day to feel of their own body and allow their minds to wander to such subjects as are only permitted to those who have entered the married state, and should only be permitted when the wife and husband desire to have children ?

Do we think so ?

Yes. We know there are thousands of these young persons, girls as well as boys, who are to-day guilty of this

142

monstrous habit of self abuse, and are guilty because there are none to tell them of its dangers and of its follies, to warn them of the horrible results which spring from this abuse of the body.

What are these girls called ?

In the medical profession these victims to this desire for unlawful pleasures are called "female masturbators."

The girl thinks she is enjoying herself by this habit, and it becomes almost a second nature.

We are sorry to say this, and if it were not our duty we should omit this chapter from this book. But we do not think the half has ever been told of the folly of the most beautiful and the most gifted of God's creatures who have the keeping of two families and so many people in their possession.

Do we think this a common habit ?

We do not think anything about it. We know there are thousands of families who have been wrecked and made the most unhappy in the world by the formation of this habit of self abuse when the girl was ripening into womanhood. We think the guilt of the male portion of the human family may be greatest. We admit that it may be greatest, but from our experience and what we can learn of the parties who are the victims to illness and to disease, we are of the opinion that there are six of one and just an even half dozen of the other.

We do not think there is any radical difference between the habits of a family, whether it is the boys or the girls.

And we have long ago arrived at the conclusion that as for the habit of self abuse, it is as bad as the worst can be imagined among the boys. This will sound strange to many, but as we are writing this in the best interests of the world, and for our own children, we have no interest in holding to or keeping up a falsehood. And it is said as deliberately as we should say it, there are as many who eat among the females as there are who eat of the males.

It is too bad to say this. We are sorry to say it and if we did not think it best for the mothers to know about their daughters, we should never have placed it on the paper.   But we believe it to be a fact.   We think after there has been one cause of disease taken out from the category of the beginning of female diseases, there is one which will take pre-eminence of all the others, and this cause is self abuse among the girls.

It is certainly a dreadful thing to say that the girl is no better than the boy.   But we think in the interests of truth there should be the truth told if it does cut some one's feelings, and it is better to know what one is fighting than to fight in the dark.

And we repeat this statement, that there are almost, if not quite, as many girls who are addicted to this habit of self abuse as there are boys.

Why should there not be ?

They eat the same food, do the same things, and sit in the house even more than the boys, and the reasons why they should do this evil are as great among them as among the boys.

Do we think this can be proved ?   Ask any physician who is honest, what are the prime causes of all the female disease and he will tell you that the self abuse is one of the greatest causes in the world

Examine now, if it suit you, the females who are sick, and get them to say whether they have ever been guilty of this habit, and it will surprise the most incredulous as to the extent of this self abuse among the girls.

We say this is the fact.   There is no one cause of the so-called "female disease" which is so prevalent as the habit of self abuse among the female sex.   When we consider that the oysters and the eggs and the tea and coffee are all of them provocative of the desires for sexual gratification, then we must suppose that the females are angels or that they are different in their composition from the male part of this earth.   We do not think this.   We know from what we have seen that the women are just as liable to have these sexual passions as the men.

When they do have them and they make a mistake and allow

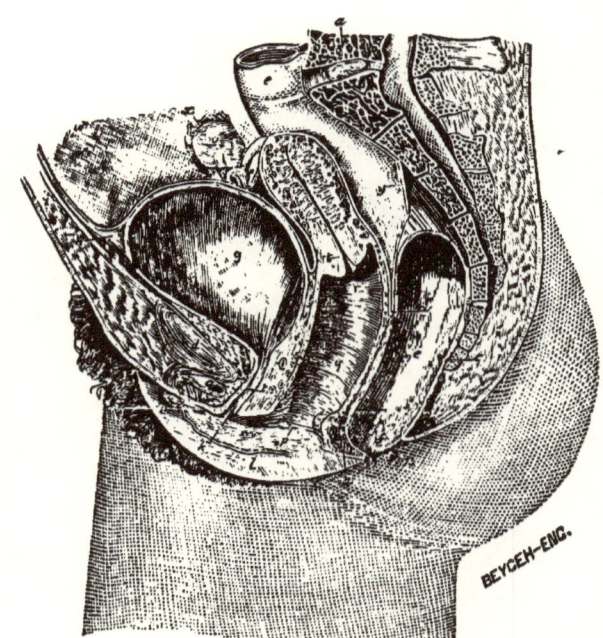

Vertical section of Female Genito-urinary Organs, giving lateral view of Pelvic Viscera laid open—right side.

a Last lumbar vertebra.
b Os sacrum.
c Os coccygis.
d Os pubis.
e Intestinum rectum.
f Anus.
g Vesica urinaria.
h Urachus, lig. vesicæ medium.
i Urethra.
k Orificium urethræ externum.
l Labium pudendi externum.
m Labium internum, nympha.
n Glans clitoridis.

o Corpus cavernosum clitoridis.
p Orificium vaginæ.
q Vagina.
r Portio vaginalis uteri, with os uteri externum.
s Cavum uteri.
t Canalis colli uteri.
u Fundus uteri.
v Ovarium.
w Tuba Fallopii.
x Fimbriæ v. laciniae.
y Peritonæum.
z Perinæum.

themselves to be persuaded into doing something for which they alone are the sufferers, then we say, ''She is fallen.'' But we should say she is but one who has shown her passion while there are thousands who are equally guilty and they are not found out.

We can not think the women who have the same make-up to the body are really any different in their feelings from the men. They certainly are not. It is one of the follies of life to think the girl can eat any and all of the things which we know will produce passion in the male, and yet be perfectly harmless and pure in thought. It could not be.

And from the experience of half a century, thirty-five years of which have been spent in direct communication with the human race, I do not hesitate to assert that the habit of self abuse is one of the greatest causes of the evils and the diseases of the female sex. The habit is one which is easily learned and is taught by one girl to another, and there is no way of finding it out, so that the fond mother and father who see the daughter go into a decline, or into consumption, fondly imagine there is some germ which, if they could get hold of, would cure their dear daughter.

While they are praying to heaven to aid them in their search for a doctor or some medicine, the girl is daily at the task of destruction which will one day lay her in the ground.

We have had some experience in this life, and we have no hesitation in saying that as far as our experience goes, there is as much of this habit among the daughters as among the sons.

How shall we eradicate this bestial habit?

Not by sitting down and complaining about it. This will not do any good. We have to take hold of the facts as we find them and see that we are educating these children so that they will not be guilty of these crimes any more. We must educate.

This is our task.

The girl who first feels the sexual passion has some changes in her body which she does not know the meaning of. When the passion is allowed to be felt, unrestrained, there is a descent of the womb into the vagina, and this is so, be-

K

cause the womb, if there is to be a sexual orgasm, will be in the best position to discharge the mucous from the womb into the vagina and lubricate all the parts, both for the sexual act, and, if there are to be children (for this act was never contemplated except for the purpose of procreating, and having offspring), the womb, having discharged all of its mucous, will be in a condition to take and to absorb the semen from the male.

There are two points at this place which are worthy of careful consideration.

First. There is the discharge from the womb, so that the womb will be empty and ready to receive the semen from the male.

Second. If this womb has no semen at hand or close by to enter the womb at the moment of its discharge, it will have an emptiness there which *will leave the womb dry, turgid and heated.*

These points are two of the things or states which are not so far as we know, laid down in any book.

(Note. There is a book which we have seen, "Satan in Society," which is written by a physician, who affirms in his preface he has not the the courage to own his name to his work. In this book there is laid down the correct proposition which is that "unless the womb at the time of the sexual orgasm has the semen of the man it will become diseased." This is the only hint, so far as we have been able to read, of the injury done to the female sex by this habit of self abuse.)

But we call the very particular attention to these two states, and ask the mother and the daughter to look at the consequences of this self abuse of the body and this gratification of the person with these unlawful pleasures.

First. The womb descends. When this womb descends and has the semen to moisten it, there is the ascent again and the womb is again in its natural place.

But if there is no semen and no moisture, there will be a permanent staying down of this womb and the woman will have *falling of the womb.*

We say deliberately, if there is self abuse by the girl, there is more likely to be the falling of the womb in her because of this lack of any compensation to the womb for its loss of the mucous which was in it before the sexual orgasm. Before the orgasm and before the passion there was some mucous to fill the womb and to keep it moist. But after the orgasm, there is dryness *in the womb* and the womb becomes *dry* and is of no account *to support itself*, as it is dead to all feeling after the sexual orgasm, or the passion without intercourse, is over. This is one of the laws which any one can see if they will reflect upon the position of the womb and the condition of this organ when it descends upon the approach of passion. While the passion is on, there is a heat in the parts and the excitement is of so great and stimulating a nature that there are no ailments felt.

When the orgasm and the passion are once over, the relapse is one of quick despondency and ill feelings. This is not said to frighten any one from the act. It is the truth, and a truth which can be seen any day by looking on the street and examining the faces of the girls who are guilty of this habit. We repeat, this is one of the important facts of this chapter that the orgasm and passion of the girl finds the womb in a full condition of mucous, which is necessary for its preservation and its supply, and when this orgasm is over, this mucous has been placed *outside* of the womb into the vagina and from there it flows away, so that there must be more of this mucous taken from the rest of the system to supply this waste and this loss.

The womb after this passion is over is empty and hard. There has been nothing to moisten it and the moisture which was there from nature's supply has been thrown away when the passion is gratified.

This habit also causes constipation and this constipation is because the rectum is partially paralyzed with this feeling of passion, and can not tell when the feces are in sufficient quantity to pass out of the bowels.

Constipation is an evil of so great proportions that all the diseases of the female sex have been laid to this one fault of the economy.   But if the other habits are good there will be soon an end to constipation.

We said the womb descends.

With this descent of the womb there is the lengthening of the ligaments of the womb, and very soon after this habit of self abuse is commenced there is a dragging of the lower bowels, and the whites follow this condition as readily as the night follows the day.

The whites is the discharge which is too well known to be described here, but it is a discharge which is common to most of the females who are in this habit of self abuse and the women who are tea drinkers.   This *lengthening of the ligaments of the womb* brings on a pain in the back, and as a consequence of this weakness of the back there has to be something to support the back, and this something is called the corset, and so the thing can be kept up until the girl is practically ruined in her body.

We are not going to be led into the habit of computing how many of the female sex are in the habit of committing this folly.   The book already referred to says (and the writer is one of the so-called "distinguished physicians") that when he "went to a boarding school there was not one boy who was not guilty of the habit of self abuse!"   This is found in that book which is from the pen of a man who says he has not the courage to own his name in connection with the publication of the book.   We will not go so far as that.   We will say there are multitudes of boys who do not know any better, and the girls are every whit as bad as the boys.   There is no use of disguising this matter and asserting the girls are all pure as the angelic host.   We know better.   The girls are so guilty of this habit that there are thousands of doctors who are daily fattening on the credulity of these same girls, and more of them will not say what is the cause of so much female disease, but they will doctor it for money and allow the girl to remain in ignorance of her malady week after week and this will be the outcome.   After the father gets tired of this paying out of any money, there will come a settlement, and then, as the case is about to slip out of his hands, the doctor may hint darkly at what he long ago knew was the cause of the "female disease" and then only in such a manner that there is no satisfaction to the father.

It may be thought that the writer is too severe. We do not think so. There is hardly a day passes which does not bring the fruits of this folly to the office of this writer.

It is not one year since there came a married man of fifty who acknowledged that his wife (over forty years of age) had been in the habit of self abuse for as long as he had known her, and he did not know how to stop the habit.

This may seem a strange story, but there are, in every doctor's experience, dozens of similar cases which come from the early habit of self abuse, and there does not seem to be any remedy.

Who are the guilty parties ? We answer, all the tea drinkers. Leave no tea drinker out from the habit of self abuse. All the coffee drinkers. Let no coffee drinker assert she is pure. There is just as much sense for a woman in one of the houses of prostitution to say that she is strictly virtuous, as for one of these habitual tea or coffee drinkers to assert they are pure.

Put them all in and assert that every coffee drinker is in the habit of self abuse, and we shall not be far wrong. A coffee drinker can not keep the body right and so we are assured, not alone by one person, but by any number of persons who have tried it, and know from experience, that there can not be a strictly virtuous life, without these sexual passionate thoughts, and at the same time drink these stimulants to the blood. And then this habit follows when the marriage tie is celebrated, because the parties have told the writer: "Doctor, I have found more pleasure from my own companionship, than from the company of my wife." Why ? Because they have both been victims to this self abuse.

The womb descends. And it stays descended as soon as these pleasures which are unlawfully gratified, are become so exhausting as to take out more of this mucous than the womb can secrete. Then the womb falls and stays descended, and the whites are present, and the back aches and all the train of evils follow which only a woman can recall. We may stop and make a few remarks on this folly and its consequences on the victim.

The first thing which happens to the girl who allows this waste to go away from her is the sleepy feeling which is almost impossible to overcome. Then follows the feeling of irritability and peevishness. Then she is nervous. Then after a little she is hysterical. And there is, in some of the highly organized persons, a danger of epilepsy. These spasms are called by every name on the calendar, but the cause is unknown to all save the girl who is guilty of this suicidal act. She can keep a secret, and she keeps this one until she is almost ruined in body and in mind. There is sometimes, not always, a kind of gumminess around the eyelids. Styes. There are some dark-colored rings around and under the eyes. Wrinkles do not always come, but they are there to stay as soon as there is any serious trouble with the digestive apparatus, which always follows sooner or later.

The victim of masturbation has a weak back. Not so uniformly as to be a certain sign, but this weak back in a young girl is one of the symptoms and should always be looked upon with suspicion. There is usually a sort of a dreamy expression to all of the girls who abuse themselves who are fleshy. But with the ones who are thin we have found a decided devilishness of spirit which is called sulkiness. And this sulkiness is sometimes followed by the most violent forms of anger. There is very little control of one's temper when one is in the habit of self abuse.

As we have seen, the womb discharges a quantity of mucous at the times of passion. This discharge comes from the general system, and is of so valuable a quality that it is soon impossible for the body to replace it, and in a short time the body can not keep up its weight and the girl grows thin and scrawny. The eyes are large and seemingly brilliant. She has a voracious appetite, but there is no such thing as any fattening of the girl, and she appears constitutionally thin in flesh, even after she has quit this vile habit. The passion, as we have already seen, is one which depends in a measure on the flow of blood to the parts of generation. This flow of blood, having been carried to these parts and there stagnated, after the passion is over is partially carried away and is in the general circulation. Some of this blood comes out in the face as dead blood, and when nature sends this to the surface, it is in the form of pimples on the face.

We do not say but what there are other causes for many of these pimples on the face. There are many other causes. But the cause of the worst pimples which often appear on the faces of youth, and the cause of so much rough skin, is brought about primarily, by this dead blood which is sent to the organs of generation, and when the passion is over this blood is dead, and so this dead blood goes back into the general circulation as dead blood and comes out in the face as pimples and blotches.

The girl may not always have them. This is conceded. But she is liable to have them, and any one who is practicing this habit of self abuse will not and can not have as clear and fair a skin as the ones who thoroughly control their sexual feelings, and see that there is no waste to their body. If the features do not become angular, as they often do in certain cases (and in these cases the features assume what is termed the features of the old maid, but which are more the features of the victim of self abuse. The long neck and the angular features are not so much the features of the maid as the features of the masturbator. The single lady who is perfectly pure in thought, never has any of the old maid features, never) there is something which is often taken for an absent air. This dreaminess is one of the most deceptive things in the world to judge by. The girl has lost part of her memory and in the endeavor to catch that which has become lost, she is trying to remember something, and this far away, dreamy expression is thought to be an abstraction of the mind. But in reality, it is the vacuity of the victim of self abuse.

And this expression is not alone found in the faces of the single women. But it is found on the faces of wives who carry themselves proudly in society. This expression seen once is readily remembered. It is the expression which comes from abused, ungratified passion. I would hesitate to say that all the Chinese nation are victims of this habit of self abuse. Yet there is in the Chinese eye and expression an expression of sensuous passion which is expressive of the height of passion. Witness the contracted eye and the weakness of the lid. A constant or spasmodic effort at winking. A sudden drooping of the eyelid which is indicative of some weakness in the nervous system. A national weakness, if you choose. If this expression is looked for in the married and is found, there is a great likelihood that there has been the habit of self abuse in the marriage bed, or that there has been the preventive from having children, which is brought about by the use of a rubber shield, and which is as bad, or worse than the habit of self abuse. How many, many families are known to the writer where these habits of preventing children have prevailed, and now in their old age they would almost die if they could have a child. So many of these sad cases could be related if we had the space and the time.

It may be placed as a fact, that a girl who is in the habit of self abuse can not look at an object steadily. We are not alluding to those who are hereditarily near-sighted because the father used tobacco. There are, unfortunately, cases in which the child may be the innocent victim of the father's passions or the father's habits of food and of drink. We may say this. The father who chews tobacco is liable to have near-sighted children. These children are not to be blamed. The parent will one day answer for this crime of bringing children into this world subject to these deficiencies of body. God will call the tobacco user to account as to the deprivation of eyesight to gratify his own tastes and his appetites. With that misfortune we have nothing to do at this time. But there is a shrinking of the eyes in the bigness, a sort of contraction of the eyelids, which is the direct effect of the habit of masturbation in the girl, and is often seen in those who live solitary lives.

On the other hand there is an open eye, with a large space of white under the eye proper, and is as if the lower lid had dropped and left the eyeball too much exposed to the light. This is usually associated with a palpitation of the heart, and is only seen after the victim has been some time at this habit. The remedy for this condition is to lead a strictly continent life and pay a strict attention to the diet; then it can be done. Melancholy has long been known as one of the results of self abuse. To be melancholy is to be at once suspected of this habit. Not that this suspicion is always founded on fact, but the habit of sorrowfulness is brought about by this habit of self abuse, and as this is known, there is an idea that all melancholy is from this habit.

The chief result of the habit of self abuse among the girls is seen in a weakness of the body, which is not accounted for in any other way, but by knowing that all the secretions are wasted when this habit is gratified without the compensation of the opposite sex. The weakness of the body is only accounted for by this habit. The girl should have as good a body and as good a mind as the boy, and if this is not the case there is something wrong in the make-up of the girl.

The facts are that there should be as good and a better constitution in the girl than in the boy; and this is indisputable. The matter of sex does not make weakness, and this should be understood. It is not the sex or the conditions of sex which makes the girl weaker than the boy. It is the habits which surround the sex, and these habits tend to weaken the body as well as the mind. The girl can not stand or endure this exhaustive strain on the body any more than the male sex, and when this exhaustive habit is formed there will be a weakness which can not be otherwise explained except by this daily and nightly loss of nervous force.

Who are the guilty parties?

Go on the street and look about you to see who are the victims and the sufferers.

You will see them by the thousands. They who are in the shops. They who work at some trade. They who are doing nothing and allowing some one else to support them in idleness, which is yet further the feeder of these sexual passions.

Look at the brown faces and the unnaturally white faces and see the marks of the secret passion and its half-gratification.

See the eyes of these victims, and watch the form, how it is stuffed with cotton or bird seed to show a form where nature has denied a shape. We call your attention to the eyes which are so sore and so weak that they are pitiable. These are the results of self-abuse or of some filth of body which is almost unpardonable.

Oh, we would be glad to think of every woman as an angel and to think she is pure and sinless. But we know better, and to help the ones who know their weakness, and are desirous of overcoming themselves and their passions, we will take another chapter which will show how to get rid of these passions and yet to have them for the greater building up of the body

Can this sexual passion be wholly controlled ? We assure the reader that all of these sexual passions are readily controlled and can be held in abeyance. More than this, we can tell the victim of these wretched habits that if they will take courage and resolve there shall be no more of this yielding to these feelings, we will do our best to show them how to use these desires so as to produce the best results for the body.

We think the persons who have these desires are the ones who are the depositaries of the good Lord, who desires them to become more than a mere human being. We think the ones who have seen and felt these desires are those who are powerful in themselves as soon as they conquer this waste and these losses.

Their very experiences with these passions are such as will give them power as soon as they are free from all of these unquenchable passionate desires.

What shall be done?

The first thing is to go to God and get his help. Then

we will examine this series of laws and see if there are no natural laws which are ready to be obeyed every day, so that we are above all passion and above all desire for anything which is not lawful and not expedient. And to help us to understand this fully, we will take up the subject in another chapter.

If we understand this matter we shall never have any unlawful pleasures to call us master or to cause us to be branded on the forehead or in the eyes as the servants of some bestial habit.

CHAPTER XV.

PERFECT CONTINENCE.

Although we have previously gone over this subject, we take it up again in a different manner to show exactly what is meant by perfect continence. First, there is to be no thought of passion. The will has to be the first to have the entire control of the mind, and if one does not have thorough control of the will the sooner one gets this control the better for her. Better for the body. Better for the mind. The method of obtaining control is to be sure one is not to have a thought of anything which will lead to the thought of passion. No lewd books. Not a picture which will bring up anything not in the best manner calculated to bring any other thoughts to the brain than those of purity. The food is the next and is really the most important, as there is no such thing as perfect virtue and at the same time a diet of coffee, eggs, wines, pork or potatoes. Bear this in mind, as if there are these foods eaten there is sure to be passion in the body, and in many of these cases this passion is stronger than the will, and when this is the fact there will come a time when the body will be under the control of this passion, and a mis-step will happen that will cause so much sorrow that all the world will never be worth living in again.

See to this food and learn a lesson from Daniel, who fed on pulse rather than to be a servant to the king and lose his virtue. For Daniel knew that if he ate of the king's meats he could not retain his virtue. This is the meaning of that food question. Read about it. Read this over carefully as it is of the greatest importance in your life to know that there is a sure way to live virtuously, and if you do not know of this virtuous way, the food will have such an effect on your body that you can not be virtuous in any manner, even though you try. The food, we tell you, has this effect

156

of arousing the passions and if you do not know of this, it is time you do.

Eggs are certain provocatives of the passions, and we do not hesitate to say that any one who eats eggs in any shape will have passions which no person can gratify while they are single.

The companionship of persons whose thoughts are bad or lewd is another source of weakness, and you will do well to get away from all of those persons who have this habit of repeating over any of the smutty stories and those double-meaning puns which are bordering on the order of lust. Shun such associates.

We say to you that you will have none of these things about you if you surely desire to have the most perfect continence. Avoid every thought which will lead to any passion, or any gesture which will recall anything in the shape of passion in any manner.

Fasting, as we have already said, is another of the best things in this world to overcome all the semblance of passion.

The cold bath is the best master of all passion, for if the bath is used there can not be a particle of passion where the body is in cold water. Soak your body and do not be afraid of anything in the shape of water as long as the menses are not on.

At that time, if the thoughts of passion bother you, go without food and walk as far and as fast as you know how. Exhaust the body by exercise of some sort, even if you have to saw on some one's wood pile. Shun the first thought of anything which may lead to passion. Avoid anything like heating or spiced food, and if there are thoughts come up that have no business in your head, fight them down at their first appearance just as you would fight down a mad cat from your person. Do anything rather than have a passionate thought for one minute. It is the first time that will tell you the story, and if you can go without having any passion for one day you can go without all passion for the remainder of your life. You can do it.

The entire secret of perfect continence is in having the

mind so under control that there will be no appearance of passion in the brain while the life is in the brain. Do not allow the mind to dwell on the person of any man or on his face any more than you would keep your hand in the fire. Do not allow any one to impress you with magnetism any more than you would allow one to impress your mind with some red-hot iron. Keep all of such thoughts out of your head and out of the brain. Keep your own hands from touching your person, anywhere. Keep your counsel and if there are such thoughts about any one come into your head, drive them out as you would drive a rat out from the meal tub. Keep the mind pure, and this is the whole secret of perfect continence. If you have the mind pure there will be no danger of being in any wise lewd or loose in your own thoughts. Purify your brain.

Much of this power dwells in your own self, and many persons think it all dwells in your own mind whether you will be virtuous or not. The Bible speaks in this manner and we think it is really true far more than the leading minds of the churches give credit for. The act of overcoming (which means all the passions, lusts and desires of the world) is spoken of as something to be done by each individual person, and if there is help to overcome, it is sent from the Lord to those who ask for that help.

We tell you this is a great point. That, in all these fights between lust and passion on the one side and the actual desire for a life of perfect continence on the other, the struggle will be of short duration if you will heed the natural laws which cause all these passionate feelings, and avoid them. Make it your business to see that your body must be pure and fight down anything in the mind which borders on the very outer verge of impurity. With the body and mind pure you can rest assured it will not be long before you will have a life of perfect continence. The angels will then camp about you to assist you. But, if we understand this matter in any way, you must be an "overcomer" to commence with. Your will must commence the inner life. Is your will ready and desirous of a life of perfect continence?

CHAPTER XVI.

FOUR WORDS.

In this chapter we shall point out some of the mistakes which men and women make in their start in life.

Some of these ideas will not be new to you, perhaps, and some will be placed before you in a different light from what you have seen, but they are all intended to do you good and not for the benefit of the writer.

These four words are Reputation, Character, Habits and the word Mentality.

These words are often used one for another, and if you can see the difference in these words and their meaning you will have a little education all to yourself.

Reputation sometimes depends upon your associates and is such as they choose to give you, or say of you, from what they know of you and from what they choose to tell of you.

When one has lived in an old village or in a town which is not changing fast, one gets a reputation which sticks to her in spite of all the changes of life, and though this reputation may be unjust and positively dishonest in its application, yet this is the " reputation," and there will be no means of changing this reputation while you live in that place.

The reputation which you have is from many sources, and if you are careful of your reputation you can have a very good one and yet be a consummate hypocrite.

This is true.

And this care for one's reputation while one is a rogue is what gives the general public the doubtful aspect towards the members of all churches.

Once there was a time when the fact of belonging to a church was enough to stamp one as having a *good* reputation.

But now there is such a wide distrust of churches that one must do something else besides being a member of a church.

"'Tis true, 'tis pity ; pity 'tis 'tis true."

The reputation is what people say of you.

And while we would not have you careless of your reputation, for the sake of friends, relations and your acquaintances, yet we know there is something which is beyond what people may say of you, and therefore we ask you to think over these four words, and see if you can not have the whole four good as well as correct all the time.

But we assure you, however you may think of the word reputation, there are three other meanings to the three other words, and far more valuable than the word reputation.

The second word is character.

Character is formed, some by the parents while you are yet small, and much more by your associates, and yet a far larger amount of this character is formed by the life you are leading.

Your character may be good or bad.   It may be gentle, loving, kind, and it may be the opposite of these.   All of these are sometimes called attributes of one's character, and you have them or you have them not.

We do not think this is correct.

You have in you, if you read the English language, a desire to have all of the best things of life, and you certainly have the desire to be as pleasant as possible to all those whom you love and wish to cherish.

Reputation is what people say of you, and the character is really inside of you.   Your reputation may be bad and yet you may really have a fair character.

We wish you to have a good reputation and we insist that your character is good.

It is best for you to have the best character possible, and to that end we assure you that every thought you may have is of some value in the forming of your character.

Every associate is of some weight in moulding that character.   Where you go is of some moment in this character formation.   All the books you read and what you have and what you wear are of some account in this character forming. You should be gentle in character, and this is a phase of character that is often called "disposition."

A gentle disposition is the opposite of rough, coarse and noisy. This gentleness of character is not wholly given by the parents, but is the result of certain conditions of the body and the mind which have resulted in forming the character as it is.

It may be said that this character is formed by the habits which one has, but the habits are acts which are regularly performed, and a habit is an act which is so often performed that we say there is a habit, because we see the act performed at regular intervals.

Passing these acts or habits, we come to the word mentality, and we find that there is something in every person which can be educated to a certain point, and this part of the body, which can be educated in every one who is not an idiot, is called the mind.

The part of the body which is under the control of the thinking part and resolute part of the body is in the brain, and is, when it is mentioned by itself, called the mind, or the *mentality*.

Your mentality is exactly as your parents formed it before you were born, with the addition of the influences and the education which you and your environments have given to that mentality.

In other words, you have a brain from the ancestors, which is capable of taking on or dropping some of the things which are desirable to your mind, and with these conditions you have a mentality completely your own.

This mentality is, after you have arrived at the age of thinking, so completely under your own immediate control, and is so completely your work, that the judges and the courts hold you responsible for that mentality, to a certain degree.

Thus, if you have educated that mentality to take of those things which are the property of another, and you have educated this mentality to conceal those things and to keep

L

them, you are called a thief, and are (if found out) punished as a thief.

If on the other hand, you have educated your mind to do good actions and to be kind to your race, you are called a philanthropist, or if the case appears to be too much of good for your own interest you are called a crank.

This mentality goes yet deeper in the matter, if you will follow it.

The thoughts you think are a part of your mentality, and they are really a part of the brain and a part of the body as much as the hand is a part of the body.

In other words, there is some change in the atoms of the brain by which there is so total a change that the mind can be and is changed from one condition to another condition which may be entirely opposite to the first condition.

This change is no doubt a change which affects the entire brain atoms so that what was a brain atom without anything on it becomes a brain atom covered all over with beautiful figures, thoughts, conceptions, memories and reveries.

Or these brain atoms may be changed to the opposite of these conditions.

During youth these atoms are readily changed and stamped, and we say youth is the period of education and of training.

This is so universally recognized that there are states where it is the law that one shall attend a school while young.

When the mind is so that it can not be changed, we call the person an idiot or a fool. Youth is the time to educate these atoms of the brain, and as they are educated, so they are quite sure to remain.

But not always is youth the period of forming mentality. Adult age changes the mind as well as youth, if circumstances are favorable. We change our opinions as we become better versed or experienced in the ways of life.

In youth we form our ideas, but these are changed or modified as we grow older. We stamp the brain atoms far more easily in youth than when we are adults. Youth is the season for rapid education, for moulding the mind.

But this is only true of certain states of mind, and there are some things that can not be imprinted on the mind to stay there until the brain is older and (presumably) harder. When these atoms of the brain are once hardened there is not much chance or likelihood of change in them.

And this condition of the atoms of the brain, as we find it, is called the mentality, and is, really, yourself.

Upon this mentality there is to be built up a new person, and a person which may be entirely different from anything which was in the brain before there commenced to be any change in the atoms.

Let us make this clear to you, for we think this is one of the most important of all the things in the world, and one on which your whole life, happiness and welfare depend.

We desire to make this so plain to you that it will do you some good, and such good as will last you as long as you live.

You have these atoms of the brain from the blood, and they are, while you are young, fresh and ready to receive any and all impressions.

Suppose you take one of these atoms this morning and stamp that atom with the memory of some beautiful scenery or some kind remembrance of some of your friends.

The atom is impressed and in the brain there is a place where this scenery or kind remembrance is stowed away so that wherever you may go that scenery and that kind remembrance will go with you.

Take another example.

You know how the domestic animals look.

Imagine yourself transported to some place where there were no domestic animals, and you would carry all the recollections of those domestic animals so that, under almost any circumstances, you would have a faculty of reproducing these animals on paper, wood, or in clay, or in any other substance which you could fashion by the hands.

This likeness of the animal would be in your head, and it would be many years before there would be any change in the atom to fade out the conditions of the appearance of the forms and colors of these domestic animals.

The appearance of these animals is said to be in your head. In reality they are on some atom of the brain and will remain on some atom as long as you live.

Your mentality possesses these animals. Their shape, color, size and habits are all impressed on your brain atoms, and it is a fair thing to suppose (although there is no positive proof, as the brain atoms have never been shown to have any or even the slightest trace of anything to show any change, so far as can be detected by the anatomists) that the brain atoms are really stamped with the things seen, smelled, felt, heard and tasted.

The five senses are then the agents which are capable of educating or changing your entire mentality in any way that you may so desire.

If this idea is in your head, then you can see that there is something in you besides the reputation, the character and the habits. You can see that there is room for the greatest change one can imagine in all the circumstances of your life.

Let us suppose this morning that you are entirely devoid of any musical talent. You have a desire to learn this branch of education and take up the study, either by yourself, or with the aid of a teacher.

The first day you learn the appearance of the notes, and the second day you are engaged on the divisions of the time and the different spaces of time between the notes, and the third day there is something else, and so on for a year.

When the year is up there is something in the brain which you can not forget if you try, because you have impressed the atoms of the brain with these ideas of the year's study, and the year's impressions will not be taken from you, no matter where you go.

In the same manner about arithmetic. You think of some mark which represents something, and the mind or the atoms of the brain are at once at work to carry out the effects of that symbol almost before you can think.

For instance, you know that the symbol x signifies multiplication. If you see 8x8 your mind flies to 64 as the solution of the figures. This is your mentality at work almost before you know there is to be any work for it.

But in the case of the untutored mind these symbols have no more effect than so much sand in a heap.

If these ideas are in your head there is nothing which you can not gain and there is no position which is too high for you.

We may say, also, that if there is not something of this knowledge of this mentality about you, there is great danger that you will descend into the lowest scale of mental life, and be in still lower mentality than you may have at the present.

You see, also, that this possession, which we call mentality, is of far greater importance than any reputation which one can possess.

One may have a good reputation, a fair character, correct habits, and seem to be everything which is desirable on earth, and yet in the mentality be a fool and a villain.

Thus you may be a Sunday-school teacher, of spotless character, the most faultless habits as far as one can see, and yet in your mentality you may be so rotten that it only takes a breath to change your whole life to the uttermost degradation.

Can we make this plain to you ?

You are a Sunday-school teacher, your life is all that is desired; if, in your mind, you will think of anything which you would do if there were an opportunity, you are as bad as you would be if that opportunity had already presented and you had done the thing which is in the mind.

Thus, if you think you would steal, if the opportunity presented, you are a thief in the mentality, and it will only require the opportunity to prove yourself to be a thief when opportunity has presented.

It is this mentality which is so seducing to youthful minds, and it is this perverted mentality or sensuous mentality which has led so many girls into bawdy houses and into the gutter, from as good homes as you and I ever had.

Their mentality was below their surroundings and in a moment they fell to the level of their mentality.

The girl who reads the novel and and wishes she were in the hero's arms, and would be in the hero's arms if the opportunity would present, would yield herself to the first hero who came along and the mentality would or could make a mistake about the condition of the hero and there would be another victim to what is called "seduction" but what is really a case of *lowered mentality*, from some cause which might not have previously been known.

In cases which are judged by the actual facts, it is seen that there is no such thing as sudden villainy or *sudden* species of crime.

No more is there what is called a "betrayal" of any girl. The girl herself has previously lowered her standard of virtue, and when opportunity presents, she yields as she did in day dreams.

This must be a fact.

The girl who, in her mentality, has previously decided that under any circumstances she would not allow any one to possess her body is the one, who, when circumstances come is not going to yield to any persuasions or any passion. The mentality can not yield to any sudden gust of passion, because when mentality sees the passion there is some obstacle in the mind as there was previously and is in the mentality, and the body follows the mentality and denies all encroachments.

It is all right for those who believe in the inherent weakness of the female sex to make excuses for the woman's fall.

We do not think it is true. It is usually the man who has fallen first, and, having fallen, then he persuades and tempts, coaxes and bullies the woman into yielding up the possession of her body for the gratification of his passion.

The point which we would make is this: If any one has a habit of thought which is not as it should be, there will come a time when this thought will master the body, and then and there, the girl will drop from the place where she is in reality to some place a great deal lower than she would be if she did not give way to any such lowered thoughts, which come of a lowered mentality. In other words, the thoughts of the sin or crime, or the lapse from strict virtue, comes previous to the fall. No woman is seduced. She surrenders herself. She is at fault in her mentality.

If one desires to have perfect control of the body, there should be a resolve not to allow any of the dreams or the reveries which are so often given way to, at the time one should be up and out of doors walking or at work.

These day dreams and these reveries of what might be—no matter on what subject these thoughts may be if they are of passion—are to be resolutely banished from the mind. Fight them down as you would fight down an enemy, and have the mind so that there is no possible chance to get to dreaming of things which should, under no consideration, take place.

We assure you there is so much in this advice that we assert that we can not conceive of any young lady ever stepping from the path of virtue and happinesss, unless she has given herself up to some dream of passion before the act comes to pass. We say to you, keep the thoughts of anything which is false or anything which is wrong out of the mind completely. Keep the mentality as pure and as sweet as if it was the only thing in the world of any value to you. Keep everything which is wrong or unlawful or out of place, as far from your mind as the east is from the west.

Do not allow for one moment anything in your mind which should not be paraded on the street. Allow no thought in your mind, nor any reverie, which you would not have the mother see. Or, if you can realize it, do not have any thought in the head which would not appear to be correct and lovely if the angels were in the room with you each day. And if this is your endeavor, you may be sure there is to be success for you in any of your walks in life. Nay, more. We can assert there is no step in the world to which you may not aspire.

There is nothing which you could imagine but what will be yours in reality and in a far greater degree than if you could reverie and dream of it all your life. The reality of love is far sweeter than any dream of it can be.

The owning of a treasure is far more to be desired than the mere dream of owning it. We say have the reality and do not dream of having it.

It is all right to dream and to study of those things which are elevating to the mind, and to aspire to something better than anything which you may have in the world.

It is all right to hold to an idea of doing some good and to do something for your own self and your family, and to think out the proper way to do these good things. These thoughts and reveries do not injure the brain. They do not destroy the mentality. It is the dream of passion and the sensuous reverie which we deprecate and which we urge you to avoid.

Fight down such ideas as soon as they get into the head. Banish them with hard work and resolute activity. If in the night these reveries approach you, get up and go to work. Or, if there is no other way, go and walk. Or take the chairs and have a silent exercise until all of these thoughts are banished from the brain. As we have already explained, these thoughts are sometimes the reflex action of the brain and the spinal cord, arising from the filling of the arteries of the sexual organism with blood, and while these arteries are filled, the brain commences to have these day dreams which are fires to burn away the intellect. Conquer this habit of sensuous reverie and have a clear mentality.

Instead of having the thoughts go out towards these material things of earth which will perish, and if they did not perish they load you with unhappiness, weakness, and a diseased body, instead of these things of earth, place the eyes on the throne of God, and have a better and a purer idea of life which will elevate you above the common herd of life and give you command of earth's treasures.

The difference between a person who has nothing of this world's goods and one who has, is often the simple result of saving a few dimes or of taking care of that which one has. You are steward of God. Will you not be a good steward?

If you desire to be a good steward, then all of these reveries must be banished from the mind, and your mentality should be as clear as the crystal lake of life.

Let the angels rejoice in your purity and your goodness.

Allow no thought of anything which is of the earth to shadow your mind. Allow no thought of anything which is of the body of man or woman to force any entrance into your mind to hamper you for one moment or to force you to have a desire for anything which is against law or justice. Keep the mentality perfectly pure, and God shall have his angels come down and camp about you. This is the doctrine of the Father, and is found in the opening chapters of Job. Your part is to keep the mentality perfect.

There is another point which is of importance in this mentality thought, and this is the fact that there is no such thing as there being any exalted thought, and very little sudden action of nobleness, fortitude, courage or bravery or anything else occurs in the brain which is not there beforehand.

We mean to say that there is very little chance to have any exalted mind which is not brought out before the time comes to have that mind tried. In other words, the idea of the act is always before the act itself.

Is this clear to you?

The house is in the architect's mind, and he plans it out before the cellar is dug. The fountain plays in the artist's eye before the aqueduct is laid to bring the water from the lake in the mountains. It is in the mentality.

Look at any bridge or any structure in the world. Do you think the architect, the one who planned the bridge or the structure, did not know in his mind just how that structure would look, before a pier or a corner stone was laid?

Most assuredly that structure was thought out in all of its details before anything was in material form.

So, too, any act of the body is always thought (although it may be sometimes in a very vague sort of a manner) in the mind before the body does the act. They have supposed such and such a case and decided how they would act if the case went a certain way.

These four words comprise yourself and the care of mind

and body. There is more thought than could be compressed into a book of this size. Let this be your seed, and foster it until you shall not alone rise higher yourself, but bring others to comprehend the value of four words.

CHAPTER XVII.

BEAUTY, STRENGTH, KNOWLEDGE AND POWER.

There are some things which every young lady needs to have, and among these needed things we class beauty, strength, knowledge and power. We will take up beauty, for that is the least understood and is the most desired.

Persons commonly suppose that beauty consists in a fair skin, a perfect form and regular features. If this were so, there would be many more beautiful ladies than there are at this time. A fair skin is to be desired, and we have already shown you how to have that. The perfect form is due in some measure to the constitutions of the father and the mother and the care of the child during infancy. But you can remedy many defects of form by exercise. So also are the regular features when there has been no accident to mar the features. But these three together and any quantity of money and artistic dressing thrown in will never make a beauty; while a person may lack all these requirements and yet become a perfect beauty in the eyes of her acquaintances.

How? We will tell you. The saying that "handsome is that handsome does" is not a myth. It is a living fact and one that is seen every day and is as little understood by the persons who see it as if it was written in some foreign language instead of the character of the person who carries the marks of beauty around.

Beauty consists in being good and kind to those with whom you come in contact. It consists in having a desire to please the people you are with. It consists in having a desire to do good and in doing good. The very fact that you have done some good to some one is one of the things which will make your face beautiful, even if you have a rough skin, irregular features and the worst form in the

171

world. There is something in this that can not be made to be plainly understood, and we shall fail to be understood in this beauty-forming if we do not make this idea plain.

We will try to be plain with the subject, although we know there will be many who will not understand this at once, because it will be new to them.

1. You do a good action and this action makes you feel happy. This happiness is reflected from the brain to the face, and this good action is shown in your face and you have a mark of beauty.

Every good or kind act goes to mark your face with these acts of kindness, and the first thing that is known is that some one is remarking how different such a one looks from what they did some time since.

This truly forms beauty.

On the contrary, if you have all of the requisites for beauty and you are sulky or peevish, every time you sulk and every time you act as if the evil spirit has possession of you, every time you get angry and have one of the fits of passion which are so common among the children who are spoiled, there will be some mark in your face which will tell on you that these fits of passion, anger, sulkiness or peevishness have been there, and you are marked as an ugly person.

We say this: Every time you think, or every time you do any act, that act is impressed on your brain and face, and you can be as easily read as if all those acts were written in a book, and when you turn your face towards your acquaintances, that book (your face) is read by some one who has had some experience in reading faces. Do you now see what is meant by the saying, "Handsome is that handsome does"?

Perhaps one of the habits which has hurt so many girls of this age is the habit of reading the smutty and indecent stories which are published so cheaply, and are so common everywhere.

The dwelling of the mind on these indelicate subjects before the body is to be gratified in a proper manner, is one of the facts which are impressed on many of the faces which are daily seen in the streets. We advise you, therefore, if you are desirous of having beauty, to keep from all these books which are so alluring to the young. We advise you not to get angry or passionate, or to have any of the fits of sulkiness that so many young ladies cultivate.

These fits hurt you. They show on your face and they spoil your countenance, no matter how fair your skin is or how regular your features may be.

The very ideas which are in your head and the thoughts you think have an impress on your brain. And they have an impress far more visible on your face. Yes, every thought is imprinted on the face. Did you ever see a policeman leading away some individual, and see how eagerly the crowd will stop and gather around the victim to see how he or she looks? Such curiosity is natural and is as common as the day. These curious people will make remarks on the condition of the criminal's face and then, after they have passed their opinion on the face, they will next and last look at the person's dress and the condition of the person.

This is one of the natural things one is constantly seeing. We are curious to know how the supposed criminals look. And when we have seen them, we judge instinctively, whether they are good or bad. So with us and with every one who has an interest in humanity. People judge us by our faces, and it will be well for us if we carry the marks of kindliness and goodness, of honesty and generosity, on our faces. We shall be beautiful, although we may be old, ugly and decrepit. We may be deformed and disfigured and yet we can be beautiful to all those around us.

Our daily habits will make us beautiful or these habits may make us ugly.

You may think you will do this one bad act and then you will stop and become good for a fact. But we do not think you can do this. The one bad act or the one bad thought is the one which is going to stick in your head and is going to mark all the brain with one impression of the act as it was. The brain is marked with the memory of that vile act and the impression is carried to the face every time you think of it. This is not a world where we can select a time and do some heroic act and go down to history as a hero or as a celebrated person, and we would not do this if we could, if we think of it in a correct light.

We have the desire to be happy now and hereafter; to be happy and to be beautiful is of more moment *now* than it will be a hundred years from now. Thinking of these facts you will desire to do good and to be good just now. Allow us to tell you something. If you so desire, the moment to do these good acts is just now. There will be an opportunity to do good and there never will be a moment more precious than right now. The God who rules this world will find you good acts to do, and if you do these good acts you will have the marks of beauty which will stay by you.

Yes, stay by you. Stay on your face and stay in your brain. When one does a mean act, that act is not gone as soon as the act is over. Not at all. The remembrance of the act is left and the act is done over and over again until the act is filling the brain. Consider of this repetition in memory. Thus you can see that any act, good or bad will be multiplied many and many a time by the memory, and so it will do you hurt or good as the act may be good or bad as long as the memory will recall the act.

Did you ever see a fat parson or a sleek priest and not think how their thoughts have run? You think of chicken pie and good red wine. These creatures carry the marks of the beast on their faces. They can not shake that mark off no matter where they go. So with the miser and the stingy person, and so with the cruel person. All of their ideas show on their faces, and we judge them without asking any questions. Do you not suppose that some one is judging your face for all it is worth?

Yes, indeed, my dear daughter, these thoughts are all impressed on your face, and there is no taking them off with any sort of paint and powder that we know anything about. They are there to stay. We desire you to appear beautiful. And we desire that beauty to be in your body. The saying that "beauty is only skin deep and ugliness goes to the bone," is not correct. Both and all of our attributes go to the bone and are passing through our circulation every minute. The very resolve which you make this minute is registered on your face, let it be good or bad.   And as you think so you will be.

Every act of cleanliness or of filth is on your face. Every act of selfishness is registered on that countenance of yours.   You may think you can conceal these private acts from the world, but it is impossible.   Some one will read you and some one will tell on you.   Get yourself right and keep yourself right by having the good Lord to keep your mind right in the truth and in the things which are the foundations of eternal life.   Be good and beauty shall come to you.

Strength.

There has been much of an idea in the past that it is not lady-like or fashionable to be strong or muscular.

This idea comes from across the water where the main idea of a women is something to sleep with and something to gratify the passions of a man.

Not that it is always necessary for these male brutes to have a woman.   For these fiends in human form do not keep women always to gratify their lusts.   They would take a boy and perhaps they would take out his testicles and then they would use this boy by having his person used as one would use a prostitute.

The Turks do this, and the Portuguese and Spaniards do this, to this day.   They have boys who are castrated, and let them out at so much a head, as the shameful woman lets out her body.   These men, who are beasts, use the rectum of the boy as they would use the vagina of a woman.   And these people do not think it womanly for a woman to have any strength.   What is your idea of the value of such a person's judgment?

You will say of no value.   And we think so.   These opinions which are based on lust and crime should not prevail in this country.   So we say the more strength any one has, the better off they are.   The next persons who do not think a woman has any right to any strength are the Chinese, and they have the faculty of binding the woman's feet in such a shape as will prevent her from ever moving about or seeing any one besides themselves. The Chinese do not think it womanly or lady-like to have any strength. What do you think of their judgment in this matter?

We believe you should be as strong and as able to bear the burdens of life as a man.

You will have enemies enough who will, if they get a chance, take away any surplus strength.

You will find that all the doctors who will be called in when you are sick will be sure to give you some poison to reduce your strength and to keep you always in the habit of taking some dope in the fool hope that some day you will strike something which will give you back your lost strength. You may as well discard that foolish hope now as any time.

No kind of medicine is able to give you an atom of strength.

All strength is from the food which you may eat and from the way the vital force is treated.

You can get strength all right. We will tell you how to get this strength. We think we know. But we desire you to discard this idea that there is any strength in any medical formula or any of the so-called tonics. What is this strength?

When a person has good muscles and good nerves there is some strength. To have this good muscular development we must exercise and we must have good food and pure drink, as well as to breathe pure air.

In the shortest time, we tell you. to have strength you must eat right, drink right, and you must exercise so as to have this strength in the proper places. Lots of people have much strength in their stomachs and then use it in such a manner that they soon wear the stomach out. You do not want to do this. You want the strength in the proper place, and under such control as will give you a power to act when the time comes.

The most familiar example is the arm of any blacksmith. When he goes into the shop at first, there is not any more strength in his arm than there is in any one else's arm. But by exercising that particular set of muscles there comes to be in his arm a most tremendous power, and a strength which is in no other class of men in the world, unless we except the brute who is a prize fighter. In your case, you want strength in your feet, in your arms, in your whole body, and especially in the arms, for any manual labor which may fall to your lot to do.

Walking will give you all needed strength in your lower extremities, and swinging the dumb bells and the clubs, or taking up two chairs for five minutes a day, will give you as much as or more strength than most people have.

You need more than ordinary people, and we advise you to take five minutes in the morning and lift up two chairs by their rounds, or take two large books from the floor and bend the body without bending the back. Pick these books from the floor and place them above the head and as far behind you as possible, and so down on the floor again.

There are many of these exercises which you will soon find out for yourself, and these exercises and walking will give you all the strength you need for anything in the world. But do not forget the daily walk, as that is the best mode of acquiring strength in the world, and one which is the most easy of access.

Walking is always ready for you to do and is always in order day or night.

With the idea that you are going to acquire strength, you will soon find that the amount of strength which you will possess will be wonderful.

All the muscles will grow larger and more firm while the body all over will fill out firm and hard.

You will see at once that any corset while you are trying to gain strength is out of place. You can not wear the corset and be well or strong, and the sooner you have this truth in your head the sooner you will have strength,

In acquiring strength you have to keep in your mind that meats, pastry, eggs, oysters, coffee, tea and chocolate are not producers of strength. The best strength-formers in the world are grains and fruits. Do not forget this, and do not

M

allow any one to change your mind from the facts that strength is from proper food, clear water and pure air.

Knowledge.

There are many kinds of knowledge which are of no use to the persons who have these differing kinds of knowledge. There is the knowledge of playing cards. This is useless and of no value whatever. It is not alone a waste of time and of space, but it is a knowledge which is rotting to the brain and excludes the other knowledge which would be of some account in the struggle of life.

We see every day a knowledge of villainy of one kind or another, which is not only useless, but is absolutely so tedious, and mind destructive, that the possessor's mind is sinking in the slough of the world's mud.

We mean this: The knowledge which is of no use in this world's battles is not only useless in the fights of the world to conquer what the world calls a living, but is more than useless, in as much as it cumbers up the brain and prevents the accumulation of such knowledge as would be of practical moment in the battle of life, and that kind of knowledge which will assist in this useful battle of earning the living is, in a great measure, crowded out from the brain of those who have cumbered their brains with this useless knowledge. Their brain is filled with rot. No room for sound knowledge.

Some of these useless kinds of knowledge may be enumerated as follows: Card playing, dancing, handkerchief symbols, games of nearly every kind, the knowledge of smutty stories, and a knowledge of the mean ways, which are thought to be a sign of one's smartness or of an education of the day.

We see the folly of this useless knowledge every day when we contemplate the people who have laid in a good supply of this brain-rotting knowledge.

We see young ladies who have had a smattering of French, something of German, and can play on the piano some, and perhaps crochet a little, with a fine knowledge of playing cards, and a knowledge of all of the dances which should or should not be used on any occasion, and we see when these persons go into the world or are thrown on their own resources for the means of making an honest living, they are unprepared for the struggle, and they go into the houses of prostitution and are wrecked on the road of life.   Their rotten brains could not take care of their bodies.

It will not do to say the gambler has no knowledge.   He has.   But his knowledge is not useful to himself or to any one else.   One of these days he will find he has no useful knowledge and his brains will allow him to kill the useless body.   He will be a suicide.

To be short in this matter let us say there are two kinds of knowledge, good and bad.

Or, the two kinds of knowledge may be said to be useful or useless.   To have the most useful knowledge we have only to reflect on what is best for ourselves or what is the best for the race.

Certainly, that which does not bring in food, raiment, and does not make us any better, is not a good kind of knowledge or a useful knowledge.

A trade is something which will last as long as we live, therefore the knowledge of a trade is a good thing to have, a useful knowledge.   The knowledge of a game of cards will never bring in anything to ourselves or any one else, and it can not be a good kind of knowledge to have for our own self or for any one else.   This is a useless kind of knowledge. The differing kinds of knowledge can be readily judged by these standards.

To gain the best kinds of knowledge it is necessary to have the brain in the best of order.   If we have the brain in good order we may be sure we can readily accumulate any kind of knowledge we desire.   If the body is in good order we may be sure the brain will be as the body is, unless there is some trait of idiocy in the family, which affects the body.

"A sound mind in a sound body," is one of the oldest and most true of all sayings.

To gain the accumulation of facts which is needed, to have what is called an education, we have two methods: instruction from books and instruction from teaching.

The young lady is not often so fortunate as to be able to have all the teachers needed at the time one can learn, and therefore the next best means of acquiring knowledge is from books.

The choice of books is of moment. Those which will give you the knowledge you desire to have, and that which is of use for you to know, are the best for you to have.

Ordinarily we do not class the books which are called "novels" as of much value in this acquisition of useful knowledge.

We think it is a fact that the novels waste time and do not place things in their true light, and so far are destructive to time and to the brain, in as much as they do not teach the truth. This error is two-fold. It wastes the time and leaves the brain in a weakened condition. We advise against the reading of novels.

If we believe the Bible we have two other reasons. The novel takes away the time from finding out of the things of God, and it also places the reader in the category of those "who love and make a lie." All lies are novels or romances, and therefore we condemn the novel in any form.

There is an abundance of other things which are useful to the young lady, and the time will be improved so rapidly that the novel will be shunned as soon as there is any understanding.

History may be very dry, but it is useful, and it will not be so dry as soon as one is able to comprehend it.

To this end let us advise you a little.

Begin by reading only a little at first. Try only a page or a half page; or even a sentence until you have that in your head. Then read the next and remember that. When the day is gone sit down in some quiet place and place all the doings of the day on a book which may be called anything you please,—a diary, or a memorandum, or a record. This will aid you in having one of the finest memories in the world.

We know of nothing which will so soon give one the memory which is so admired in the circles of scholarship and of intellectuality, as this habit of daily recording all the events

of the day, correctly repeating and impressing the brain
with the events of the preceding twenty-four hours.

This is a habit we strongly advise to any young lady,—
this keeping a daily record of all the events of the day and of
recording them as accurately as may be possible on paper.

We do not now speak from what some persons have told
us of this habit. We tell you this from a personal knowledge which was commenced when the writer was no more
than twelve, and has been continued to a late period of life.

It has been the foundation for what has been termed "a
good memory," a good head, and a perfect comprehension of
things as they were.

We do not say that the keeping of a daily record of one's
doings will certainly give one the brains one would have had
if the parents would have daily educated the child as it
grew up, educated the child by a judicious conversation.
We think there is nothing in this world which would compensate for the loving and educating talk of the parents
while the child is growing up from childhood to manhood or
to womanhood. But if there is anything which will more
than repay for all the defects of an early education, it is
in having the habit of remembering everything as it passed
and as the day went by, adding to the stock of knowledge in
the head, fastening and nailing this knowledge into the
brain atoms. This is one of the surest methods of placing
that knowledge safely on the brain that we can advise.

It is Bacon who says, "Reading makes a full man, speaking makes a ready man, writing makes an exact man."
And by the method which we suggest, you can have all
of these desirable conditions in yourself. You can be full,
ready and exact. In short there is nothing but what can be
learned by applying one's self to a steady pursuit of knowledge,
and this knowledge can be so firmly placed in one's brain,
that there will be no possibility of its loss.

The most useful kind of knowledge for a young lady is to
have those facts in her head whereby she can readily place
herself in any position of earning her own way in life and
be able to adapt herself to any surroundings.

Such knowledge is invaluable, and without some of these kinds of knowledge there will never be any happiness, never any contented or peaceful mind.

The knowledge of making good light bread; of making good and palatable soup, and cooking the various kinds of meats as well as of making gruels, toast, broths, and some of the simple infusions, are among the most useful kinds of knowledge.

As soon as one can wait upon and help an invalid, there is always an avenue open for profitable (in a sense) kind of employment. We do not advise any kind of nursing as a profession, because if one desires to learn nursing, we should advise the study of medicine. Nursing, as commonly practiced, destroys the bodily health, and is not a desirable avocation for any young lady to go into. The practice of medicine is all right for the young lady who desires to do good.

The many branches of a good education demand that any one who expects to make her way above the condition she is now in, should be possessed of a good and rapid hand of penmanship and should be a good speller. The lack of these two accomplishments will sometimes debar a young lady from being in the society she would like to be, and is hers by right. And if she does not possess these two accomplishments, she will have some bitter moments when she will regret not having given sufficient time to these branches.

As to the penmanship, we have no hesitation in saying that any one can be accomplished in these two branches by placing aside an hour each day, or, if there is no time in the day, an hour at night, or early in the morning, and placing the mind on the acquisition of these two branches, and become so proficient that there will never be any lack of the knowledge of spelling or the means of placing it on paper.

Correct writing is not so important as it was once, but there is still room for the best pen-writers in the book-keeper's departments, and when one can write plainly and quickly there will be no lack of employment.

Other branches will be spoken of under the head of earning one's living. While we think there is no knowledge which one can not acquire while working every day, we think there are some of the by-paths of knowledge which are well worth the trouble of going after, and we will mention a few of them.

Knitting, sewing, darning, canning fruit, making jellies, cutting and fitting one's dresses, mending a shoe, if one lives in the country the knack of mending the harness, are all parts of a general knowledge which is of the utmost value in the daily life of this America.

The art of growing a garden is one of the things that is little thought about by the city miss, but it is one of the arts which is soon learned where there is a will and the opportunity.   The garden is of the greatest value in the country, and if the young ladies of the country knew their advantages they would never envy any person who lives in the city.

The place where the berries grow is the place where there should be no consumption.   The place where there is pure milk and good air is the place where there should be a long life and a sweet companionship with nature.   The reason why the country home is dull is because of the lack of educational advantages of the country, and an inability to pierce through the glamour of a ready tongue and city accomplishments.

Life is harder to earn in the city and health is harder to keep.   Knowledge is as easy gained in the country as in the city, if one will commence aright.   But, as there is a magnetism about the city which can not be found in the country, there will always be some who find the city the most pleasant and most desirable to live in.   Solid knowledge is not gained by any ready stroke of chance but by continued application.   Hard work is the price one must pay for any knowledge which is above the average.   The parrot gains his little sayings in a few days.   The man who makes a profession a life-long study, will not get through his studies until he is certain the tomb is waiting for him.   But the knowledge of how to live happily and successfully has already come to the reader.   Will you profit by this knowledge?

Power.

By the term "power" I mean the something that will captivate the persons who are around us and make them our friends. It is indefinable. It is called animal magnetism, and is often mistaken for something which any one can acquire and is to be acquired by being polite and easy and graceful.

Sometimes this power is called by the name of accomplishments. I think this is not correct.

Personal power is something which is, to a certain extent, in every one, and is something which we think every one can gain if they will strive to have it.

The power which we have can be used for either good or bad, and if we use our power for good we shall have it in a greater degree than ever after we have done some good action, and if we do not use this power for the good of those with whom we come in contact we may be certain we are going to lose this power sooner or later.

It is said that there are some persons with so strong a personal magnetism that they can influence almost any one to do their will.

This is true. Animal magnetism is of so pronounced a fact in many persons that it can be felt. They are filled with fire. We should not be so weak as to be influenced by any one who possesses this power, and we should have enough of this power to ward off any evil effects which may come up from those who may wish to use their power for evil over us.

Power is one of the results of knowledge and strength over ignorance and weakness. A sound body is one of the beginnings of power. A conscious power lies in the mind that is determined to do right in all things. The great secret of true power lies in the fact of one's having the smile of the Heavenly Father on all of our work, the feeling that we are really the children of a king and that we can not want while our Father is alive. The power which is of value to us is the power to know the right from the wrong, and to do the right at all times and to flee from the wrong. This doing right gives us conscious power.

CHAPTER XVIII.

DEPORTMENT OF YOUNG LADIES.

A sculptor, if he desires to form an exquisitely beautiful statue, searches among the people about him for a lovely face and form, then copies it in marble or bronze.

One who really wishes to be well behaved would do well to follow his example. Choose from among your acquaintances those who are well behaved, and learn, by association, their ways.

This essay is devoted to the motherless girls who are liable not to be taught the snares that are laid for the unwary.

A few thoughts for those who are seeking a higher plain, or who wish to know what their mothers might wish them to do.

To begin with, I would rise early. This will be necessary in order to take your bath, comb your hair and clean finger nails before breakfast. Try always to look neat. Some one will remember your looks. After bath hang up towels throw out water and set pitcher in bowl. Throw back bed-clothes and open window to air your room. Do what is required of you in a manner that will not annoy your friends. If you set the breakfast-table, have a pretty way of doing it; don't throw victuals and dishes at the table. One can learn much in this matter from seeing it nicely done.

If you wash dishes, have a certain righteous pride about you. Try to feel that you and your friends are too good to eat from half washed dishes, too good to go about on half cleaned walks.

But suppose there is not much required of one, as there is not when there is hired help in the house Then learn something useful. Attend the public school. Your chances of being a free American citizen center in the public schools. They are fostered to root out superstition, vice and ignorance. We have no slaves in this country bought and sold.

The only slaves are those bound down by superstition and ignorance.

If it is vacation, learn to sew. The course in plain sewing is as follows: First, patchwork sewed over and over with edges of cloth folded back. Then learn to hem neatly a narrow hem. Hem ruffle and gather it on to a piece of cloth and face back. Gather a puff and face it back on both sides. Run up a seam and fell the edges. Get some one to assist you a little, and if you apply yourself you will do nicely. Make wide hem with measure. Then shirr, blind hem, etc. Keep samples of your work to convince your friends of the deftness of your fingers. By all means learn to mend neatly.

Read good books, especially the Bible. Learn some passages and chapters by heart. Read it well for there are things in it you have not dreamed of; things you ought to know. There are coming soul-trying times, so treasure up some comforting passages. "Come unto me all ye that labor and are heavy laden and I will give you rest." There are multitudes over the river who have thus rested, and about you in the daily walks of life a multitude more.

As early as the age of thirteen, at farthest, join some church. Those who have the care and management of young people will agree with me that there is nothing equal to the love of Christ, the leading of the Holy Spirit, in awakening all that is lovely in the manners of young people. The disposition to do unto others as you would that they should do unto you will make up for many defects that may arise from inexperience. Then strive for that purity of heart that will admit us into the presence of Him who said, "Before Israel was, I am."

Minor matters in manners are easily learned. Be observing. At the table cut your food with a knife and eat with your fork and spoon. When returning from church or a walk put your gloves in your box or drawer, your hat in a hat-box, your cloak on a hook. Try to be orderly, it will save you time and make others happy.

When sitting in company, keep your feet close together,

and as nearly as possible for comfort out of sight. Sit erect. Before leaving the house to appear on the street, tip your mirror, turn about before it and see if your skirts hang as they should, and your suit is properly sponged and dusted. Loud talking or laughing or handkerchief flirting on the street are bad form. I would not learn to dance. I have known of many instances of bad colds taken from overheating in this way. The air is bad in a ball room, both morally and physically. Don't. If you intend to visit a friend answer your invitation promptly and in a cordial manner. Let them know you appreciate their kindness and are grateful for it.

While there, if they do not hire help, assist with the housework. Wipe dishes, help stem berries, string beans, by all means make your own bed. And now about yourself. Remember there are some subjects no one but your own mother should talk to you about, or an older lady whose advice you need.

No man, however saintly his profession, has any right to ask you about your courses, or passionate nature, or private matters of that sort, unless wedded to you.

If it is necessary to consult a physician on such private matters, take an older lady with you.

Young ladies should learn to guard themselves. Persons who want to talk or act improperly can be avoided. Strike for your liberty and honor as becomes a young American of the nineteenth century. You do not live in a country where any one need be a slave.

If the young person who poisoned herself over the way had attended school till she learned there was no purgatory, and that Christ was the only mediator, she might have been alive to-day. The light is beginning to shine in the dark places. Don't spend all your thought on your own pleasure and amusement nor always follow your own inclinations.

Try to act wisely in whatever you do and you will not regret the effort though you do make some mistakes.

LINCOLN, NEBRASKA.

CHAPTER XIX.

THE CHOICE OF A COMPANION.

I do not know that the subject which is to be thought out for this chapter was ever in print before. And, moreover, if it has ever been in print the writer has never seen it, although there was a time in his life when he made very diligent search for it.

The choice of a companion. The choice of a mate. The choice of the father of your children. The choice of a master. The choice of a helpmate and the choice of one to whom all your body will be in subjection. This is only a part of what is implied in the choice of a companion.

Somewhere in Cobbett's life there is a passage where he says he chose a wife because she was out on the porch scrubbing down the stairs early in the morning.

This was a good wife for Cobbett, but we should as soon think of drawing the grand prize in some bogus lottery as to think of choosing a wife by her scrubbing qualities.

And it is the same with the selection of a husband.

At this outset I hear some one say that the women do not choose the men, but the men the wives.

Let me say right here, and I will say it again after a time, this is a grand mistake and one which should not be placed in the head of every young lady. In reality, she is the one that chooses and the man is a cipher in the case. It appears to be the other way, but I am assured it is the attractions of the woman that always make the match if there is any love in the case.

The objector will be the one who will assert that the woman does not have the chance to pick out the husband, that the husband has to pick out the wife. I think this is also a grave error. The wife has the same opportunity. But I will not answer any more objections but go at once to the root of what I consider the evil of nearly all of the present marriages, and an evil which causes all the divorces and all of the unhappiness in this world, and especially among the civilized world so-called.

The generality of all classes appear to think if they get some one who has some property, or something to do, to make what is called a living, there is to be a good match.

Indeed, I have heard this ever since I was a boy, and hear it now to my great disgust, and when I do hear it I am thinking of the fact that there are so few real love matches and so few happy homes.

Many of the homes of America, to-day, instead of being the happy places which they should be, are really and truly, the abodes of misery and of discontent and adultery.

Children are brought up in an atmosphere of want and in a discontented spirit, so that there is no great happiness in the family, while the head of the house has to slave out his life to support this show of happiness. This family of two or four, as the case may be and as the woman is smart enough to kill off her brood, is one nest of quarrelling and unhappy wretches who are at war with every one for the purpose of making a living, and then they do not know what it is to live in any sense. The children being hated before they are born, hate others when they are living. It is simply an unhappy gathering with no more of the home than there will be found in a stable, and often not half as much, as the animals in the stable love their progeny, and the people in the house hate their children, while the children are waiting when the older ones die off so that some of the money saved up can be expended on themselves.

This is wrong, foolish and wicked. It is needless. And if there is anything which is of value in this book, this is the chapter where there is value. We are not telling you anything which we heard from some one else; as we have already said we have never heard or read one word on this subject, as we shall place it before you.

We are just as sure we are right and that we have the combination on all the happy marriages in this world as we are sure the sun shines, or that there is any daylight.

The great key to all the happy marriages and to all the
the happy mates, is to get the one who was designed for you
in the day you were born. We know the only happy marriages are those where the wife and the husband are perfectly mated in love and point of serving God. And without
this fact as a basis there is no such thing as a happy match,
no matter what all the world may say.

There are two things which will right themselves. One of
these things is the possession of property. The other is any
disparity as to age. We can not tell any of these things
and it is none of our business to know anything about these
two things which the world and the hens in the world make
so much cackling about.

Property is one of the things which makes much unhappiness, and we think other things being equal, the persons who
marry and do not have much to go on when they start, are
the best and the happiest. But that has nothing to do with
our theory of happy marriages which we will proceed to
show as plainly as we can.

In the first place, we think and know there is a God who
has made this world and all that therein is, and, while He
has placed us here and in the possession of love and the desire to love and the desire and passion and the longing for
companionship, there must be, and undoubtedly is, some
provision made for all these possessions to be used and enjoyed.

Very well. If he has made one of a pair he knows where
the mate is. And we say with all reverence which a child
can give the Father, there is no such thing as an unhappy
marriage where there is the man and woman made to be
joined together as Eve was joined to Adam by the Lord
Himself. This must have been a true marriage of hearts
and love, as the Father must have intended when He made
the first "Isha," the first wife who was "bone of my bone
and flesh of my flesh."

To select this mate is not the work or the handicraft of any
human being and there has long been acknowledged that
there is no possible chance for two persons to become ac-

quainted with one another before they are married and live together for one or two years. We think this is true. We know it. There is far more love in the third and even the twentieth year after a true marriage than there was the first year. But in the actual life how few there are who ever find this marriage of hearts.

How to find this mate is the thing which we are going to show. Let the young lady who thinks she desires a companion, commence to ask God, who is her Father, to keep and to care for and to make known in His good time, longer or shorter, the one who is truly her companion.

We say, commence to pray to God this very day for the one who is to be your companion and who is the one who is to be the father of the children and to be the companion of all of the journey through life. We know this is the true way of selecting a mate, and when there is one who has been selected by the method of prayer and formed for you by God, there will be no unhappiness and never a diverse action or any of the cross things that make so many of the homes on this earth a perfect hell.

This prayer to God is not to be thrown aside as an impossible thing because one is in society. There is the more need of the supernatural help than ever, if one lives in the states of society which are so artificial and foreign to nature.

These unhappy marriages and the divorces are among the questions which puzzle the world and which the world is always putting right and always getting wrong. All of these things, as equality of temperament, states and castes of this earth will be made right if the match is from the Lord, wife and husband born of the Spirit of God.

There is yet more to this trust to the God for a companion than can be said here. There is something which the world does not look at until it comes into court to have the law's redress and then it is laughed at.

We allude to what is called "conjugal infidelity,"—the case where a man finds out, after marriage, of course, that the woman he has taken as a wife, is unfit for him sexually, and that some other woman will suit his body better. This

is the work of the devil, and is (I wish I did not have to say
this, but it is true and I think every one of the young
ladies who are to take husbands should know of it and the
proper prevention) it must be said, one of the most common
things in the world of sin.   No matter where one goes, this
vice of adultery is one of the most common and glaring of
sins.

Yet I say if there is a love match, there is no more danger of the man proving unfaithful than there is of his being
struck with lightning.   The very remembrance of a lovely
wife will keep the biggest fool of a man virtuous.   I say,
and I know what I say, when I say that I have never known
of any man proving unfaithful who had a wife whom he
loved.   And I also say that any match which is made with a
fear of God and a desire to serve God in this selection of
companions, will always have love in it and have love
enough to sweeten all the cares of this life.   In such a
match there will be no outside influence strong enough to
mar anything which is of and belonging to the happiness of
the family.

The traditional mother-in-law and all the things which are
put up as explanations of the unhappiness of the families,
will have no groundwork to base anything on in a family
where there has been the love which is from God.

How shall we know?

I think it is true that when one commences to pray there
is something which brings an answer to those prayers.   And
there will come to the one who is praying for the keeping of
her mate, a serene and peaceful content which is above all the
cares and wiles of the world.   A love match which can be and is
made in the heavens above us and is not alone a match for
this earth but for all eternity.   To explain all the particulars
of such a love match would be impossible, as there are no
two alike.   But we will say there will be no doubt of such a
match when the right parties are together.   If there is the
least doubt about the matter there will not be love.   Wait until
the times and all the affairs are at some quiet time and the
one whom you think you love is out of sight, so that there is

sure to be no passion accelerating the marriage, and then ask God to help you to decide about the fitness and the selection of the companion who is to share all the sorrows and the joys of life. God will never fail to answer this prayer.

But, as we have said, if there is any doubt there is a certainty that God is not in the match. Consider this and appeal to God.

If any doubt exists in the mind, do not consummate the marriage. Break it off or hold it in abeyance and tell the man frankly why you wish to wait.

If there is anything in the personal habits of the man that is disagreeable to you before marriage, you may be certain those habits will be tenfold more unbearable after the marriage has been solemnized and you are alone with the object of mastery to you. We may mention a few of the points on which the wife has been so often wrecked, that it seems a wonder that any one could ever go on in the same ill-fated road as long as the world stands.

One of the most common of all things is the idea that marriage will break up a man's desire for drink.

Now it is certain, and of a truth which is inherent in the brute man, that marriage will not break up anything, much less any desire which it implanted in the body of the man.

The drink habit is the worst which is in the body and is to be dreaded more than anything which is on the face of earth. If a man drinks any liquor, there is an end to any happiness and any contentment in this life. So, if there is any leaning toward any man who is a drinker of beer or any kind of liquor you may set the thing right down that there is no love from God in this match, and if there is any affection for such a person it is an affection from the devil, and the sooner you root it out from your heart the happier you will be.

Oh, he may promise and assert that he will leave it off, and make you the most solemn of all promises on his bended knees, but you will curse the day you ever saw the man if you allow him to persuade you into marriage. He may make these promises with all of the faith in the world, and he himself will really believe he will leave off, but that appe-

N

tite will control him and all of his fine promises are so much
sand on the sea shore at the mercy of an angry ocean.
They will not stand and can not stand a moment in the face
of temptation. That drink business will appear and claim
him as sure as you are mortal, and while you are bearing
your children, that is the time he will come home drunk, and
your dreams of peace will all be shattered to a million of
flinders. Sooner than marry a man who is addicted to the
taste of liquor, go down to the river and soak yourself until
there are only a few of your bones left. You will be better off
to keep the man in your heart as a remembrance, than to try
to live with him after he has lied to you as he surely will lie.
Mind this before it is too late. A drinking man never tells
the truth unless he is drunk. Your husband, when he
drinks, is a liar; there is no truth in a drunkard and never
was and never will be any truth in one who drinks.

You may think this is severe and so it is. But there is
no such thing as anything being too severe for the drinker.
The drinker will pawn your clothes and your children and
sell you for the drink. He will go down to the saloon and
gamble away your supper and come home and kick you to
bed.

He may look nice to-day. He may wear good clothes at
this time, but the time is coming when he will be a pauper
and you will have to get a divorce or go to the poor house.

You may have one or two nice children. Your drunken husband is as liable to take an ax and knock the brains out of
them as he is to drink. More likely. It is in the drink
and there is no telling what he will do. Your other children
may be idiots or drunkards. The man who goes into the saloon is the one who is not the one whom you can think of as
a possible husband.

He will tell you, of course, he is going to reform. If you
think of him in any possible way, try him for two years.

But wait. We will tell you a surer way. If this man becomes converted and has the grace of God he can change,
but there is no other way that can change any man from the
habit of drink except the power of God. This is certain.

You may think he only drinks a glass of beer once in a
while. That is all right now. But as sure as he drinks
beer now, there will come a time when he will drink something stronger, and then you will curse the day you were
born. Sure. We tell you in the plainest manner that any
man who drinks, or who touches anything in the shape of
liquor is not fitted to be the husband of a hog. The sooner
you are free from all of his temptations, the sooner you are
a free woman. Shun the drinking man as you would shun
the one who comes at you with a club to beat your brains
out.

No matter how specious his plea now, there will come a
time when that plea will be laughed at and you will be
scorned, when he will be bloated in the face, and you and
the children will be ashamed of him. That time will come
as sure as he now drinks. The taste of liquor in a man is
something that is so hard to understand that there are mil-
lions of unhappy homes now existing without your throwing
away your life on a beer drinker. Shun him and go the
other side of the street. Go to the other side of the world.

Do you think you can change him? No. A million
times, no. All the blandishments of a woman's arms are as
nothing compared to that taste for drink, that love of a
whiskey glass. He loves it. He can not love two things, and
therefore he can not love you. He may have some passion for
you. Most likely he has. All the drinkers have more or less
of this sexual passion, but that is a short lived passion in the
drunkard, which is soon satisfied, and the return to drink
comes on worse and more exacting than ever. Then is the
hour of your punishment, and like Cain you will cry it is
greater than you can bear.

Oh, by no means have any thought of one who is a drinker
of beer or wine.

Leave them as they are and if the Lord is not able to send
you a better husband than a drunkard, then you may be
sure that God is dead. But this may strike the eye of some
one who is already tied to some drinking brute. What shall
I do?

We do not have a minute in saying to you, get down on your knees day and night and ask the Lord to perform a miracle for you. We tell you to have nothing to do with any one who drinks and we say to you that cohabitation with a drinking man is crime before the great God. If the great God does not heed your prayers and perform that miracle for you, then we say get a divorce and place the continent between you and him. You may have children. Take them and fly. Go anywhere.

Do anything rather than submit your body to the embraces of a drinking man. It is not wholly for your own sake. That is bad enough. But the moment one contemplates the consequences of the union of a drunkard with a pure woman, and the ill-fated offspring which are the result of the union, you will hasten to fly from the embraces of a drunkard as one would flee from a whirlwind of destruction.

Do you think you love a man who is the user of tobacco?

We desire you to do well. But as you value anything which is of the earth, and as you value the brain, marry no one who uses tobacco in any form whatever.

The tobacco user is not so bad or so degraded as the man who drinks whisky or beer, but there is the same destruction of life and the same destruction to your body which is in the association. We do not think you will understand this assertion, and we do not think it is of any use to tell you of it, but it is our duty to tell you of the evils which will result from the union of any one who is pure to the one who uses this filthy weed, tobacco.

The woman who is married to a man using tobacco is not quite as likely to have children as if she were married to the man who does not use it, but she is likely to have some sort of children, and these children will be the fruit of her womb, and she will carry these children, one or two at a time for the space of nine months.

When the spermatozoon goes into the uterus the "living thing" commences to grow.

It takes its growth from the substance of the woman as that blood goes to the outside part of the womb.

After a little while, say about the fourth or fifth month, there comes a time when the .blood from the child, which is in the uterus, is carried back to the general circulation of the mother, and the blood of the child and the blood of the mother are in a measure one blood, although they are never really commingling with each other at any place in the body.

The blood from the child finds its way to the mother from the uterus, and then, as these bloods commingle there will be an interchange of the blood. Then the time comes that your blood will be impregnated with tobacco from the blood of the chewing man.

But wait a moment. The child takes on the same character-istics as the father had, and any of the diseases which were in the father are surely reproduced in the the mother as well as child. This is certain and as sure as anything can be on this earth.

Now, if the father has had the syphilis, although he may have gotten over it in a great manner, yet when the child is born it will show these traces of syphilis, by its teeth, by the shape of the jaw bone, and by a humor on the surface of the body, or by something in the eyes.

In case the syphilis is not wholly eradicated, there will come to the mother who is carrying the child for the hus-band or man who has not this syphilis wholly cured, a com-mingling of the blood, and as a result from the commingling of the blood, the mother will have, about the fourth or the fifth month, a humor about her and a fever, and possibly the hair will drop out so that she will wonder what is the matter with her hair, or with her person, and being an ignor-ant, innocent woman she will naturally lay it to the carrying of the baby and say nothing about it to any one but the hus-band, who will quiet her fears; and she goes on until she loses this child or brings it forth as an instance of the per-fidy of man.

In the case of the tobacco chewer there is the same com-mingling of the blood, but with a different result.

The syphilis has a certain course which is uniform. This disease will cause the mother headache, an eruption, loss of teeth, and a fever. But the tobacco in the child from the tobacco user, will act in a different manner.

The pregnant woman will be sick at her stomach. By the way, this woman who is in the pregnant condition by the tobacco chewing man, is far more likely to have a severe attack of sickness at the stomach and all the other ills which afflict the pregnant woman than the woman who carries children by the man who does not use this weed. And it is a fact, as I can testify from my own experience, that I have never seen a case of hard labor with a woman who had a child by a strictly temperate man. I do not consider any one strictly temperate who uses coffee, tea or cocoa shells. The man who drinks beer is a drunkard, no matter if he only drinks one glass in ten years. And she will have all the other ills that any one can have from the effects of pregnancy. After the third to the fifth month there will come some of the symptoms of mild tobacco poisoning, and then the woman will lose all her ambition and become a dragged-out old creature.

This is no hypothesis and some fancy sketch, although you have not read this in some of your works on physiology. Nor can you learn it at your card parties. It is a fact from the observation of one who has looked at this growing curse to women, and does not have to bite his tongue or become frightened in the saying of anything which is a fact. We repeat this. The woman who is pregnant by a man who chews or smokes is going to be poisoned by this tobacco user's body, when she carries a child for him. And the more children she carries for this tobacco user, the sicker and weaker she will become. She becomes tobacco poisoned.

Why?

Because this tobacco has pervaded the semen, and the spermatozoa in the male are already impregnated by this poison, and when the child commences to grow there is some quality from that tobacco which will poison the mother as she carries that child in the uterus and absorbs the poison from that tobacco through the uterus.

Do you think this is a fancy, or far fetched? Do you

think this may not be so and you can marry a man who uses just a little of this poison and yet you can be well and strong?

We tell you to look around you and see the women who have borne children by tobacco chewing men and see how many of them are well and strong.

This is something that claims all your attention before you make any step towards marrying and bearing children by a tobacco chewing or a tobacco smoking man.

There is no end to this thing if you will look at it in a correct manner. The man being poisoned, his seed is poisoned. This seed in growing takes on new life and is going to grow in the same manner as the parent-poisoned seed. This poisoned seed in growing will surely poison the nest it is grown in, and so this poison material grows and spreads itself through the body of the young mother, who does not know what is the matter with her, and surely goes to destruction. We do not ask you to take our word for this astounding statement. We ask you to look at the wives of the tobacco users all over the country and see the effects of tobacco on the wives of men who use this poison weed.

It is a series of facts which are not hid in a bushel. But the facts are not spoken about, as people are afraid of hurting somebody's feelings. We do not care so much for hurting the feelings as we do for getting at the truth and finding out how to remedy these misfortunes which are placed on an unsuspecting girl. Why should the girl go to destruction just because a man is a fool, or because the man is wicked?

Some years ago there was a lady in this state of Minnesota who had a boy; she allowed the boy to do as he had a mind to do, and the boy had a mind to do almost anything and had his way at all times and in all places. After this boy grew a little older he had a gun and went hunting, and one day he hunted after something in somebody's store. They caught him and sent him to the penitentiary for two years.

I saw his mother when he came out and a more woe-begone creature I never saw. The wrinkles on her face, and the white hair would have melted the heart of a stone. She was an invalid in every sense of the word, Yet, as she had some money, she was in the rotten caste gatherings which are called society. And in this society she was intriguing to find some good young lady to be a wife for her dear boy and reclaim him.

Oh, this is a fact, as I knew the lady, and she tried to get one of my acquaintances to intercede for her with a certain young lady to go home and spend a few days with her.

What kind of a life would that young bride lead? What kind of a body would she have after bearing children for this young brute?

There is more to this. The children of tobacco users have the worst temper in the world. Among the intemperate and the insane the tobacco users come first. Always the tobacco users are the ones who have these sudden deaths and the shocks of paralysis which break up a man's family and leave them to the mercies of some one else.

Even if there are no children, there will be the contact of the body, and it is impossible to keep the body in good order which is placed every night in the intimate companionship of a man who is in the habit of steeping his body in tobacco.

Yes, there is yet more. No man, I do not care how good he is. can ever become a true child of God who is in the habit of stuffing his mouth full of tobacco. His brain is addled and he can not think.

He does not fast and pray to God, as there is nothing in his mind which can allow the tobacco to be let alone. He is a slave to the using of this article, and there is no use to try to make him quit.

When you consider these facts you will see that a tobacco user is one who is out of the question to have any love for, as a love from the God who made you. It is impossible for him to love you, as he can only love one thing and that thing which is his love, his idol, is the tobacco. He is wedded to that weed and when he becomes married to you, it is quite plain to understand that you are the second wife; not a legal but an actual bigamy, that will bring the bitter salt tears from your eyes. His first wife is yet living, and the first wife's name is tobacco. Think of the matter yet farther down and you will see that all the children of the tobacco users are short lived.

All the tobacco users will deny this, but it remains as a fact. Tobacco shortens the life of the children as well as shortens the life of the parent.

It is a law which no power on the earth will efface. It is a law which will follow all of the children, and we do not wonder the tobacco users will hate to have you read this book. We have no idea that you will heed this. But you will think it over, and after you have raised a family of sickly children and seen them die, then you will be converted; and although this writer will be in the ground awaiting the final trump of the judgment, you will be converted and be as anxiously fighting this evil as the writer is now doing. You will now think this is only an idea and a whim about this tobacco. By and by, when you see the little babe die and see some of the evils arising to yourself from this curse of tobacco, you will begin to think, and this little thought will be a leaven which will work, and you will not have to get some doctor to talk wise to you. You will know for your own self, that tobacco is a curse to the body and to the mind and to the wife of the tobacco user, although she has only gotten the tobacco second hand as it were, but she is poisoned all the same. And so we tell you, don't marry, don't love, don't touch a tobacco user. And if we could still thunder in your ears, we would thunder, don't touch, taste or handle the child of a drunkard or of a tobacco user.

Tender bowels, piles, weakness, lassitude, epilepsy, paralysis, peevishness, feeble mindedness, nearsightedness, and idiocy, together with organic heart disease, all follow the use of tobacco, and will follow in the children as sure as the night follows the day.

When you have married this tobacco user, and see the flesh of your body turning from firm to tender and flabby, then you can call to mind what is told you here and it will not do you any good as it will be too late. But then you will know what is the matter and if by that time you have some of the virtues for which Christ was so noted, you will be trying to do some good to others and this will be your cry: "Don't touch or fondle or love or marry a man who uses in any manner the filthy weed, tobacco."

We will pass from the drunkard and the twin brother, the tobacco user, to another class who are not to be touched as husbands, if you know what you are trusting.

The gambler.

We have no means of knowing who are the gamblers and we are unable to say who are and who are not the victims to this vice. But we think each girl as she gets acquainted with the people she is in company with and those whom she trusts can readily find out very much of any one's character.

Besides this, we think if one is praying to God there will never be allowed, only for a wise purpose, the union of a pure woman with a gambler. The gambler is bad. But he can not be so bad as the man who uses tobacco or drinks. That is, not so bad to bodily contact.

We think of the man who is mean, and would caution any young lady against marrying a man who is mean towards himself and towards his own blood relations. We should say, don't touch a mean man. Do not take any one's word for this meanness, but see that you know in what his meanness consists. Many a man is said to be mean by others, but who is only saving and prudent. Be sure one does not influence you in any way against a person without a cause. As we have already said, do not take any one's word about things which are of themselves indicative of some gossip or of some tale which one may tell, but see that you know quite certainly what you believe, and why you believe it. Get the truth and then do not allow any one to rattle you out of it.

We can not tell you whom to marry. No one can do that. But we can tell you that if there is to be a happy marriage there is to be something in that marriage besides the desire to be married and the fact that the other party wears man's clothes. If a man's breath is bad you do not want him until that breath is better, until it is sweet. If the man's teeth are rotten, see if you can not change his ideas and have his teeth fixed. These minor things can be remedied and love will do wonders. Love will refine a man and make him better all over. But it will never reclaim the drunkard or the gambler. You are not the one who can so change a man's nature that he will not be the same person after the marriage as before, but he can be cleaned up and made to look a thousand per cent. better after marriage than before.

If you have a little fortune keep this out of sight until the marriage is over. Never give up the possession of any of your property, and do not sign away the mortgage of your home after you are married. But all of these things will regulate themselves as the time rolls on, and you need not worry about them if your stay is on the rock of belief in God. In all of these things see to it that God is the first refuge, and do not take any one for a husband unless you are persuaded that the Lord is in the match. If there is any doubt, be sure there is something wrong and the sooner you allow a postponement the better for your peace and happiness.

I now come to the last class of men who I think always make unhappy mates.

This class is well dressed and this is all right.

They always have some one they are "going with."

Their reputation is good enough, but they are reckoned a little "fast." If this fastness is in the gambling line or in the drinking business, you do not want to think of them. If this "fast" reputation comes from some girl who has lost her character by this young man, we say to you that all the blood in the world will never wash out this stain, and all the wealth will never be of any value in making a happy home, as the young man who has ever ruined a girl is cursed for all of this life. His children are cursed, and if you marry a man who has had the reputation of having ruined any one, you may as well make up your mind at once that with him there is to be unhappiness, and no matter how much there may appear to be some prospect to reclaim him, there is in reality no actual prospect of any change in the man; and you want to understand, in spite of all the talk to the contrary, that on that man rests a curse, which you, and the children by him, will share to the end of life. All the excuses of the world will never wash out the fact that there has been a soul ruined by this man and that God has cursed him. This curse is not seen, it is felt. And if you are desirous of knowing how it is, you have only to pray to God and he will show you in his own way how it is possible for one to look alive and yet be dead. We tell you that to shun the man who has already seduced a girl is to save your life and to save your soul. Besides this, there is a curse attached to this man which will descend to his children, and thus, in spite of all the things which appear on the face, you and your children will share the curse which always follows this betrayal of womanhood.

If a man loved a woman well enough to seduce her, and would not then marry her, it does not take any prophet to tell that the disposition which accomplished this evil will go with him all the days of his life, and you can not afford to be the companion of one who has wrecked a woman's life.

I have personally known of such marriages and I have seen their children grow up and become men and women, and I can say, with these examples before my face and in my memory, I would rather be dead and nicely covered up than to have anything to do with the man who is alive after such a breach of faith and humanity. The seduction of a woman is worse than murder.

If there is anything which is cursed of God, it is one of these men or the semblance of men who think that the possession of a woman's body is to be desired to be used and thrown away.

So we say, if you have any regard for any future happiness, do not think of loving or of marrying any man, no matter what his position may be in life, who is known to have seduced a girl, or who has lived with any woman without the rite of marriage being performed.

There is one point which is of interest to every young lady, and which there is always a diversity of opinion about, and which will always be discussed by all the persons who think they should be consulted when a marriage is to be made. We allude to the age of the parties who are the ones making the marriage.

As to age and temperament, social position and all the other questions which are so complex, we do not think any one is able to decide about this for the parties themselves.

The young man may be very old, and the old man will be quite young if his youth has been well and kindly taken care of. The woman of any age who marries for a place and for a home is always going to be unhappy. We think this is true because the swapping off of one's body to get a place to stay or to be dressed and to get something to eat is not one whit better than to sell the body for money. It is a species of prostitution which has its reward on this earth and there is not very long to wait for it.

The lady who will do this under the influence of friends or of her relatives is sure to be unhappy. There is no such thing as the love coming after such a barter. There has to be a love which is not like any other feeling in this world, and this feeling will not and does not come where there is a loss of self respect in either party.

So we say, do not be changed or influenced by any one outside of your own mind and the instincts which are implanted within you.

But at the same time there is the marriage between opposite nations. We do not think this is usually a happy match, for there are so many conflicting ideas that these are always sources of discord. This is true also of the differences in religion. But as for all of these things we say as we did at the outset, if this match is good in one's sight, and the blessing of the Lord has been asked on it there is no danger of unhappiness.

There will be a perfect freedom in the family and that freedom will have peace, which is the first requisite of happiness.

The fact should never be overlooked that a passion for one is not love. The passion for one is one thing and the love is another and an entirely different thing in the world.

The meanest reptile on the globe has this sexual passion for the' opposite sex, but the love which is born in heaven has no passion about to make or mar it. There is no passion with pure love. It is a self abnegation which can not be understood by half the world, and there are many people to whom love has never come, because they have never seen the one to whom they could give their affections.

There will never be a happy match for the girl who takes her father's coachman as a husband. She is not honest; she has taken something which is not hers and she will not be happy with what is stolen. The coachman who will steal a girl because of her youth and inexperience would rob the girl if he had the power. This kind of a match starts out with a lie. It is not the match of unequal parties in rank which is the whole wrong, but the fact that there is no honesty in either of the parties. The girl owes something to the parents and she denies this debt when she gives herself away to one who is beneath her in this world's station and in this fact that she has been brought up by those who were her owners until she became of age.

All these stories about happy love matches with such unequal standpoints are lies. There is nothing in them; there can be no happiness in any family unless there is the blessing of God upon it. And there will be no blessing upon any match which is so ordered that there will be no honor to the parents. "Honor thy father and mother;" and there is no honor to be found in the fact that the cherished daughter has run away with a man who is a menial in the servants' room.

These matches are all passion and are always unhappy. They always end badly. The offspring go to make up the criminal classes. They are already weighted with the wrath of God which abideth upon them. There can not be a happy match which will not have time to pray over it and do honor to the father and mother.

To any such young lady who may think she has fallen in

love with some hero in the guise of some menial, we say, stop and pray to God and God will listen to you and show you the way out of all these dilemmas. No girl has any right to think of one who is in any position where she would bring reproach on her parents, if there was marriage. Take this to your own self and act in these matters as if you were in their places and they in your place, and then you will soon get over any ideas which would drag the parents' heads down to the grave with sorrow.

Another thing which is to be said in the choice of a companion; do not hurry. There is so much rush in these latter days that we had almost said, do not rush. There is so much haste in all of these quick and hasty matches that there is always sorrow in the near future. Then the saying comes in "Married in haste and repented at leisure." Don't do this. Keep all these things safe in the distance, and think of marriage and the choice of a companion as the work of the Father who doubtless has some one for you in His eye, and do not allow anything to persuade you into anything which is to be borne by others as well as yourself.

Go to the Lord with these things which are too hard for man to decide, and wait until the Lord sees fit to answer you. There is some one for you who will be everything to you; will be all love and kindness to you. All your desires will be satisfied, and there will be such sweet trust and confidence and such perfect union, if the match is from the Lord, that all the rest of this world will be as dross compared to the love and devotion which you will bear to him, and he to you.

You can often be made to feel ashamed of some person who is of menial blood, especially if this menial is one to whom you are tied. But of the husband whom you will love and cherish there will be never a possibility of any shame, to you or to your parents. All will be love here and love beyond. The love will increase with its growth.

CHAPTER XX.

HAIR, HANDS AND FEET.

The hair.

Any person's hair can be made lovely and thick if they will take pains with it.

The two requisites are *cleanliness* and *exercise*.

The hair should be washed once a week by rubbing on the whites of three eggs, making a thorough lather, rubbing it in thoroughly and rinsing the head in warm, clean soft water. Dry the head thoroughly with a coarse dry towel and do it up in a net (not a night cap; a night cap is apt to heat the hair and render it musty) or else have it spread out on the pillow.

It is best to do this washing at night, as one is liable to take cold if the head is washed in the day and the person goes out afterwards.

Cut the ends of the hair once a month certain—no matter if you do cut but just the tips or a fourth of an inch, cut it. Cut off the dead ends every month as regularly as the new moon comes round.

This cutting off the ends of the hair will give it a stimulation which is better than all the hair "vigors" and washes in the world.

Brush the hair three minutes slowly and thoroughly from the roots of the hair to the ends and do not leave a spot of head which is not thoroughly touched from three to ten times by the bristles of the brush.

Never use for any purpose the fine comb on your head.

If you become populous in the hair, use the carbolic acid soap daily or put three large spoonfuls of ammonia to a basin of warm, soft water and wash the head thoroughly every night before bedtime until the intruders leave the premises.

Another good thing to take out bugs in the head (or in any other part of the body) is a wash made of three tablespoonfuls of ammonia, and two quarts of soft water,

208

mix well, and wash the head thoroughly, and dry it with soft towels before the fire, or wrap up the head at night so as not to get cold. Then let some one look the head over. Keep the fine comb away from the head if you desire nice hair.

The ammonia wash just spoken of will also overcome the offensive odor which comes from sweaty feet and the armpits. It may be used every day during the hot weather.

Persons who are in the habit of taking a daily bath will not have any offensive odor about them.

Oils, musks, pastes and hair dyes should be kept from the hair at all times.

Any hair can be made beautiful by exercise and cleanliness. Keep the follicles of the hair, just under the skin, in good condition and you will not need any hair dyes or hair oils.

It may take you six months to change the condition of the hair, but you will succeed if you have continued care and do not get discouraged the first week. The happy results will agreeably surprise you.

I am sure there is no head of hair that will need oil if that hair is properly taken care of. There is no special objection to bangs or curls (if one desires them), but there is an especial objection to a bushy, shocky head of hair.

Brushing will correct this bushiness, so also will this brushing correct the ugly appearance of the bushy eyebrows.

Have a toothbrush as an eyebrow brush, and brush them twice daily, morning and night.

It is the daily and thorough brushing which will secure a good circulation of the capillaries under the skin, and secure nourishment for the hair. Without the daily brushing any head of hair can be spoiled.

The hands.

If the hands are coarse, rough or cracked, look for the cause and remove it.

If you are a working girl, there is no disgrace or shame to you if the hands are coarse and rough, but we think we can assist you to keep them better. Have an old pair of gloves, and after washing the hands in warm water, in which you have placed some bran, wipe dry and wear the gloves to

O

bed. This covering the hands with the gloves will soften the skin and keep the hands in much better shape.

Of course, when you go to hang out clothes after washing. you should place mittens on the hands. When you go on the street put on gloves. The secret of keeping the hands right is in keeping them from the sudden changes of moist to dry and hot to cold. Protect the hands while they are exposed to these sudden changes of the temperature. Cold days are destructive to the skin if the skin is not protected.

Five cents' worth of gum benzoin with two ounces of alcohol and four of glycerine will make a compound that is much sold by druggists under different names. It can be used at night to soften the hands after washing.

Pears' soap has a reputation for softening the skin. It is worth fifteen cents a cake. We have used it and think it an excellent soap. The common yellow soaps, composed of fat and potash, are destructive to the outer skin. and this causes cracking and drying of the skin and "chapped hands." Rubbing the hands with glycerine and then dipping them in cold water and after that putting on the gloves to sleep in will soften the hands in a few nights.

If one wishes to have soft, white hands, wash in oatmeal and soft water without a particle of soap.

When one wishes to use a cold cream for chapped hands and cracked lips, try the following:

℞   Oil of almonds..............4 ounces.
       White beeswax..............2 drachms.
       Spermaceti.................2   "

When this is melted add four ounces of rose water and one ounce of orange water. Stir it while it is cooling and pack it in some covered glass or earthenware.

A wash to take off freckles, tan and sunburn is made as follows:

      Ox-gall ....½ pound.
      Burnt alum...................½ drachm.
      Camphor......................¼   "
      Borax 1   "
      Rock salt....................2 ounces.
      Porto Rico molasses..........2   "

Mix all together and shake up thoroughly in closely stopped bottles. It can be put on at night and washed off in the morning. If closely stopped it will keep for months.

We think the wash of oatmeal or corn meal in warm water is much better than any of these compounds. If one can get soft water to use and keep the hands from sudden changes there will seldom be any "chaps" or roughness of the hands.

If the hands are very bad make a pair of large mittens of cotton cloth, fill them with wet bran, so as to have room for the hands, then insert the hands and have some one tie the mittens close (not too tight) about the wrist, so the bran will not get out.

We can tell you this will make the hands as soft as a baby's, and when you get up the next morning and have these mittens off and wash the hands in cold water you will have as nice a looking pair of hands as you have owned for some days. If you keep up this practice there will be no nicer hands than yours.

What we already have said in regard to the keeping of the body virtuous is as applicable to the hands as to any other part of the body. If the sexual organs are kept under the most absolute control there will come a beauty which is hard to understand, and although we can not understand it, we see it and see the want of it at each turn of the street. If we desire the hands and the face and the entire body to become a mass of beauty and filled with strength and power, we have to begin at the foundation and keep the powers of life in ourselves at once. If we do this we may be sure we shall have beautiful hands and become beautiful all over.

There will never be any shyness or any bashfulness about us if we are strict in line of bodily continence. Heed the warnings of nature and have all the body under the most strict control of the mind. If this is done we can do anything which is in our way and have every part of our body as pure as a lily and as fragrant as a rose. Our hands, face, feet and every part of our body will be beautiful. Without this virtue all these appliances will be in vain.

The feet.

While the body should be bathed wholly every day, the feet should be soaked once a week in warm water (soft is preferable), in which there is a heaping tablespoonful of soda, or a couple of large tablespoonfuls of ammonia dissolved. The water should be warm, and the feet may remain in the water until all the dead skin is readily taken off. Then brush the feet, heels and between the toes with a brush and wipe them dry. Trim the toe nails close and cut off the corns at this time, if you have any. The toe nails should be scraped down a smooth as possible. If corns are painful, soak the feet in warm water and soda (two heaping tablespoonfuls to three quarts of warm water), and after paring them down close, touch them with a drop of the oil of origanum.

It is a misfortune to have anything like corns, but if you have them do not lose any time in getting rid of them.

The origanum oil is one of the best things we know of, but sulphuric acid in little doses, touched with the fine point of a match, will soon cause the corn to disappear.

After the feet have been cleaned once a week for several weeks there will be no danger of any further corns appearing.

The Israelites were ordered to bathe their feet often, and it is quite certain there was never a fairer skinned people on the earth than the ones who obeyed the Mosaic law.

When it is considered that all the feet have a circulation which is changed to the head every two minutes and that the blood in the feet is the same as the circulation of the face, and that all of the circulation of the body is completely interchangeable, it is seen how important it becomes to keep the feet clean.

If the feet are kept clean there will be much less mending of the stockings. No stocking can be kept whole where the heels are filled with dead skin and the toe nails are allowed to grow until they are sharp enough to scratch gravel.

There is also another item concerning the feet which is not seen in print It is this: When the feet get cold there is a cold all over the body. When the feet are clean there will be much more warmth in the feet and the general circulation will be better.

If we put these two items together we can see the great intimacy between unwashed and uncared for feet and a disease of the lungs. Filthy feet are sure to bring diseases to the lungs. If one's feet are filthy there is filth all over the body. It is true the feet are out of sight, but the circulation of the body comes to the gaze of persons on one's face and hands and on the neck.

CHAPTER XXI.

PERSONAL HABITS.

Whatever may be your education or accomplishments in books, or your lack of them, never allow yourself to eat with your mouth open or to form any habit of making any noise with the lips, mouth or throat when eating. If you have any of these habits break them up and overcome them at any cost whatever. Eat alone in some place, or go without your food until you can thoroughly masticate the food without drinking, and swallow without making any noise whatever with the mouth or throat.

While you are at the table never sup or suck your drink, whatever it may be, out of a spoon with a sucking noise or a supping sound which is so painful to hear.

Do not trust yourself in company to eat a mouthful until, in your own chamber, alone, you are competent to eat any article of food without this disgusting habit of drinking while eating, and to take soup without making a particle of noise with the lips or throat. Refuse every invitation to eat at any place until you are mistress of your own body in all its parts.

If you have any impediment in swallowing, or if there is any gulping, practice drinking alone in your own room small swallows of water, until they can be taken without a sound. If this does not do, fast and totally abstain from water and food for twenty-four hours and commence again. This is almost a certain cure. Usually where there is any trouble with the throat there is trouble with the sexual organs. Think of this matter. Never pick the teeth in the presence of others, or show your toothpick.

If you make any noise with your mouth while you are eating, it is one of the best methods to take a good drink of water before you go to the table, and so have the stomach filled with water and have moisture enough to keep the

glands soft and filled with moisture while you are eating.
This will help to keep you from drinking at the table and
will also assist you from making any noise while the fluid is
going down the throat. Keep away from the swallowing
habit with the mouth open.

We say to you, do not go to some one's table thirsty, and
have to disgust all the others at the table with some noise
that you are as much ashamed of as they are. The noise
can be broken up and overcome in a very short space of
time, if you will take a little time and attempt to overcome it
while you are away from every one else, so they can not hear
you.

By practicing on this habit while you are out of sight and
out of hearing you will soon be able to swallow without a
murmur of noise. There are some habits which will be disgusting to you the moment you see them, but you will be
too well bred to make any demonstration or notice them in
the least particular while you are in their presence. Think
over all you have seen in others and avoid all things which
would be unpleasant to others in you and are unpleasant to
you in others. Note how the best bred people eat, drink
and act, and, if necessary, copy their manners.

So act as to make yourself agreeable, but do not try to mince
or to make mouths or to cast sideways glances at one in any
part of the room or street. Look straight ahead and have
the eyes open. Downcast glances and those little sideways
looks are such as the girls of the town make toward those
whom they wish to ensnare, and there will be some one who
will see you and these things will be remarked about you
when you are absent. But this is only the least part of it.

You will know why you made the sideways glances and
this knowledge in you will be worse on your own mind and
degrade your own self respect far more and hurt your countenance far more than it would do to have persons talk about
you a thousand times behind your back. It is your own self
respect that keeps you clean and sweet, and not some one's
else self respect. What some one else has is hers. What
is yours should be **your** own. In these personal habits there

is nothing which will give you so much stability of mind as to know you are correct, to know you are doing right. This knowledge will come to you at once when you feel assured that you know how to act.

While there is any habit about you which is uncertain there will be an element of uncertainty in the mind and you will feel badly. Then will come the bashfulness and the shyness and all of the unpleasant feelings which make one so miserable.

There are the habits of etiquette that should be learned and the best method of learning these habits is to have some elderly lady friend to whom you can go and ask and let her tell you where your faults lie. Happy is the girl who has a mother who can tell of these little things while she is growing up.

There are many things which you should never do, or if you think of doing these things banish them from your mind at once, for the very thought of them will burn you all the way through and leave you in a much worse state than you have ever been before.

Never try to get anything for nothing. Never take any gift or any present from any one (unless a near relative) who is in any way acquainted with you. Do not accept any attentions from any one whom you would not introduce to your mother or to your father and to every brother you have. Allow no strange man to talk with you. Do not get easily acquainted. The acceptance of any present makes you a person in some sort of debt to the one who has made you a present. "A gift turneth the heart." No matter how trifling the thing which is given, do not accept it, but decline positively with all the apologies which are needed.

Do not accept it in your mind for a moment. Do not handle anything belonging to any one else, and we may say with much emphasis, don't touch anything which you do not have from your parents or your brothers or sisters, and under no circumstances allow yourself to covet or to glance at anything, to long for it, that is not yours and you can not afford to buy and pay cash for at the time of the purchase.

In the matter of nuts and candies do not take them from any one and do not eat them if they are forced upon you. No matter how much you may desire them, do not touch them from a stranger.

If you are in a strange place and want paper or pens and ink and can not afford to buy them, go without until you can buy them. Accept nothing from any one else unless it is water for the needed washing and the loan of a towel. But you are and will be subject to all sorts of dreams if you use some one's towel. Have your own.

There are no circumstances in which you should be made to borrow any article of dress unless you have been drowned and resuscitated, and in such case it will be allowed that you may wear some garments until you are at home again. If you have borrowed anything, take the first opportunity to wash the garments and return them as soon as there is any chance to get the things returned. When you return the things which are borrowed, do your best to thank the parties who have been kind enough to loan you their things, and try not to be drowned again.

We urge you to let this matter sink deep into your heart and resolve that, outside of your own intimate family circle, you will not have anything which is not your own, and that which is bought and paid for and is your very own.

You should learn at the very outset of life that there can be but very few more unhappy persons than the ones who are in the habit of borrowing. This applies to all things and every condition of life. It is an old and true saying which runs: "He that goes a borrowing, goes a sorrowing." Don't borrow, don't beg; starve in your shoes before you take anything which does not belong to you wholly and solely. A thief has the direct curse of God upon her. With these resolves and the grace of God in your head you will have an independence which the world will bow down to and which will conquer the world.

Your associates.

There are plenty of people who will wish to associate with you as long as you are well dressed and are supposed to be in good society. These people are everywhere and it is impossible to get rid of them wholly. There is this in all of your associates which will keep you very near right, and, if you take the advice given you elsewhere about the asking of God for everything, there is no danger of your getting into any difficulty about them.

There are some things to be said which you will do well to heed. There are some persons who will wear your shoes and your hat and your socks and your underwear, and of such associates the sooner you are clear, the better for you and your fortune.

You can never do this. For you already believe that there is something in every person which is different and if you put on some one's clothes, you will be apt to catch some disease sooner or later and which will make you very sorry. Even if no disease is caught there will be some smell or odor, which comes from some one else's clothes. More than this, we advise you never to allow yourself to accept, unless from some very dear friend of yourself or your mother or some relative in whom you have every confidence, any garment or article of wearing apparel or anything which has ever been on the body of any living human being. Do not touch, much less wear, any person's old clothes. Do not touch them and above all do not wear them on your person. Let this lesson go a little farther and avoid any picking up of anything which you may find on the street or in any place whatever. We even go farther and say it is quite bad policy to read some books which have been handled by other parties and which may contain disease germs ready to fasten themselves in your flesh and form the most unsightly sores. If you do not catch them for yourself, you can transmit these disease germs to others. This may seem to be carrying this matter too far, but the more one thinks of the possibility of the absorbents and the prevalence of frightful forms of contagion there is no limit to the care which should be exercised to prevent one's body from these pests.

As long as you are a *young* lady there should be this care

exercised for yourself and your parents and your relatives. When you are the mother of children there will be the same necessity for this supervision of one's body so as not to take any of these diseases, and there will be an increased care needed if one has children. Then your thoughts will assist in preserving them. You should take care whom you embrace and whom you kiss. Kissing is a foolish habit unless among one's own relations and even among the relations there is the same objection to all forms of intimacy which we deprecate. A contact with any other person's body is liable to give you some disease. Keep your body pure as snow and as chaste as ice.

Always late.

There are some people who are always late and who think some one else is to blame for what they have neglected to do themselves. They are good enough girls (and there are boys in the same song) and appear well enough when they are dressed up and are out on a call. They can sing "When the dewdrops fall," and they are good when there is not much of anything to be depended upon. But when there is anything to do or anything to be depended upon, these late girls are anywhere but in the place where they are needed. And they suffer for this foolishness. They suffer untold agonies for the things they have neglected. They have their bread burn at the very time when that bread ought to be the very best. They have their underclothes soiled at the time when they ought to be cleanest. And when they are to go to some place it seems as if all the fates in the world are against them. They are late in getting up and late in going to bed. They are always late at the train and they are always late at an entertainment and late to the church. They are late everywhere. We see these girls always, everywhere, and when they are gone into their old age they are sitting in some one else's chimney corner and sewing or mending for some one else, or they are in the poverty house. I never saw a woman of the town but what was one of the late girls. Oh, it is one of the very worst things which can happen to any person on the earth—to be late. This being late to the train, late to the school and late to the table and late in going to bed and late in getting up and late in all the good things in this life. It is simply a habit, but it is more than a habit. It is in some persons' blood. They do not seem to be able to help themselves. They mean to do better and they do try, but the idea that there is time enough seems to set them wild as to the time to do the proper things which are really needed to be done at once.

Can this foolish habit and this misfortune be corrected?

Yes. It can be corrected by the most persistent effort only. It must be taken up and eradicated just as a garden should be weeded. One thing has to be borne in mind all the time, and that is to do the next thing. *Keep doing* and do not stop to rest a moment if you have that dreadful habit. Go to bed early and go to sleep. If you can not sleep at the time you put yourself on the bed there is something wrong with your habits. Get up and wash in cold water. Get up and walk. Get up and read. Get up and do something.

Napoleon's idea of getting to sleep was to put one of the fingers over on the pulse of the other wrist and count "one two, one two, one two," until he was asleep. This will do it in some cases as the writer can speak from experience. But the best thing to enable one to go to sleep, is to go without any supper. Drink a glass of cold water and do not eat anything. This will give you a quick sleep. But if, after trying all of these things, you find you are not able to go to sleep at once, you want to take notice that you do not need to take any medicine. The specific is in your mind. You must help yourself, and there is no one that can help you but your own self and the God who made you.

Coffee and tea are great things to make you keep awake. Don't touch them under any consideration, and if you do, and wish to get out of the most unlucky habits in the world, stop taking them at once. But if you do not touch these drugs and can not go to sleep and you find the night is passing without your getting to sleep, and the washing of your body does not do you any good, then try the counting and try to recall the events of the day as they all occurred. This will exercise the mind and give some good thoughts, especially if you are on the right desire to do some one some good and beginning with your own self.

Putting the feet in cold water for the space of two to ten minutes is a good thing to do if it is not near the time of the menses. Not a bit of danger of your taking cold, as we have explained in another place.

However, we hope you will get to sleep at once and be ready to jump out of the bed the moment you wake in the morning. Don't wait a minute after you have become awake. Make a start and go to the washbowl and plunge the arms and hands into the water and then to your head carry a sufficient amount of water to wash your brain clear of all the cobwebs which sleep sometimes brings to one.

Wash the body all over and wipe dry and quickly.

Put on clean clothes all over if it is a possible thing each day. Whatever you do, do not wear the same things which you have worn in the night. Keep a separate suit; if you have only two suits, see to it that one is worn in the night and one is worn in the day time. Never, *under any circumstances*, wear the same thing in the night and in the day time. It is ruinous to the body and ruinous to the brain. You can not be clean while you do this filthy act of wearing the same thing in the night which you are carrying around in the day time. The filth which has been accumulating on your skin in the day time should never have any chance to be reabsorbed in the night time when you are asleep.

Sign-boards.

.When one is traveling along an unknown road and finds at certain distances a sign-board on a tree or a post which says, "to such a place — miles," one is sure of being in the right way.

In this chapter we have grouped a set of sign-boards which will be of value to you as you read them.

Never tell a lie. Do not do this lying in a joke. It can not do any good and this habit soon shows itself in your face. After you commence lying there is a sign-board on

your face which says: "This is a liar." It may be done at
first as "a good joke," and all that, but the habit of lying,
when once formed is one of the hardest things to be unlearned.

It is a common habit. This is a lying age. The children
who go to school and are taught to write "compositions"
out of their heads and are given prizes for the best "story,"
are in reality practiced liars. We do not think this is a
correct or a good education, and we know this is not the
way to have the brain in one of the conditions of success or
of advanced invention.

Besides, this habit grows on one, and while it is only a
harmless joke to-day, to-morrow there is some need to tell a
lie to shield one's self, or to save some one else and the case
becomes one of hopeless lying.

If you can not tell the exact truth, do not say anything.
Keep the mouth shut and have a thought of the throne of
God and of your own self rather than to tell or say anything
which is not exactly true. Above all, the one who lies is one to
whom the face of God is hid. When the storms come down
and the reliance on something which is of greater power
than all the world becomes absolutely necessary, to keep
one's mind steady, then there is the darkness which is always
in a liar's mind, and sorrow which will not be comforted.

Teach your tongue to tell the exact truth or else do not
talk. Keep your mouth shut, unless it is to be opened to
speak the exact truth.

Look, listen, reflect, place all facts together, but do not
allow your tongue to make a motion which is not precisely
the truth, and you will have one of the fairest complexions
and one of the clearest minds in the world. Truth is a mind
clearer. Truth is a mind strengthener. The exact truth is
one of the attributes of God. You can not become God, but
you may be like Him, and we are sure He will love you if
you are striving to follow His ways. His ways are strict
truth. Do you follow exact truth, and if you can not tell
the truth, shut the mouth.

When you find out that a person is wrongly informed and
yet is honest in desires, wait and you will have an opportu-

nity to correct the person and you will have gained a friend. But, if you find a person who is wilfully blind and does not wish to know the truth, or will not obey the truth, do not associate with him, or have any business transactions with him or her.

This will also apply to all of those who are ready to take advantage of some one else. If they will lie or steal from some one else there is only an opportunity needed to do it by you. Shun any intimacy with all of this class. Keep them from knowing anything of your affairs and your mode of thinking. Get out of their way and do not go with them if there is any way of avoiding it. If you find out a store to be tricky, let that store alone. Have nothing to do with anything in the shape of lottery winnings or their habits or any game of chance. All these thing are destructive to the mind.

If any of your associates are lying for anything, leave them. Allow yourself no company, rather than to be in such company, which will have you in the same class sooner or later.

Do not commit any of what are called practical jokes on any one; or have any companionship with perons who do. If you do not heed this, there will come a time when one of these so-called practical jokes may take away your best friend, and then you will have a lesson which will be burned into your head as with a red-hot iron. But it will not bring back your friend. The friend will be dead to you. Practical jokes kill the strongest friendship.

Have the habit of looking a person directly in the eye while you are talking to them. You can thus learn to read what is in their mind and so stop the moment you find your talk is going for nothing. If a person doubts your word, say nothing and do not allow one of the class to question you concerning anything; say that you rather have nothing to say about the subject which is before you, and keep your own counsel. Especially is this to be followed about the concerns of a third party. You have no more right to discuss the affairs of some other person without you know all of the circumstances (which is almost impossible from the nature of this world), than you have to place your hand in their pocket and take out the money they have earned.

Never allow yourself to make any remarks on the dress of the passers-by or of your acquaintances, or of any one. Never turn around to look at any one; never look behind you; look ahead. Think what you may, but do not allow your tongue to utter it aloud. Keep your thoughts in your head and they will return to strengthen you.

Wherever you may be, do not allow anything to cause you to giggle and to laugh at circumstances which may be ridiculous or seem to be funny or annoying to some one else. Be careful how you open the mouth and remember, while you are laughing at some one else, there may be others laughing at you.

There is a sure rule which will always help you to find the thing to do in the exact time and in the exact place. "Do unto others as you would that others should do unto you."

"When you are in doubt, do not act." This was a Roman maxim, and is probably much older than Rome. It is good to remember. But there is something still more sure while in any uncertainty. Think how Christ would have acted if He were in your place. This will be your guide and there will seldom be a mistake in any situation you may be placed in.

Never laugh on the street. Never look at a dog-fight. Avoid all the crowds of the street. If it is in you, do not seek to go into the dances or ball rooms; banish these desires. There is no happiness there and there is much unhappiness. You can not gain anything in these places and there is much to be lost which can in no way be regained. One night in a ball room with the crowded breaths and the dust, as well as the excitement of music and refreshments, is not such as will assist any young lady in preserving her health of body or her equipoise of mind. The so-called "sociables" are another species of jams that are destructive to happiness and to good health. Keep away from them unless you have so much money and so much time that you do not know what to do with them.

It may appear to you that acquaintances are to be desired. We do not think so. What is wanted is a friend who is true as steel and as pure as fine gold. These true friends are not to be found in these gatherings. People go to these places for the same purpose that they go fishing, to catch something, and to have what is called fun. You do not have to be caught and you should be no subject for any fun for others.

As for acquaintances, they will be made anywhere, and at any place they can be judged better than at a place of jams. Besides if we are correct about the Lord ruling this earth, there will be all the acquaintances which are for you, if you keep away from these places and strive to do some good to some of God's poor. If you have any time which is heavy on your hands, go and see some poor persons and do good. You shall be blessed.

When you have more time, write down what you know in your daily memorandum, and if that is filled, read from the Bible. Fill the mind full of good knowledge; so shall you become wise in yourself and blessed of God.

PARTHENIA.

Some things are so patent to others and we can not see them ourselves that a few words concerning them will not be out of place.

Sulkiness is habit as much as talking. Some children are naturally sulky and take it from the mother's milk; others have acquired the foolish habit and while they have some good sense they should break the habit up at once and thoroughly. Sulkiness consists in thinking we have been abused, and we are going to punish some one by spiting ourselves. A child will go without its supper to spite some one and be as mulish as a pig, just because it can not have a certain article to eat.

A girl will spite some one of her acquaintances by refusing to do something or to go somewhere, or will say some hateful thing which will rankle in the minds of those who

P

hear what is said, and become a source of fear and of distrust, when she could, by the refraining from these habits, be a source of pleasure and also be happy herself. The going without the supper and of pouting are habits of sulkiness which are in themselves sources of unhappiness to the girl who is the unfortunate possessor of this habit.

The best way to get out of this sulkiness is to think that one wants to be happy, and the best and only way to be happy is to do good to some one else and not to think about your own self. It is the good we do to others which brings us happiness and not the good we do ourselves. If we say a thing which makes some one else feel badly, we do not so much hurt the person to whom we have sent the angry word, as we do ourselves. The angry word returns to us and we are more unhappy than the person that has received the blow. This is the secret of all happiness, to do good to others. The moment we think we can be sulky and punish some one by some act of ours, that is the moment we are supremely unhappy.

No matter if we have been insulted, or abused, or there has been something which does not please us our way, let it all pass as pleasantly as we can and have nothing to re-member as a folly of our own. Say nothing which can re-turn to us as some of our sayings when we were angry. Control the temper and keep the sharp word in the mouth unspoken; we shall be happier. And if we have been in-sulted and abused, leave the place and do nothing which will prevent any one from saying we have lost our temper and are foolish when we are angry. Let no one see that we are ever angry. Above all things do not allow any one to know that you may think yourself insulted. If you are in some one's house shorten the visit as much as possible but do not pocket the insult nor the sharp repartee nor retail some goss'p about others. Shorten the visit and resolve in the future not to have anything to do with the party who you think has in-sulted you. But say nothing. Do not do anything which could be retailed in any place or among any of your ac-quaintances to your detriment, or for the purpose of having any fun or laughter at your expense. Be a lady above all things and be a lady under all circumstances.

KANSAS.

Friends.

A great many people have an idea that the life we lead here is of so much importance that all they have to do is to live well and be happy here and the next world will take care of itself. These people live for themselves, and to gratify themselves they are ready to do anything and to say anything, even if it is against their best friends, so they may gain something for the present. A lie in these people's mouths is to them of no moment, so that they can accomplish their ends. Their object being themselves, the friends, the honor, the truth, and all the finer and nobler feelings, are put out of sight so that they can just now accomplish their ends. And it is but truth to say that they usually accomplish their ends. But when they have all they go after, they find that they are not as well off as they thought they would be when they had succeeded in their undertaking.

We hope you will learn early the fact that a friend is a gift, and a gift of such a nature that all we can do to retain that friendship is not too much, if the party is really a friend. A friend is priceless. We have known of parties, who to place themselves in a different light among their acquaintance, have told lies on their best friends and received a temporary benefit. But they lost their former friend and after all they were worse off than they were when they were in the original position. Oh, no, do not tell a lie. Do not betray a friend. Do not betray any confidence. If you have a friend who you think has misused you, say nothing. Let time cure that wound. Do you keep that wrong in your own breast and sooner or later that friend will come to you and the matter be settled in a manner that will give you great comfort. But if you tell a lie—if you betray all the confidence that was once between you and that friend, the time will come when you will want to make up, and the wounded friend will be so hurt that there will be no making up in the world. Cherish every friend that you may have. A friend is a gift from God. Your wants in this life may be great. But see God for those wants and do not burden your friend, who may have all the burden that it is possible to bear. Go without something your own self and bear a part of the burden that falls on every man, woman and child. Do not shirk your burden. Do not get in such a place that you have to think that you must tell a lie or betray the confidence that was once between you and your friend. Keep your own counsel and see if the cloud does not blow over and let the sunshine in by and by.

If your friend has betrayed you, never let it be known. Bear the betrayal without a murmur. Lock up the secret in your breast and keep it between you and God. Remember this—Christ is the nearest and dearest, ever-present friend you can have. He will never betray or leave you. He is love, strength, power and eternal life. Go to Him for a constant friend and whatever comes to you He will never betray or leave you. Oh, what a powerful, loving friend you leave when you forget that Jesus is your owner and master who has bought you with a price and waits for you to turn your feet and heart to him. If you have earthly friends thank him for them. If you have no friends remember Him who is surely your best friend.   INDIANA.

———

Not so nice, but useful to know.

When a young lady goes into the world and thinks all the people whom she meets are the same clean and healthy, sweet persons as her own people, she is liable at certain times to find the difference to her great discomfort and to some cost before she gets through the life and the acquaintance.

To obviate some of these things which are so unpleasant and so very disagreeable to the inexperienced, and who may be never so pure and yet come in contact with these pests of society, this chapter is written.

We know there are many persons who will read this and

condemn the entire book and say it is not fit for any young lady to read, but as I have some daughters myself, and I wish them to know of these things, I am quite sure that the knowledge which comes from the reading of this chapter will more than outweigh the disagreeable things which will come up before we have done with the chapter.

Among many of the reasons why a young lady should know of these things is because the very persons whom she may trust and whom she will trust are the ones who will never aid her in this knowledge, but when she is afflicted, will give her the cold shoulder and talk about her behind her back.

So I am convinced that every young lady should know of some of these disagreeable things so as to keep clear of them. She will find enough of things to fear which are not and could not be laid down in this book. With these preliminary remarks, we will commence our advice.

When you go visiting, or to work at any place, always take your own toothbrush, your own towel, your own hairbrush and comb and soap. Under no circumstances, allow your body to come into contact with the garments which have been worn by any one else, and for this reason always take your own nightdress and what napkins you may think may be needed while you are away. Think over all of these things in detail and supply yourself while you have the opportunity, and see that all of the things which are to be necessary for the use of your body are well supplied before you start to leave your own home.

Make a sure thing that you will not have to borrow anything while you are away from home. Feel certain that there is to be no contamination of your body with other bodies while you are away from the home roof. Your towel, flesh brush, soap, tooth and nail brushes should be in a little leather case, or in a linen case which you can make your own self. These can be kept in a compact form and where you know you can put your hands on them in the darkest room. So you should also take a drinking cup with you on the cars, and never drink after the rest of the passengers. Take an extra collar button with you and always have something to protect the hands on the train and yet not wear your best gloves on the smoky and grimy cars.

Night caps have gone out of date, but we advise you to have a night cap and to wear it in a strange bed. Also, if you think of any waste to your body, you had best have a napkin and see that it is properly fastened before you go into some one's strange bed and wake up in the morning and find the bed soiled. Think of these possibilities and act so as to prevent any of these annoyances which you will feel if anything happens while you are asleep. These are small things, but they show the well bred lady as differing from the ordinary miss who has never received anything of an education. Think of yourself as a perfect, well bred, educated, thinking lady. We have said for you to have nothing in common use with any other person. We will make a yet more particular assertion and tell you never to use the things any one else has used. To make this assertion in detail, let us particularize.

Never use the same towel. Rather not wash the body than to wipe on a towel where one with the itch or the leprosy may have wiped just before you.

Do not use the same seat when the closet is to be used. When you go to a strange closet, take a piece of a newspaper with you and place that paper on the seat so that any portion of your body does not touch the seat which some one else has been sitting on. Do you think this is a needless precaution? Listen. There are three kinds of causes of diseases which can be transmitted through the medium of the closet seat.

1. Bugs. Under this head come the lice, crabs, pinworms and tapeworms.

2. A plant or a series of plants of the fungus variety which will cause the most intense itching and also worry you a great deal in getting rid of this cause of disease.

3. A venereal disease which can be and often is transmitted to some innocent person who unconsciously uses the same seat that some public woman or some unfortunate

wretch has used just a moment before. So we say to you, *never use the seat* of some public closet without taking some paper and covering that seat so that your body will be free from all these sources of disease.

Should you be so unfortunate as to contract any of these miserable things, we will tell you how to get rid of them at this time, and not have to refer to them again.

Bugs. The proper way for any ordinary case of lice is to wash the parts in a solution of carbolic soap-suds, made rather strong, and after you have dried the parts, apply the following solution :

Carbolic acid..................... 1 ounce.
Glycerine......................... 6   "
Water............................. 6

Mix well and apply thoroughly to all the parts which are affected by the burning and the itching.

Never apply any preparation of mercury or any preparation which is sold under the name of "blue mass" or "mercurial" ointment, as that will cause a much worse disease than the bugs.

The carbolic acid is a poison and will certainly kill all the bugs as well as all the plants which may be caught by an unwary person.

The ammonia wash which is spoken of under the head of hair and feet is most excellent to cure these "caught" diseases. Should this not cure at once, and should there be little sores which appear as if they were eating down into the flesh, you have caught a venereal disease (which is not so uncommon as the readers might suppose), and this sore is called a chancroid.

To cure this, get some pure calbolic acid and wipe the sore out dry. Then have a pointed match, dip the end or the point of the match into the acid and touch all of the sore, a little at a time, until it turns white. Then dry the sore and if there is any place which is not touched, touch it over again. When this is all white, dry it and apply an oil as follows: Olive oil, twelve parts, carbolic acid, one part; mix together and shake up well.   Apply this on some absorbent cotton, and keep the sore wet with this oil until it heals up. If it has any smell, touch the carbolic acid to it two or three times a day, and then apply the oil as before.   Keep it from chafing and keep it clean, but do not wash it too much, as the washing is not what is needed.   It needs to have this foul poison and this parasite, killed by the acid.

Should the urine become scalding, drink freely of a tea made of flaxseed and lemon.   Two heaping tablespooonfuls of whole flaxseed and a whole lemon, peeled, mixed together in one and a half pints of warm water.   It may be sweetened. Should this not relieve it, try the drink of a strong infusion of slippery elm bark.

Three heaping tablespoonfuls of soda to three quarts of warm water will make an effective wash for nearly all of the pests which one may catch in the cars, but it must not be placed in contact with the hair of the head, as it will soon take out the hair and it will take a long time to have it grow in again.

It is to your interests to have your body pure rather than to have to do any doctoring afterwards.   Think of what you are doing.

Shoes and buttons.

There is a passage in the Bible which reads, "Obedience is better than sacrifice."   The meaning of this verse is that it is better to do the will of God at once and at the time one can do it than to be contrary to God's will and then try to sacrifice afterwards.

You can read the story in Samuel.   We wish to impress on you something of the sort in a far different sense from the way this passage was written, but we wish to tell you of what seems to us a part of the divine law.

The taking care of that which we have is a duty which we owe to God, who has furnished us with our goods and our breath and the water we drink, as well as the pleasures to our bodies and good to do to some one else.   It is a duty to live aright.

Our shoes are, in reality, one of the most important of all

the things which we wear on our bodies. They are the groundwork of all the dressing we may have, and if we do not have good shoes or good boots, we are not dressed well or comfortable.

Besides this, we are to find that if the shoes are bad or if they are tight or if they are run over on one side or the toes are out, we shall have some feeling as if we were in some sort of pain. Mentally we shall be in pain. We do not think it is possible for one to be happy and have on worn-out shoes or worn-out slippers and be liable to have some one come in and see them, or to have to go to church or to school or to do some shopping on the street and have on the shoes which we know do not look well to others.

There is some sort of magnetism about having good shoes which is catching. We can not explain it, but when we see a person on the street who is well dressed on the feet we say, "Such a one is well dressed on the feet," and we instinctively look at the rest of the body to see how that corresponds with the well dressed feet.

Let us try to have well dressed feet. To do this we have to take care of the shoes we already have, for if we do not care for them, we shall have to keep buying new ones.

The shoes should never be placed near a fire to warm the feet. When the shoe goes near the fire it will be ruined, as the leather is from the hide of some animal, and the moment the fire is come close to the shoe to burn or even to heat that leather, it becomes rotten and the next time it is wet there will be a shrinking, and the leather (which is the tanned hide of the creature from which it was taken) cracks, and there is an end of all usefulness and all wearing qualities to the leather. The shoe, although it does not look so, is at once destroyed. The next time it is worn there will be some trouble in the fibres of the leather because it will be so dry, or because the grain of the leather is broken, and then there will be an open place in the shoes and the shoemaker can not mend it, because the leather is rotten. The shoe is spoiled. We say heat is the great destructive agent in wearing out all the shoes which are made. We tell you, keep those shoes away from the fire, as you would keep your eyes away from the fire. The fire as good as burns that shoe rotten in two minutes, and although you may not be able to see the burn, it will be in the shoe and no matter how good the shoe may have been, after it is introduced to fire, it is ruined.

I have seen girls place their feet over a register in the school room and have actually known of some girls who took a pair of shoes which cost $3.50 and had them ruined in a day. I have known of two girls who had the same kind of shoes which were made to order, and one of them wore the shoes a year and the other one would not wear them six months. The difference was in the introduction of the heat to the leather. If you desire to burn anything burn your fingers. Place your naked feet in the fire and burn them, but do not burn the shoes which have cost time and labor and skill to make and which to destroy is to steal from some one. Yes, steal. You have no right to waste and no right to destroy some one's labor.

You say you wish to be warm; very well, be warm. Do not heat and ruin the shoes in trying to get the feet warm. Take off the shoes and place the feet near the fire if you choose, but let the shoes remain in the cold, and do not ruin a day's work in one minute because you have not brains enough to think of where that shoe came from.

Think of placing a two-dollar bill in the fire and burning that bill up. Think of working all day over a shoe and then to have some one come along and place all your day's work in the fire. Think of having your body taken up and having your skin tanned and then after it is all fixed for some animal (a monkey, if you choose) to wear, and that animal places the part of your hide which is in that shoe in some fire and burns it up. How foolish! Yes, it is folly. But the burning of the shoe is a far greater folly. The waste that is annually on a family for the not taking care of the shoes is enough to pay for their flour. The taking care of the shoes is of as much importance as the taking care of the bonnet. More, for the bonnet does not keep the feet from water, and the feet are of more importance than the head in the matter of the care of the body. You can get a cold in your head and soon have it over, but if you get a cold in the feet there is far more danger to the general system than if you had a cold in the head.

There is yet another thing to be thought of when you take notice of the shoes. You need to walk to exercise all of the body, for when you walk you have nearly every motion of the body in full play. You must have shoes to walk with. If these shoes are not in good condition there will be some time when you can not do as much walking as you should, and then you will blame the shoes for not allowing the rest of the body to be well exercised. The shoes are important. Take care of those shoes. No good, honest, industrious girl will burn up her shoes.

If there is anything which will tell of your personal habits to the outsiders who do not know you, it is the habit of not having the buttons of your shoes and the buttons of your dress or the buttons of your jacket or wrapper sewed on and fixed tidy to go out on the street at any time.

If you are in the habit of leaving off these important adjuncts to your dress, allow us to tell you that you are now on the way to a very great unhappiness. No one can keep house, or can keep herself clean or sweet, who will not keep the buttons sewed on her clothes and on her shoes.

She is called names behind the back, and it is of no consequence how well she can sing or how well she can play, the fact that she will not have the buttons sewed on is enough to condemn her as a bad woman. I never knew a happy or a long-lived woman who would not sew the buttons on her clothes or on her shoes. When I see a button off from a shoe, I think of what I heard a man say concerning the character of one who always had the buttons off or dangling about her. "She is an unhappy wretch." You may not be able to talk but one language and you may not be able to play on the piano; but if you can find time to sew the buttons on your clothes you will have some of the joys of this life. But if you are too much engrossed in this life to sew on the buttons which should be used every day. if in their places, and if you *will not* sew them on, we think the day of grace is past and there is no use to say anything more to you. Good bye.   MAINE.

Colds.

While we have given you our ideas of the skin we have not told you of the great importance which arises from knowing how to keep this skin in good and working order.

When once this skin gets out of order there is a great frequency of what the common people call "colds."

What is a cold ?

A cold is a condition of the body where the pores of the skin are contracted and the insensible perspiration can not find its way out through the proper channels, and so the entire system is out of order.

There is too much to do for the lungs and so there is a cough.   There is too much to do for the kidneys and so the urine is more frequent than it should be.

There is a running of the nose because the mucous membrane which lines the nose has too much to do in carrying off the material which should have gone through the entire skin and out through the entire body.

There is too much of an effort to get rid of this material, and this effort of the vital force to expel this insensible perspiration is called a fever.

If, now, this effort of the vital force is not aided by your assistance, there is going to be, as soon as the vital force gets ready to make a more strenuous effort, a chill.   You will know it when this chill comes to you.

As we have already spoken of our method of treating these chills, we will give you the method of speedily curing this condition of the body which is known as "a cold."

The cold is a contraction of the pores of the skin, which can not throw off its accustomed perspiration.

The thing to do is to open the pores of the skin and keep them open until the circulation is fully restored.

While you may take some warming teas, as of ginger, or Canada snake root (infusions), there are still two of the more important conditions which are too commonly over-looked.

1. The condition of the temperature of the room in which the body is to stay.

If you open the pores of the skin and then go into the air so as to again rapidly shut up the pores of the skin, the condition of the skin will be worse than it was at the beginning of the cold.

Therefore the best thing to do is to make it a point when you have a cold to be certain you can stay in one temperature until that "cold" is over and gone.

The failure to know this fact is what prolongs the condition of the skin and so precipitates the body into that condition of effort which is called a "fever."

When you have a cold and desire to be wholly rid of the effect of this cold there must be some provision to keep the skin in a proper temperature until it is able to retain its equilibrium.

The skin should be educated to hold its circulation under as many different circumstances as possible.

2. The second best thing to be rid of this cold is to have the daily cold bath.

The next best thing is to have all of the body clad in an equable set of garments. Cotton stockings on the feet and a thick undershirt on the lungs do not leave the body equally protected from all the inclemencies of the weather alike. So the sudden changes of high to low shoes is one of the most frequent causes of colds in the early fall and winter.

And the change of one kind of underwear to another is often a cause of taking cold. The sudden taking into the body of some kinds of hot drink and going out into the cold air is another method of "catching cold."

But the skin which is not educated is the one which is to be found with a cold.

The skin should be washed every day. It should be rubbed every day as early as one gets up in the morning. Then with the daily rubbing and the change of clothes as we have spoken of, there will come such an education of the skin as will withstand nearly all of the ordinary conditions known as the changes of the weather.

If the skin is an *uneducated* skin there is every likelihood that the least sudden change will give one a "cold." We repeat what has already been said. Every young lady should take the daily bath in the morning every day when the menses are not on and possibly a day before and one or two days later, if there is any doubt about the real cessation of this flow.

This education of the skin, will, in nearly all ordinary cases of life, prevent the "catching" of all kinds of colds.

We should not be awake if we did not mention the fact that the habit of wearing the low shoes and the habit of having the ankles unprotected are two favorable habits for catching cold and having this "run into quick consumption."

The reason for this condition is as follows :

The blood starts from the heart and goes to the extremities of the body, and when it gets to the extremity of the body this blood passes through what are known as capillaries and then gets into the veins and so back to the heart.

Now, if there is any clogging of these capillaries of the skin, as in the feet or in the head, there is going to be some stoppage of the blood as it flows through these capillaries, and there is going to be some dead blood corpuscles. When these corpuscles of blood die, there is going to be some congestion, and soon there will be an effort of the vital force to overcome this obstruction, and this effort will be called a fever.

If this effort is continued and the death of these corpuscles continue there will soon be more dead blood corpuscles than the vital force can carry away, and some of these dead blood corpuscles will be deposited in the lungs, and sooner or later there will be a sure case of consumption. This is called "quick consumption."

And we have no hesitation in saying that the senseless habit of wearing low shoes, and the wearing of the slimsy shoes that are so commonly sold, are two of the great reasons why there is so much of this kind of consumption in the eastern states.

To have the feet clad in the best manner is of the first importance, and there can not be too much pains taken in stamping this fact on your mind before you are booked for the consumptives' route.

The next fool habit is the one of having the underwear of insufficient texture. Underwear should be of the best. It should be changed when the body is laid down for the night, and under no consideration should the same garments be worn in the day time which are worn in the night. All of the underwear should be made tight during the winter and it is far better to have a little trouble to unbutton two or four buttons than it is to cure a cold after the cold is once started.

The habit of female dresses has been an endless theme. There can be no two persons who will think exactly alike on these matters, and you cannot afford to be odd enough to brave the sneers of your own sex and the shafts of small wit that would be sent at you if you should attempt to dress sensibly. But in regard to your underwear, that is something that is under your own immediate control and you can fix it as you please. We say, therefore, do you have your underwear so that in the coldest days there can be no possibility of catching cold because the draft comes up on your intestines when the underwear is open. Have all of the drawers made tight in the winter and fall and have them long enough to tuck into the stockings and to have some to spare.

See to it that you know how to wash your own flannels, and do it when you are not perfectly sure that they will be washed soft and nice. If it is possible, have your shoes made to order and have them cut high and cut wide in the soles. Have good, thick soles on them and have a pair of insoles in them which will protect the feet as much as another pair of stockings will during the inclemency of the the weather. If these things are seen to properly it does not matter so much what you will wear on the outside.

It may be calico or silk, and if your body is warmly clad there will not be much danger of catching cold by these most common methods.

But if you have a cold.

The first remedy is slippery-elm-bark infusion. This is one of the best things in the world, and one which will, in the large majority of cases, cure your cold by opening the pores of the skin and carrying off the impurities of the body which have been lodged in the intestines and in the cells of the kidneys.

See to this, also, that you are not obliged to stay in a draft during the time you work. See to it that your feet are not exposed to some draft of cold air from the bottom of the door and so keep the pores of the feet contracted. All these little things are of importance while you are having a cold, because this care of your body will *prevent more death* of the blood corpuscles, and thus assist your body in soon recovering its wonted state of health.

If you are a servant girl and cannot take the proper care of your body, that is, if you have to do washing and all that sort of work during the time the menses are on, it is best for you to promptly leave the place and stay at some friend's until you are in a condition to go again into service. You have only one body, and when you lose that body it is unlikely that you can get another of the persons who are perfectly ready to use up the body for their own personal gratification.

Take good care of your body while you are young and it is likely that the body will stay with you to an advanced age.

If you think you can overcome any of these diseases more readily than thousands of others who have tried the same thing and are now out in the graveyard, reflect if you are not mistaken in your ideas. Ask yourself if there are not some things which are of more value than money.

Your complexion. Your continued good health and strength. Your will power. And finally the preservation of the body in more senses than one.

If you decide that your body is of more value than some one's work, and you have a cold, take the most prompt steps to overcome this condition of the body which is known as a cold and get yourself into good shape before you attempt to do any one's washing, or their out-of-door work.

One of the best remedies for a cold as well as a remedy for a cough, and painful or scalding urine, is the following:

Take two great spoonfuls of whole flaxseed which has been picked over clean, one-half of a peeled lemon, four ounces of white rock candy, a large handful of raisins which have been cut twice in two. Place all of these in one and a half pints of boiling water. Let them stand half an hour and then when they are settled you can drink off the top and fill up the ingredients with another pint of boiling water. This can be drunk freely if one is in a warm room. But if one is engaged in washing, or is in some draft of air it should not be taken.

Put your body in a temperature of 70 to 74 deg. and stay there until you are well.

Q

CHAPTER XXII.

COMPENSATIONS.

There are some subjects which are better untouched. We would be glad to leave this subject which we now are about to commence, unspoken of, but we can not do it and finish the book.

There would be some things which would not be seen and some things which come in daily notice which would be always obscure. And we would not wish to think that one of the pitfalls of life had been left open and we had shunned to mention it, while there are some which will fall in, no matter how much the way is guarded. We have already said that the young lady who permits any man to take any liberties with her person, is a fool. She is, but there are those like the fly, who think they can do anything and yet come out all right and be as well off after their experiment as before they tried it. We know ahead that there is failure in all of these lapses from the strict path of virtue, and we have had our say about what we consider the proper way to do in these cases. Our idea of preventing all departures from strict virtue, we repeat most emphatically: Never allow any familiarity with your person, and above all never allow yourself to do in the dark that which you would not have your mother see you do in the broadest daylight.

But while we say this, and we know this is the best advice which we can give, yet we know there are cases which are not right and which are called anomalous and which any one will say are almost foreordained, and that is in cases where after the young lady has been so imprudent as to allow any liberties with her person she is to become in a condition which will call for tears and sighs and regrets, but there will nothing be of any avail and the young lady will be in a condition from which she would gladly go to death. She will have inside

242

of her a new being, and that will be, without the marriage rite, a condition of shame and disgrace to all of her friends.

With the marriage rite this will be the normal condition, and a desirable condition for the wife who loves the husband; yet, when this condition comes from an intercourse which is illicit, this child will be most unwelcome to all, and the state of the young lady who is in this condition will be most deplorable. We say this with all the leniency which we can have, there is no condition on earth which will be so bad as the condition of the young lady who has permitted some trifling familiarity at the first and this goes on until she, in a moment of thoughtlessness or a moment of passion, allows the fatal familiarity (which is certain to follow the least surrender of the deportment), by which she surrenders the body to the passion of the man.

All the moralizing in the world will never be sufficient to keep a young lady from making a mis-step, if she is not in the right line of thought at the very beginning of her life. She should be able to think for herself before she yields in the slightest particular.

More than this, she should be ready to think for her own self, and be ready to stem and repress the passions of the man, who will tempt and promise her anything to gain the control of her body. She must think and act for herself and also stem the passions of the lustful man. All this is true, but in spite of what has been said there will be some who will forget all of these resolutions and sayings while the fit of passion is on, and when the result of their passion is come on them, there is the greatest remorse and the most abject despondency.

They see no way out of their mistake, and the man usually leaves at this time, and then, in their ignorance and their terror to hide the first sin or the first folly, they think or are persuaded to kill the growing evidence of their shame.

They desire to commit an abortion and to bury the little life which is dependent upon their will, but which really has as much right to live as if born in wedlock a thousand times over. Their hearts are filled with murder, as it is the same as murder in any way it is looked at. To these unfortunate women this chapter is sent.

Compensations. No; we can not tell you any royal route out of your distress, nor can you be helped from the birth of that child. It will be born somehow; and if not allowed to be born in the proper way, there will be some compensation you will think of in a degree still harder than having a child.

First. Your idea should be to see the man to whom you have given your all and see if he will not make you the wife he has probably promised to do.

While we say this is the first object, there are some objections to this step, which we will briefly name.

Do you really love the man?

If you do not, then the life which you will lead after you are married will be one continuous hell. You had better have the baby a dozen times over than to be obliged to live with the man who has had the heart to betray you. He will never cease to throw up this slip of the judgment and there will always be some doubt on your part, which will be the very worst unhappiness, and which you will have to bear without any repining. For there is no one to whom you can go and tell the griefs which come from the one to whom should be confided every care of this life.

So we say, think of this a little and do not have the man if there is any doubt of your love for him or his love to and for you.

Again, if there is any unfaithfulness on his part, we advise you not to have any marriage ceremony mumbled over you, but to resolve to bear your own shame rather than to be tied to some one who will not be faithful to you after the marriage. While the unhappiness is great now, there is no comparison to the unhappiness which will be on you when you see the same unfaithfulness carried out with others.

As a happy wife you must have a virtuous husband, and if you think you are to have a man who will not be true to you, do not marry him for all the inducements of this life.

Second. If there is any chance, if your mother is living, the one whom you should make your confident is the mother.

She is your best friend at all times, and will shield you longer than any one on the earth.

The next thing is to see where you can go and how you can act so as to cause the least shame to you and your relatives. All this is to be considered and it must be thought of seriously. You have not only yourself to consider, but the condition of all of the relatives and their standing and their rights. When you fall, you disgrace the name of the family, and by this you pull all of the family down to a lower level than they were before, and you yourself are the object of detestation.

This must be acknowledged.

But can all this be overcome without killing the child and hiding the evidence of your shame in the graveyard?

Let us see.

Suppose you have the child killed?

The child is dead and in the ground. You have committed a second crime against nature to hide the first mis-step which you were guilty of. Will this second crime do you any good?

You have killed the child. It is dead. You are held guiltless, and possibly there may be no evidence of any of your folly on the earth. But there are three who know of this, and there will be more whom you do not know who will know all of these circumstances, surround them as you will.

You will know for one. And that this thing has happened will always be on your face to the longest day of your life. I say this murder of the child will be on your face to the day you are dead. Consider whether you desire the crime of murder to be written on your face in such characters that any one who can read your face can tell of this crime as soon as they can see your face.

The woman who has committed the crime of abortion has already this criminal face, and any one who has seen the kind of face which is represented by these abortionists will know this face anywhere it is met. This is a compensation. You may think this is unjust. But it is not. Nature imprints all of these thoughts on our faces and an act is doubly impressed,—impressed on the face and impressed on the lineaments of the countenance. This is one of nature's compensations, and although every one is not able to read this countenance there are those who do, and those who do read this countenance are the ones whom you will desire as friends. Kill the child, and as sure as this is done there is murder written on your face. As long as you are on the earth this murder will remain on your countenance, and no soap or washing will take it off so that it can not be seen.

Nature can not prevent you from murdering the child, but she can and will put a brand on your face that will prevent others from trusting you in your relations in life.

Third. The considerations of the body which you may possess are of some importance.

When you have produced an abortion there will come to you such marks on the inside of the uterus as are only known to the anatomist who is familiar with the bodies which he examines. These marks are such as we have no time to speak of, but which consist in an injury done to the lining of the womb. The mucous coats of the uterus are so injured that there is a scar there where it was all a smooth surface before. As there was a loss there in the uterus there is a loss of muscular contractility in the whole body.

You will no longer be the same person, and for all the purposes of this life, for all the enjoyment of this life, you are practically dead. You can never be as strong as you were before, and the greatest of all probabilities exist that you will have much shortened life. It is true that this does occur as well to those who are married and have the abortions performed on them as those who have abortions who are unmarried. The ceremony of marriage does not make any difference as to the crime against nature. Nature's laws do not depend on any will of man or on what man says or thinks. Nature's laws are above all of the work of man.

So the effects of all abortions are likely to be and are the same. In some cases, under favorable conditions, the laws may seem to be in abeyance, and the abortion may be successfully carried out and the person pass on through life to the apparent and outside eye as good as if the abortion was never committed. But nature never makes a mistake. She keeps a correct account, and when the time comes she exacts one hundred cents on the dollar, and if there has any wrong been done to the body, nature exacts the full payment for all of the injuries done to the body.

I call to mind a case which occurred nearly thirty years ago. There was a young couple, and the young man had been too intimate before marriage, and they thought when the baby came it would tell of their time of intimacy previous to marriage.

So it would, of course, and there would be some of the old hens who would always rake up such things and detail them in all of the societies where they went, and they would make the days very unpleasant for all who were concerned.

So the young husband went to a doctor, and the doctor was too big a coward to do this killing himself, and he loaned the instrument to the young husband, and the husband went to work on the wife and soon had the baby killed.

It was all passed over as one of the things which will occur. But nature is not to be fooled. So one day this young wife woke up with a cough, and then it grew worse until they had all the doctors around there, and among others was the writer of this article; and the wife who had been afraid of the hens was soon in the fast stages of consumption, and was laid away to await a judgment where there will be no dictum of the black-dressed crows of the so-called society. That is, she will await a judgment if she does not remain in the congregation of the dead.

I saw another young girl who was in this unfortunate condition of " loving well but not too wisely, " and she went to a distant state to have the baby killed. She went to one doctor who was afraid of her surroundings (she was rich), and he would not do it. So she had recourse to an old lady who did not hesitate to do these little murders, and this fine old lady gave her a hook. With this hook the young lady went to work and hooked out the baby in the most literal manner. There was a sudden flooding, and this writer was called but could not attend, on account of other patients, and soon the other doctors with ergot helped her—to die; and they sent the body home in a nice coffin.

There was a Catholic woman, the wife of a barber, who had the idea that having a couple of children was enough; she did not want any more, so she proceeded to a lady physician and the lady doctor went to work and made an operation of the uterus to produce abortion, and having done this the woman went home satisfied.

But when the child came away there was a flooding and the symptoms became so alarming that there was a hastening for the nearest doctor and the nearest priest. The priest was there first and absolution after confession was in order. The priest stayed long enough to know the lady was dead, and then went to the mayor of the city and told him to arrest the lady doctor. But the husband of the lady physician was a mutual friend of the mayor, and in the early train the lady doctor went to a distant city.

These are only samples of thousands of cases which have come under the observation of the writer from the acts of abortion. These are compensations for breaking one of the great laws of nature. We say, do not kill that baby. Wait a minute.

One of the most eminent senators ever in the United States and one who never had a spot on his character, was a child born out of wedlock. May it not be possible that the child which you are so anxious to kill will or would prove to be a blessing? Don't kill it.

Let us tell you a much better way of doing. There are thousands of places where that child can be carried, and where you can live by aid of some friend until the child is born, and then the child can be kept in dozens of ways so that the disgrace will not fall on you or your family. Look at this well, for upon this fact hangs a chance for your reputation and your child's life. It certainly is not needed to kill that child when you think that child is a part of yourself and that there can be no such thing as a quiet murder with-

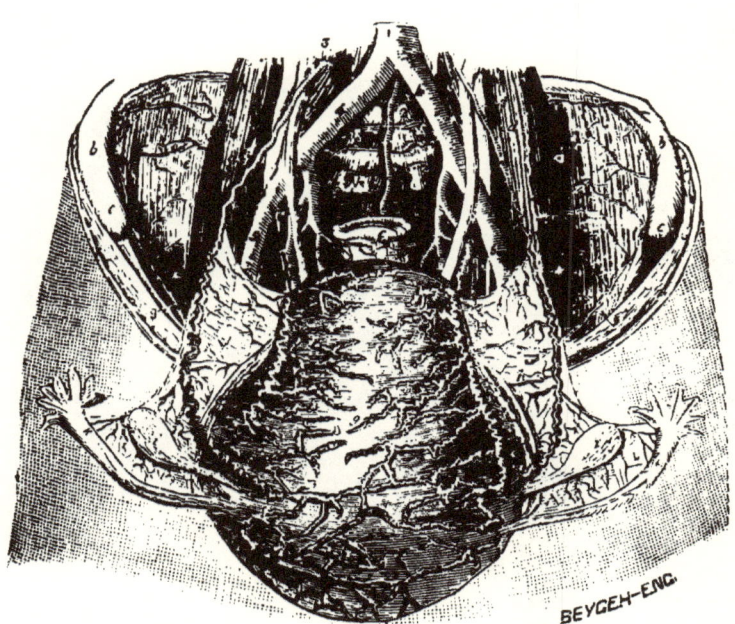

Arteries of Pelvis and internal Genital Organs in the Female subject.

a Os sacrum.
b Crest of ilium.
c Spina ilii anterior superior.
d Mscl. psoas magnus.
e M. iliacus internus.
f Intestinum rectum.
g Uterus.
h Ligamentum uteri latum.
i Ovarium with ligamentum ovarii.
k Tuba Fallopii.

l Ligamentum uteri latum.
1 Aorta descendens abdominalis
2 Art. sacra media.
3 Art. spermatica interna.
4 Art. iliaca interna.
5 Art. iliaca externa.
6 Art. iliaca interna.
7 Art. uterina.
8 Art. hæmorrhoidalis media.
9 Art. circumflexa ilii.

out any compensation. If you murder, the compensation comes sure. On the other hand, if you choose to allow this child to live there is something to look at on the other side.

God must live; He must reign, and if, in his wisdom, He has allowed a child to grow in you, do you not think there will be some blessing attached to the obedience of His laws? We tell you there is an obedience in these things which brings you a blessing and a blessing which is a compensation for many of what are called disgraces.

If there has been any surrender of your person so that you are with a child, we say take some way to preserve the life of that child just as if it were from God, and trust to Him to take care of you; but do not think, under any circumstances, of killing the baby to hide the supposed shame which the birth of the baby will bring upon you and your family. We acknowledge it can be done. But every one knows it or will know of it. Think over the best way to have the baby with the least publicity, and have it. God will certainly compensate you for your trouble ; and go and sin no more.

CHAPTER XXIII.

DURING COURTSHIP.

We who look forward to a life beyond the grave believe that our present existence (rightly improved) gives us sufficient spiritual strength to fully meet the wants of that future life. Our mistakes may injure *us* the most deeply, yet they are so far reaching in their consequences that it seems as if no act, however trivial, could affect but one person alone.

When we see lives go wrong, we feel that early training and early associations were not adapted to their individual needs.

Our object in the present chapter is not to clear up all existing evils, but rather to touch upon one period of our existence. The question often arises, How much do the misunderstandings of wedded life depend on the association of the parties before marriage?

Chinese custom does not allow the betrothed to see each other until their wedding day. Then if the bride elect does not strike the groom pleasantly, he can slam the carriage door in her face and there is no marriage.

This, however, seldom occurs and the marriages are as happy as they generally are where the woman is an absolute slave and the man has authority to beat her if aught in the cooking goes wrong or she in any way displeases her lord.

Among the Hindoos a girl is married when only five or six years of age, and she goes at once to live with her husband's parents, who give her whatever training they wish until she is old enough to live with her husband as his wife.

These two extremes do not strike us pleasantly, and we rather incline to the Europeans who allow betrothed lovers to meet only in the presence of chaperones; but even this custom (liberal as it may seem in comparison with the Asiatics) conflicts with our ideas of independence and self-respect.

Each of the three customs has its advantages and would be beneficial with some natures wherever found. Our country has in some respects the best type of civilization, and it behooves us to reflect on these questions and instruct those who look to us for counsel that they may not abuse the privileges of a life which has the freedom of Eden.

It often happens that a young girl who is in doubt will go for counsel to one scarcely older than herself, and thus the young become counselors of the young. These remarks are, therefore, not inappropriate as a preliminary to the question, How far does the conduct of a young lady during courtship affect her life after marriage?

There is one special admonition I would give to all young girls, *be natural*. It is often remarked that young ladies with brothers are much more popular than those without, because they are not so overawed by the presence of a gentleman as to lose their conversational powers and natural voice.

Young ladies who are guilty of affectation are generally disgusting, and even if they act their part well enough to deceive the very elect, their success proves a sorrow when unmasked.

Talk sincerely with your lover and other friends, for thus you are less likely to be deceived. The atmosphere of heartfelt sincerity is hard to resist and seldom proves attractive to the hypocrite.

Do not imagine that coarse, unfeeling speeches are a proof of sincerity. A perfectly sincere person is apt to be just and kindly at heart; and with such there is a charming courtesy which rises above mere conventionalities.

There is here a word of caution to be given to those who are engaged; *don't flirt*. You may succeed in bringing your lover to your side with flattering protestations, but you can never be quite sure what volcanoes lie beneath.

On the other hand, you are not to ignore all other men simply because your preference is made known.

Be courteous and lady-like to every one. You are at liberty to converse with your acquaintances, but not to accept *special attentions.* Any reasonable man would be contented with this; an unreasonable man you do not want.

A dignified women with good conversational powers often helps a man to a position from which he might otherwise be debarred. Society is glad to retain those who have something besides the mere conventional chatter of the day, but education *alone* does not enable one to converse acceptably.

In all this, be careful that there is no undue familiarity. There should be no intercourse even between betrothed lovers which would cause a tinge of shame if each were to marry another. These things may seem trifling now, but they are remembered in after life with possible exaggeration; and even if nothing is said they weaken the confidence which each might have for the other.

"Familiarity breeds contempt," for the too-free talking person soon grows lax in other respects. The girl who loses her modesty loses her birthright and deprives marriage of its sacredness.

It does not pay to associate with immoral people or to ape them in any respect. I once knew a girl who was attracted by the flashy manners of an unscrupulous woman, and she copied some of her ways, little knowing the absurd wrong she was doing herself. By this means, the impression was given among strangers that she was bad. Being innocent, this knowledge was a great grief as well as surprise to her.

Perhaps I am old-fashioned in my ideas, but I detest anything like chasing after the opposite sex. I dislike to see young people go to prayer-meeting for the sake of having some "feller see 'em home." The female of doubtful reputation does this, therefore every right-minded girl should avoid what may seem a slight appearance of evil. Come home with your brother or parents or neighbors, the ones you go with.

Some years ago, I had a servant in whom I was much interested because, although ignorant, she was sincere and faithful. I once remonstrated with her on the variety of her lovers and on her standing at the door an hour or more to talk with the one who had escorted her home from some evening entertainment.

"Well," answered she, "you don't like to have me ask 'em in an' set up with 'em, an' I don't see how else a girl is goin' to get engaged. Of course, I want to get married some time."

She listened with an incredulous stare to my assertion that a girl was more likely to receive eligible offers who would not accept these promiscuous attentions from Tom, Dick and Harry.

Undue familiarity cheapens a girl even in her lover's eyes and lays the foundation of future jealousy and possible murder. There is plenty of time for familiarity after marriage. What you most need during your engagement is to learn each other's dispositions and general tastes.

It is said that long engagements are not judicious. They are apt to be broken; but a broken engagement is not always a calamity.

I once knew of a man who had very rigid ideas about woman's sphere, but he fell in love with a young lady who bade fair to eradicate some of the old whims. She was a charming woman and a treasure in housekeeping as her father could testify.

As Dr. Porter sat with his bride elect a few evenings previous to their wedding day, he thought it wise to explain some of his peculiar views in regard to a wife's submissiveness. "Why," said he. glancing at the large fire-place, "if I should tell my wife to put her head under that fore-stick, she ought to obey me instantly."

The young lady rose and said with quiet dignity, "You must look elsewhere for a wife, Dr. Porter, for you can't find one here."

Nothing could change her determination, though it ruined the doctor's life; but who could blame her? Had she married him, her servitude would have been life-long.

Take the case of a certain young man whose heart was in the ministry. He married a wife whom he thought a gift from the Lord. She proved worse than Delilah, for her home life was a constant sneer at religious subjects.

"Overcome such prejudices," some one says. Let me tell you that the lion can conquer an ordinary enemy but he is powerless against the gnat in his nostrils.

This was a long engagement broken at intervals. The man's love had proved constant, but the woman had probably failed in her attempts elsewhere and, regarding him as her last chance, accepted the duties of a wife with but one ambition, to outshine her neighbors.

But long engagements are not always unhappy. One of the pleasantest homes I ever knew was that of a couple who were engaged several years. The lady occupied her time, from the first, in making articles for use in her future home.

She was an exceptionally fine artist and painted many beautiful pictures for the decoration of her house. She also learned to cook and became skilled in every other department of housekeeping, so that now her house shines whether she has a girl or not.

There is one more thought which it would be well for maidens to bear in mind. Do not seek to appropriate your affianced wholly to yourself. Introduce him to your grandmothers, and any one else who may be at your house. There is no surer index of a man's character than the way he speaks to elderly people and children. A man may be ever so punctilious in regard to little matters of etiquette, but there is something in the eyes which betrays the cruel man when he looks at the very aged or extremely young. This expression is hidden when he looks at the woman he expects to marry. Love's passion naturally obscures it for a time, but the disguise is thrown off after marriage; then girls wake to the consciousness of their situation and grieve that they had not learned the truth before it was everlastingly too late.

It is better to learn all these things before engaging yourself to any man, but it is wrong to marry in ignorance of each other.

Also if you find out after marriage that you have got a boor instead of a gentleman, try by your own courtesy to win him to a higher plane of existence, but never let him know the tenderest spots in your own heart. A coarse nature will seek to probe every wound, and your only safety is in silence.

These mistakes made before marriage are sure to follow us, a life-long curse. There was a custom among the ancients, when a man had killed another, to bind the corpse securely upon the back of the murderer, and thus he was obliged to carry his victim around day after day until death released him. Very horrible, and yet no worse than many tragedies in daily life.

Some seek relief in divorce, but the *weight* remains the same. Laugh it aside who will, there is in each heart a regret for the past, the wasted years.

The woman is apt to look back with sorrow as she remembers the months or years previous to her marriage, and she will say, "Then was the time I could have made him respect me, but I gave him reason to think all women were vain and thoughtless." She acknowledges with a blush of shame that she dared not avow her more serious thoughts for fear he would think her dull and prosy and leave her for more brilliant acquaintances.

The man's retrospect is no happier. "If I could have married a woman whose highest desire was for something besides a good time and a great display, I might be having a *home* now and a name in the world instead of being the wreck that I am."

"God pity them both and pity us all
Who vainly the dreams of youth recall."

X. X.

CHAPTER XXIV.

SOME CONDITIONS AND HOW TO TREAT THEM.

For any sort of weakness in your body, first think what has caused that weakness and proceed to remedy or to avoid that cause. In short, *remove the cause.* If it is accompanied by a bad breath, have the bowels clean and take some bitter tonic. Read the chapter on constipation. Among the best of tonics, chamomile blossoms stand first in order. Place forty blossoms (or, if it is German chamomile, which is yellow and smaller blossoms and much finer, a tablespoonful) in a pint of boiling water ; let this stand for an hour and take a swallow or a wineglassful three times a day.

This is one of the best tonics which is in the world. It cleans the stomach and is also a good but mild vermifuge. It destroys germs.

This infusion may be taken for all sorts of weakness and for a chronic cough and for any form of dyspepsia.

It is good for faintness at the stomach, and for what the doctors commonly call "female complaints." Another remedy for faintness at the stomach and a voracious appetite, is an infusion of the sassafrass bark made with one-half teaspoonful to a cup of boiling water, and take half a cupful before every meal. Sassafrass is said to "thin the blood," but we do not know that this is true. (Unless it thins the blood in the doctor who could get a fee from you.) It is a good vermifuge and is of service in relieving the stomach and intestines of the slime and the germs which accumulate there after one has a diet of meat, potatoes and coffee.

For pimples on the face, avoid all kinds of grease and have the bowels kept loose. (See constipation.)

Make an infusion of the common burdock (*arctium lappa*) and take a cupful three times a day.

Do not eat anything in the shape of flour bread, but eat

256

graham or corn meal bread or the mushes. Take the daily bath, and if there is any such thing as parasites in the skin, use some of the washes advised in another chapter.

For any spitting of blood; drink freely of bugle weed and nothing else. This is the *lycopus Virginica* of the botanists and is a specific for any bleeding. It is also good for fistulas and falling of the bowels and for some forms of palpitation of the heart.

In cases of shortness of breath, use the injections of water daily and eat vegetable food.

In cases of asthma, use the tincture of wafer ash (*ptelea trifoliata*), ten to fifteen drops three times a day dropped on a lump of sugar, and avoid any food which is of a starchy nature, as potatoes and corn starch and rice, sago and pastry.

Many of the present brood of diseases are caused by the common use of fine flour. Biscuits and baking powder are disease breeders.

Pure graham flour made from whole wheat is far the best, and it will only take a little effort to get it made into bread. Or, if one is boarding herself, have this graham made into mush and eat it with honey or sugar or syrup or milk.

Do not drink any milk if constipated. Make it half water or do not touch it. If faint, add a little pinch of salt. This drives out the worms.

Much of the milk sold in the cities is not fit for use. The milk usually found in boarding houses and in restaurants is slop-fed milk and contains the germs of consumption.

Never retain the urine or prevent a natural movement of the bowels as soon as nature calls. The retention of the urine has often destroyed the power of the bladder and left the unwise lady in a state of weakness from which there was a slow and imperfect recovery.

Attend to all calls of nature at *once* and see that the body is kept perfectly in order.

A good remedy for scalding of the urine will be found to be an infusion of slippery elm bark. Have the bark whole and place a handful of the whole bark in a pint of warm water; let it steep an hour. This can be drunk freely, and

R

will prove one of the best things to relieve a cough, as well as to remove the conditions which bring on the scalding of urine. There is no danger of taking too much, as it can be taken with advantage day after day until all the obstructions are removed.

For anything which is the matter with the back, think out what is likely to be the cause; then remove the cause. The greatest cause of a weak back often lies in having a mass of material in the bowels which should have passed off long ago. Take the injections to the bowels and see that the food is coarse enough to pass through the bowels readily.

Sometimes this backache is caused from some worms which are burrowing in the intestines. For these worms, take an infusion of sage three times a day, a cup full. Tansy is a good vermifuge; have a cup half full of the infusion (the infusion of these herbs is usually made by having one heaping teaspoonful in a cupful of boiling water). Let this steep an hour, strain and keep warm. Take a table-spoonful every time before meals, and if you are faint and weak go to the cup and take a teaspoonful. It may have sugar in it.

The doctors have called tansy a poison; it appears to be a poison to worms and to the doctors. As long as our mothers could use tansy the doctors did not have so much to do as they did the moment they could warn the people away from the use of these simple remedies.

An excellent remedy for worms is the balmony (*chelone glabra* of the botanists). Make an infusion as of the others and drink before eating, one-fourth to one-half a cupful. This is also an excellent remedy for all forms of bad breath. Balmony is a tonic and a vermifuge as well as a cleaner to the stomach and to the intestines.

Gentian and capsicum (red pepper) are two of the best remedies for pin worms. They should be made into an infusion or into a pill. This pill can be taken after meals, one or three grain pills.

An injection to the bowels every night will remove all the

worms in the intestines and will soon have them out of the body if the diet is correct.

There are hundreds of young ladies who are sick and do not think what is the matter with them.   They are sick because they have a body which is not clean on the outside and not clean on the inside.   And to cleanse this body there must be a change in their habits and a change in all their actions.

They should think out what is the matter—what causes their aches—and resolutely make up their minds to live according to the laws of good health.   The body should be clean on the outside and washed out on the inside as much as possible.   The visit to the ordinary doctor will leave so much mystery about them the moment the doctor commences to talk that the young lady will not know what to believe.   In some cases she will think of something which she should have done, and in these cases the doctor finds a willing victim to believe the lies he will tell about the trouble with her womb.

She will commence to think there may be something in what he says and then submit herself to an examination of the doctor.   We think this is one of the worst things in the world for a young lady to do,—to submit her body to the gaze of the doctor while she has no disease of the generative organs.   We are sure this is a foolish and common error. We do not think there is one time in five hundred that there is anything the matter with the uterus while the rest of the body is in order.   We think the uterus is out of order when there has been some diseased condition which has been placed in contact with the uterus, but that the uterus should so commonly take on any form of disease, as an organ, while the rest of the body is cleanly and well preserved, we do not believe.   It is the doctor's teaching and that teaching is erroneous.

The same may be said of the troubles of the back.   One of the lady writers whose name is in all fiction readers' mouths, has said, "Wear a plaster on the back," and then she states the kind of plaster she prefers, and goes on to say that " this plaster is like the pressure of a great, warm hand."

We have a pity for the young lady who is needing a "great, warm hand on her back" until she is married.

The facts are somewhat different from what this lady writer suggests. The facts are that this plaster contains some kind of a narcotic poison, and this narcotic will kill the living matter and thus the pain will be relieved, because the nerves of the spinal column will have been killed or destroyed by this plaster. All of these commercial plasters contain some narcotic which kills the living matter, and although the pain of the back may appear to be relieved, yet the causes of this unpleasant message (pain) will remain in the back, and the body will be worse off than before the plaster was applied. There has been some destruction to the blood and the nerve corpuscles and the body will suffer in proportion to the strength of the poison plaster, and the length of time it is worn.

We say, therefore, for all of these troubles, think out the cause and do the best to remove the cause of these aches and pains, and do not allow any one to tell you about applying a poison plaster to any part of the body to get rid of some pain, while the thing which should be done would be to remove the cause of the disease. Remove the cause of the pain in the back and do not kill the nerves in the back so they can not send you any more messages of obstruction.

A wet bandage over the back is of far more actual value in taking out the cause of aches and pains than any plaster or any examination which the doctors can make; and then have their bill out of you beside.

If the doctors were honest they would tell what is the matter with the body. We say they are not taught to be honest; their teaching has been to make a bill and to "lead silly women captive." So there are thousands of women to-day who are suffering from some form of disease which could be easily cured, if they would have the patience to look after the cause and go to work and remove that cause. The placing of these poisons as of belladonna, aconite, opium and strychine on the body to kill the living matter, is a far more dangerous practice than is commonly supposed.

It is one of the reasons why there are so many weakly women. We say to you, keep these poisons away from your body and out of the system. Keep away from these poisoners. Keep away from a doctor as you would keep away from any one else whose business it is to make money out of the necessities and the ignorance of the people. Keep the plaster and the so-called remedies of the shops away from your body as you would keep away from a snake's fangs. They may have done something towards keeping the minds of some people from a grievance, but we declare to you that all of these things which are sold in the shops are only so much detriment to the body, and the use of water, hot or cold, is of far more benefit to the body and will leave the body in a better condition than any of the so-called plasters will do. Every plaster, lotion, liniment and wash which comes from the drug store is a poison and will injure your body.

After the body is once poisoned there is an end to health. We may go a step further and tell you that every regular doctor and every drug store is in league to poison your body. Shun these allopaths as you would shun the coffin or the pest house. The curse of Almighty God is upon them. God will never save or raise up an allopathic doctor. This is sure.

Weak legs and weak ankles are to be overcome by a continued exercise. Walk in the morning and at noon and whenever you have the time to walk. Walking is the best of all the exercises and will do you good like a medicine.

If it is convenient after you have the walk, have a good wash all over and change the underclothes.

For bunions change the foot wear (shoes) every day. or three or four times a day, and see that the feet feel pleasant. It is a dirty habit to allow the feet to wear the same shoes and stockings every day. If it is possible do not allow yourself to wear anything on the feet which bears on the bunion or corn. Have it trimmed off closely twice a week and apply a drop of the oil of origanum. This will soften the corn or the bunion so that it will come out and vanish.

Soaking in weak lye water will be found very useful, if you have something which has annoyed you for a long time.

The secret of getting rid of these corns and bunions is in getting a good circulation in the parts and not allowing anything to be there which should be passed off through the pores of the skin. Therefore when one tries to get rid of these bunions or corns they should be ready to wash the feet three to five times a day and wear the softest of stockings and the widest and easiest of shoes.

The constant changing of the foot wear while one is trying to remove the corns is imperative. Stockings should be changed every day and the shoes every day if the ones which are on do not feel easy and comfortable. You can change them in the middle of the day and any other time of day when the feet do not feel easy. Attend to the feet, as they are your best friends.

Headaches are nearly always caused by some habit of the body which prevents a good circulation of the blood, and the best and the quickest remedy is to take an injection to the bowels large enough to bring away all of the old material which is lodged there. This injection can be of warm water and may have to be repeated twice or three times before one will get the injection far enough in the bowels to bring away the offending material.

After the trial has been made, and the bunches of old material come away, there will be no trouble in taking up four or five quarts of warm water and this may give one a pain but it need not matter as it will soon pass off and bring away masses of old material which will prove by its smell that it should not be in the bowels torturing and smelling to the rest of the system.

If there is a periodical headache take a pill made of the extract of Culver's root rolled out in pure capsicum. You can buy this extract of a druggist and make them yourself. Take one after meals and do not eat but two meals a day. This will relieve ninety-nine cases of headache (including the various forms of sick headache) which are on this earth.

For diarrhea take large warm water injections and drink

freely of the slippery elm tea.   If this does not fix it right
in three hours, and there is any pain, drink an infusion of
blackberry root, or take the infusion of wild cherry bark,
rhubarb, prickly ash berries, Culver's root, pleurisy root
and peppermint, and steep up a cupful and drink a half a
cupful after every operation of the bowels.   A raspberry
leaf injection is an excellent article; repeat after every operation of the bowels.   A wet band wrung out of warm
water is good to wear over the bowels all the time one has
the diarrhea, and the body should be kept warm.   Eat soft
food.   Avoid all foods of gravies and meats while the bowels are out of order.   The worst cases of dysentery may be
treated in the same manner and will be brought safely through
by this means, and the body will be much better than if
treated by the poisons of the doctors.

During the diarrhea or the dysentery one can drink all of
the soft water that is desired.   Lemonade is also to be allowed, if there is no cramp in the bowels.   Crust coffee is
the best drink, if one can have it made properly.   The wet
band around the bowels is an excellent thing to know in all
cases of bowel troubles.

We have now come to the end of this book and if you
have learned anything new and of use to yourself, we ask
you to try to help some soul that is lower and poorer than
you, remembering that God is the same yesterday, to-day
and forever, and that He has said, "As ye would that others
should do unto you, do ye also to them likewise."

It is happiness for us to do good so far as we know it, and
if we do good so far as we know we may be sure the promise
is good to us that we shall not be forgotten.   Blessed be
God who has helped us, who has bidden us to come to Him,
and who has said by His apostles, "If any lack wisdom let
him ask of God."